SEAHAWK BURNING

A THIRD NOVEL *of* THE CIVIL WAR *at* SEA

RANDALL PEFFER

a division of F+W Crime

Published by
TYRUS BOOKS
an imprint of F+W Media, Inc.
10151 Carver Road
Suite 200
Blue Ash, Ohio 45242
www.tyrusbooks.com

Hardcover ISBN 10: 1-4405-3316-4
Hardcover ISBN 13: 978-1-4405-3316-7
Trade Paperback ISBN 10: 1-4405-3315-6
Trade Paperback ISBN 13: 978-1-4405-3315-0
eISBN 10: 1-4405-3175-7
eISBN 13: 978-1-4405-3175-0

Printed in the United States of America.

10 9 8 7 6 5 4 3 2 1

Library of Congress Cataloging-in-Publication Data
is available from the publisher.

This is a work of fiction. Names, characters, corporations, institutions, organizations, events, or locales in this novel are either the product of the author's imagination or, if real, used fictitiously. The resemblance of any character to actual persons (living or dead) is entirely coincidental.

This book is available at quantity discounts for bulk purchases.
For information, please call 1-800-289-0963.

For Patience Wales,
Jon Wilson, & Captain Bart Murphy,
who started me on this course . . .
as well as Captain Paul Zychowicz,
Captain Ned McIntosh,
& Captain Noah Peffer,
who helped me sail it . . .

Prologue

CSS ALABAMA
January 27, 1863
South of Hispaniola

Captain Raphael Semmes grabs the seaman by the arm, delays him as he prepares to climb the ratlines to his lookout perch at the main truck. He stares deep into the sailor's face, a pale mask in the moonlight.

"Look sharp, man. The Yankees are abroad."

"I hate the buggers, sir." The seaman cocks his head as if to say he must go aloft. Eight bells have just rung. The night watch is starting. The man who has been aloft for the last two hours is no doubt shivering from this stiff northeast breeze, cursing with each plunge of the ship into the head sea that his relief has not yet arrived.

But Semmes still has hold of the young man, whose broad shoulders remind him of his son Oliver. Squeezes with his right hand above the Jack's elbow, feels the cords of sinewy arm tightening beneath his fingers. Impatience, maybe even anger, here. This Jack and his shipmates only had five days ashore back in Jamaica—their first real liberty in six months on the *Alabama*. He's one of the many men in the crew whom Lieutenant Sinclair had to pry by bribery and threat of force from the arms of the molls in Kingston's bawdy houses two nights ago. The night Semmes got word that Abe Lincoln had issued his Emancipation Proclamation on January 1st. The night Old Beeswax, as the crew calls their Reb captain, suddenly felt a sharp impulse to flee Jamaica. To flee the pleasures of the harbor.

To bolt before Charles Wilkes's Flying Squadron or any of a dozen other Federal warships arrived at Kingston intent on making kindling of the *Alabama*, homeless ghosts of her men, her master.

"You'll not go dreaming of a cathouse wench up there now?"

"No, sir."

"We must feast on the Yank before he feasts on us, sailor. And . . . mark my words, he comes."

"Yes, sir."

"Do not leave me unsatisfied." Another squeezing of the arm.

"No, sir."

"What will y'all do then?"

"Sing out with the first sight of sail, sir."

The waxed tips of Semmes's preposterous mustache twitch. A sad, little smile rises on the face. At fifty-three he feels ancient. Old enough to be Maude's grandfather, not the gladiator who left her two years ago in Washington. Not the lover who held her like life itself last June in Nassau. Even after she told him she carried another man's child.

He lets go of the arm. "That's a good man."

The sailor lifts his hand to his face, points to his eyes with two fingers. "Winkers like an eagle, sir," he says with a Scottish brogue.

"Show me the bacon, son . . ."

Lest my country starve. Lest all that we have wrecked has been for nothing. Not just the enemy's ships, twenty-eight so far on this cruise aboard the Alabama. *But the torn hearts of loved ones. The rent souls of children.*

***

"Jesus, look at that!" The Jacks are pointing at the flames.

Semmes's masthead lookout has been more than good to his word. In four hours the eagle eyes have brought *Alabama* twice to prey. The first, four hours ago, was a Spanish brig bound from

Montevideo to Havana. Released. An hour ago a sweet, little Yank. The hermaphrodite brig *Chastelaine* out of Boston, sailing westward tonight from Guadeloupe to Cienfuegos, Cuba, for a load of sugar and rum. Now, it's after midnight. Her crew already made prisoners on *Alabama*.

The brig is a phantom to spark night terrors in those gathered here off the little Dominican island of Alta Vela to bear witness to her death dance. Semmes's firing squad has lit her up with all sails set. Something they have never done before. It's the captain's idea. The *Chastelaine* is a black hull in a halo of light. She's bound westward, moving well, at least eight knots of speed. Following a river of moonshine, running before the easterly trades. Putting distance between her executioner and herself. A mindless specter spouting golden fire. Flames flare in windswept columns from the doghouse companionway, the main hatch, the cook shack forward, the fo'castle scuttle. Just now they have begun to weave into the rigging, sparkle on the sails.

Semmes has told his first officer—the luff—Lieutenant Kell that he aims to give the Jacks a thrill with the *Chastelaine*, a new spectacle to take their minds off the rum and the women that they left back in Jamaica. To take their hearts off yearnings for home and hearth.

He does not tell Kell that he, too, needs this distraction from the bittersweet memories of family and his lover. Does not say he wants to give himself and his crew a fresh taste of the fiery glory that must surely be their future. Possibly their deaths. The *Alabama* has barely begun her reign of terror. She has hemispheres to span, oceans to cross, tens of thousands of miles to put beneath her keel. Brazil, Cape Town, Singapore lay ahead. Unless, or until, she runs afoul of a Yank with the speed of a thoroughbred, the teeth and talons of a tiger, the wit of a bloodhound.

Certain, there is such an enemy. *But where, when?*

Now, standing alone on the windward wing of the bridge deck watching the *Chastelaine* sail nobly into the good night, into oblivion, Semmes feels phantoms from his memory circling, descending around him. Scores of them. The dead. Faintly calling to him . . . as if his own mortal end is being weighed by cosmic forces. Calling to him from ghost ships. Like the sinking decks of the USS *Somers.* His first command. The one he lost in the squall off Veracruz during the Mexican War in '46.

The burning ship is no longer the *Chastelaine,* but the *Golden Rocket.* His first victim, July 3, 1861. The wraith that hounds his sleep.

The flames rush up with a fury. The draft of air sucking into the ship is like the whir of an enormous winged creature beating against the sky. On the waves the reflection of the burning ship sails again, a second ghost.

Tongues of fire race up the rigging into the tops, then to the t'gallants and royal mastheads. In a moment more they are at the trucks. Currents of flame flash along the yards, igniting sails. A t'gallant sail, ablaze, flies away from a yard, drifts downwind and lands far off, a patch of flame on the dark sea. Yards, long strands of thick flame, drop, pierce the water with wails, glowing as they dive down beneath the waves.

Then the network of the ship's rigging traces itself, golden threads against the night sky. The threads part, whipping in the breeze. The ship lets out a cry and the mizzen mast crashes to the deck, cartwheels over the side. A mast totters, collapses with a loud snap. Another falls, crashes. A plume of sparks churns, rises fifty or sixty feet into the air.

He used to think he must be returning to these ghost ships—the *Somers*, the *Golden Rocket*—in his dreams, hoping to find something he had lost, some part of himself that once labored face-to-face with the gods of fire, wind, water, war. But that was months ago. Now he wonders if the Almighty has been sending him these nightmares of burning, sinking ships as an omen of his own fate.

In the aftermath of these dreams he used to pray to his God for forgiveness. *Lord God Our Father, it is only the war that has turned me into this destroyer, not my immortal soul.* After the prayers he would turn his mind away from the images of the burning ships, the drowning men, and think of Maude, his beloved. His West Irish selkie. He would remember lovemaking in the glow of her coal stove on a bitter St. Valentine's night in Washington. The scents of fire, lavender, the mustiness of her hair.

He can barely picture her face, except in fragmentary glimpses. Green eyes, freckles across the bridge of her nose, copper hair falling in ringlets over her ears.

Perhaps he has lost, is losing—or *needs* to lose—everything in his life except this ship and fire. Word of Lee's great victory in December at Fredericksburg has given him hope for the South. But now with the black man free to join arms with the Yank against Dixie. . . .

He turns his gaze once again back to the *Chastelaine*. She's just a fading glow, a prick of light on the moonlit horizon to the west.

"What if my sense of duty and honor, my loyalty to the cause, is sending me on the worst kind of gull's mission?" He wants to shout after the vanishing ghosts of ships and men. "What if I am once and forever to be fortune's fool?"

Do I have the courage to fall on my sword?

1

DISTRICT OF COLUMBIA
Late January, 1863

"We can't go on like this, Gideon. The country cannot take it!" Abraham Lincoln presses his hands together beneath his nose as if praying. But the black-eyed stare he casts at the secretary of the navy is anything but spiritual. "Damned even is the name of Raphael Semmes to my ears."

Welles feels the weight of accusation crushing his chest. Feels the sneers, the scowls, the judgments of the other men seated at the large walnut table. Especially, Secretary of State Seward, Secretary of War Stanton, Attorney General Bates.

It's a Tuesday morning cabinet meeting at the executive mansion, and Welles has had the unhappy duty of informing the president and secretaries that he has just received dispatches from the Gulf Blockading Squadron standing off Galveston. The attempt to seize the port from the Rebs failed January 1. Confederates drove back three companies of soldiers and seven warships. Confederate gunboats succeeded in capturing the USS *Harriet Lane* and forcing the USS *Westfield* aground. The Union fleet commander William Renshaw and a number of his men died attempting to destroy the grounded *Westfield* with explosives, rather than let it fall into Confederate hands. Then on January 11, the *Alabama* swooped in from nowhere and lured one of the remaining ships of the blockade, USS *Hatteras*, into chasing the raider offshore. There Semmes engaged and sunk the *Hatteras* and made prisoners of her crew.

"How does such a thing happen?" Bill Seward's voice has regained almost all of its arrogance. It has been six weeks since the president refused to let a band of jealous senators drive the secretary from office.

"My god, there are just two entrances to the Gulf of Mexico, Gideon." Edwin Stanton rolls his eyes. "Did you not send Charles Wilkes and a special Flying Squadron off to block those entrances and catch that rascal Semmes months ago?"

Welles looks to Lincoln for a signal. Can he tell them about conversations he, Lincoln, and the president's chief of security, Major Allen—the current alias for detective Allan Pinkerton—had about Rear Admiral Wilkes back in December? Can he say that sources here and abroad have given them serious cause to believe that a well-organized ring of Confederate spies and agents have been at work in Washington and beyond for more than a year? Not just Mistress Rose Greenhow's women warriors, but a well-placed military officer and possibly someone high in the Lincoln government known only as Iago. Can he say that Allen has evidence that the traitorous officer may have the initials C. W.? Can he say that the name Wilkes has come up more than once in Allen's investigations of what he's calling the Iago Plot?

The president bites his lower lip, gives a subtle shake of his head.

No. Welles must say nothing. Not about Wilkes or the Confederate agents. And it goes without saying that he must keep quiet about being blackmailed by Semmes's Irish tart back during the first months of the war. The woman is long gone. Dead according to Allen, drowned in an escape attempt on the way to prison up north. He must keep mum, too, about the more nebulous, more serious threats—those damned little red envelopes—that came to him a half-dozen times last year, promising harm to the president if he, Welles, did not resign his job.

"Really, Gideon," says Ed Bates, "do you not weary of bringing us all such horrid news at such regular intervals about your navy's failure to catch this pirate Semmes? Do you not just yearn to quit this town and take that lovely family of yours back to Connecticut?"

Damn you, Welles feels the sword pierce his side. The threats in the red envelopes had often posed the same question in slightly different words—would he not be happier back in "little Connecticut." He feels the need to adjust his long gray wig, lift his thick beard to bleed off the heat rising in his neck as he tries not to shout at Bates, or look at him. Or any of the other smug buggers at this table. *Damn them all . . . and Charles Wilkes as well.*

Lincoln clears his throat. "Please give me confidence, Gideon. The nation and our merchant fleet crave good news."

"The navy will do better, sir. I promise." He folds his hands on the table, stares at them. Tries not to do anything that will expose his stratagem for catching the seahawk. The plan must be kept totally secret. No Iago can suspect what he intends. He's putting a new man on the hunt. John Ancrum Winslow. A man who knows better than Semmes's wife and girlfriend how the seahawk thinks. Winslow has been Raphael Semmes's contemporary in the Federal Navy . . . and his friend. The men have been shipmates. Twice.

2

FAIAL, AZORES
February 1, 1863

How does a good Christian warrior behave at moments like this? Does he resign or does he do his duty?

Captain John Winslow can't decide. He's following the footpath, as he has every day for more than a month, the one he calls his *thinking trail.* It leads out of the town of Horta at the southeast corner of this small island. Among sheep, cattle. Through upland pastures to a brilliant green hill that is the collapsed remnant of the volcano Conceição. Even though it's winter, all he needs for warmth is one of the wool fisherman's sweaters the local women knit.

He has no ship here. Nothing to do but to wait, walk. Buffeted by the salty winds, he swings-and-plants, swings-and-plants his cedar walking stick. Feels like an exile . . . with his imagination running free. When he first arrived in the Azores aboard the *Vanderbilt* more than a month ago, he was fat, paunchy. Every bit of fifty-two years old. A man in decline. But these walks have helped him start to get a bit back in trim, to feel some vigor again. It would be best that he lose another fifteen pounds. *Still. . . .*

He carries orders to take command of the nearly new screw sloop *Kearsarge,* 1,031 tons of speed and thunder. But the ship has been delayed in a Cadiz shipyard. She's having repairs made to her propeller for speed and efficiency. He wishes he could have an active role in her fitting out. But if he takes passage from here to Spain, he might sail right by his ship on the high seas while she's coming here to the Azores for him.

So he remains among the whitewashed churches and townhouses, the red roofs, of Horta. An outcast. All he does is walk and worry. He fears that the malaria and this infernal infection in his eye—both contracted while serving on the Mississippi last fall—may never fully leave him. Fears he may lose the sight in his eye entirely. He also worries that Gideon Welles has sent him here, not to await his ship from Cadiz, but to punish him for a disparaging remark about Abraham Lincoln that he made to a Baltimore newspaper reporter. Sent him here for some other mercurial reason as well.

Did "Grandfather Welles" know that with all this idle time, Winslow would stew, would find himself torn by the most hideous orders a sailor might ever get? He's charged with one duty only. He must find and destroy his shipmate and friend Raphael Semmes. Burn and sink the *Alabama.* Annihilate a brother. Become a Cain. Because Gideon Welles wills it, Abe Lincoln desires it.

Every day on this walk he witnesses peregrine falcons circling high overhead, sometimes sees them—as today—preying on the canaries that flit among the hydrangea bushes. The hawks drop, dive. Black missiles hitting the canaries with such force that nothing but a puff of yellow feathers lingers in the air after each attack.

These acts of obliteration, this killing—even for food—makes his belly tighten into rock. Must he strike and kill Semmes even so? Or take him prisoner to be hanged? Semmes who was once his cabinmate aboard the *Cumberland* in 1846 off Veracruz in the war against the Mexicans. Semmes who was to him then a man of good fellowship and infinite jest? A soul mate? Semmes who, a few months later, was the very man whose wit helped them both recover emotionally from the sinking of their commands?

Winslow lost the *Morris* on a reef. Semmes lost the *Somers* in a squall that fall. Both men were reassigned to the *Raritan* to lick their wounds while the navy decided their fates. And here they shed anxiety over facing a court martial, eased their melancholy and guilt with endless teasing.

I say, Captain Semmes, they are going to send you off to learn how to take care of ships in blockade.

Captain Winslow, I shall go only after they send you out to learn the bearings of reefs.

Shall we have a duel at sunrise, sir, to decide this matter of who goes first?

I prefer we meet at noon, good sir.

Hardtack biscuits at twenty paces?

Make it fists of salt-beef at ten.

Who knew then that they would come to this? That a then-unknown lawyer from Illinois would be the agent of this schism between the North and South. That Lincoln's election would force Semmes and his beloved state of Alabama to secede? That Winslow, Carolina-born, would side with his Puritan forefathers of *Mayflower* fame because abolitionist sentiments run deep in his blood?

And yet, when both men were not jesting . . . when, as here on Faial, they had a chance for liberty ashore to walk and talk—it was in Tampico while a band played "Blue-Eyed Mary" in the plaza. . . . When they followed a trail into the hills such as this path to the volcano . . . had they not confessed to each other that above all they believed in the same three things? That human freedom is an inalienable right. That honor and duty go hand in hand. That nothing can touch a man's heart so deep as his bond with his shipmates and his ceaseless wonder at the richness of womankind.

Winslow stops near the green crest of the volcano, turns and looks to the sea. He inhales the moist air, carrying just a hint of fallen grapes from a vineyard. He remembers nights in the wardroom on the *Cumberland* when the captain broke out the wine for his junior officers. Remembers Semmes smiling with the first taste of vintage, that silly rapier-tipped mustache flicking.

"What if it is not Gideon Welles or Abe Lincoln who sends me after you at all, Raphael?" His voice is low, trembling. "What if it's God? What if the Almighty has been weaving our fates together so that something of greatness and good fortune may yet come out of this awful war?"

What if I must find Raphael Semmes not to kill him, but to save him? What if I must hunt him—must face his guns—not to make war, but to secure peace?

He hears the cheeping of a falcon, looks up. A raptor's circling overhead once again. And a canary has risen from its hiding place among the hydrangea hedges, is fluttering among the cattle in the pasture again. Falcon and canary. Both winged creatures. Both free and admirable. But with different destinies.

For some reason he finds himself thinking of biblical brothers. No longer the story of Cain slaying Abel, but the story of Jacob and Esau. Twins in youth, estranged as adults. Bound by God to long trials of hardship and loneliness. But fated to reunite.

A cadence, a drumming, quickens in his chest.

"Jesus, son of God, grant me strength. . . . Take me to my brother."

Wherever can he be?

3

BEAUFORT, SOUTH CAROLINA
February 2, 1863

Maude Galway feels the soft pinch of babies' mouths, one on each breast. Opens her eyes. Feels someone watching her.

Her. A lost soul, displaced person. The pirate Semmes's West Irish selkie, nursing a white daughter, an adopted black son, too, in a cane rocker. Creaking softly on this warm winter afternoon. The sun just low enough not to disturb the babes or burn the freckled skin on her nose. Low enough that the blue cotton shawl feels just right on her shoulders. Low enough to cast the shadow of a small black woman across her knees. Here on the third-floor porch of an Italianate mansion, the woman who saved her almost five months ago, saved her from a Federal death sentence for spying for the South. Her friend "Minty," Harriet Tubman, steps behind the rocker, puts two hands on her shoulders, her neck. The fingers are dry, calloused but warm. Kneading her tense muscles.

The magnificent Low Country spreads before her gaze. She sees the brilliant blue-and-white reflections of sky and clouds below in the Beaufort River. The mix of green and rusty-golden marsh grass on the shores of Ladies Island to the east. Her nostrils inhale the tangy scent of tidal flats, oysters, blue crabs, game foxes. And something the locals call Frogmore stew, boiling in a nearby cookhouse. Shrimp, potatoes, corn on the cob, smoked sausage. Spiced with sea salt, mustard seeds, black peppercorns, red pepper flakes, celery seed, dried chives, oregano, ginger, bay leaves.

"Sometimes I just plain forget about the war," she says to Minty. Nearly adds that she almost forgets at times now about her Raffy, too.

But she thinks better of it, considering her present company around whom the name *Semmes* must not be mentioned. Considering, too, the promise she made to him last year. And makes again every day in the letters she writes to her seahawk in secret. Nothing could destroy this love I feel for you. . . . Every day I hold you to my breast and kiss you in my mind, my heart, my soul. It seems odd to her how she makes these promises even now, even though the last five months of living with Minty among black refugees has brought on her a complete change of heart about this civil war. The Irish lass who was once one of Rose Greenhow's Southern spies in Washington, a confidante of the First Lady of the South, Varina Anne Banks Howell Davis, a Confederate nurse in Richmond. She has come to hate the war and the institution of slavery that provoked it.

"I could sit here all day long . . . just rocking my babies."

"I don't have that luxury, Missy," says Harriet Tubman. "And, truth be told, neither does you."

"You need me down at the church, then?"

She means the Baptist Church on King Street whose cookhouse Minty uses to make food for the hundreds of black refugees who have come to town since the Federals wrenched the Low Country from the Rebs in the Battle of Port Royal fourteen months ago. They are former slaves whom Minty and Maude—with the encouragement and support of the Massachusetts Anti-Slavery Society—have come to help get on their feet. The two women are here with about twenty white nurses, teachers, and a doctor from Boston. They call themselves *evangels, Gideon's Band, Gideonites.* The white evangels live here in this mansion, the Oaks, that the Yanks confiscated from a rich Southern patriot. Harriet Tubman has her own place near the church she calls Savan House.

"It's time already to get started?" Maude rises from the rocker, adjusts the babies in the African-style slings she wears on her shoulders.

"That's why I come up here."

Maude feels her children slipping off to sleep, drunk on mother's milk.

"What do we have to do?"

"We got to make more of that stew and about fifty pies."

"Then what?"

"Only Jesus know for sure."

***

What she likes best about baking these apple pies, besides the scent of stewing freshly cut apples and the rhythmic rolling out of the dough into crusts, is the company of other women and the singing. Minty and the seven other women who prepare the food, all black, sing as they work. Songs about swinging chariots, about following the drinking gourd, about the promised land, about the gospel train, about Moses. She particularly likes singing the one called, "Michael, Row the Boat Ashore."

When she sings it, she feels hope that someday she will not be torn between two worlds. The white cavalier's world, Raphael Semmes's world. And Harriet Tubman's world. When the song of Michael rises in her throat she has hope that her Raffy will be coming ashore for her. That he will leave his wife. That he will accept Fiona, this daughter. The baby she conceived with the French diplomat who helped her escape Washington, escape the wrath of the Federal detective.

Major Allen would have most likely killed her in Washington for trying to blackmail Secretary Welles, trying to stop his hunt for the seahawk. When Allen caught up with her a year later in Maryland, where she had come to tend to the Confederate wounded after the battle at Antietam Creek, he beat her and her Irish friend Fiona to within a hair of their lives. Then he sent them off to prison up north.

On the train to prison, Fiona admitted to Maude that when Allen caught her she had been carrying a coded message for Southern partisans, a page torn from Shakespeare's *Julius Caesar*. Her contact was to be someone named John Surratt and a person known only as J.W.B. It was shortly after this admission that Fiona lost her life in a shootout, trying to escape the blue coat guards on the train to jail. She gave her life so that Maude might flee, might mother the new life growing in her belly, the baby who bears her name.

At moments like this in the cookhouse—when her song joins the other women's—she can imagine that a time will come when all the blacks are free. When this most hateful war is over, when people in both the North and South will affirm that all men are created equal. Then . . . then, Lord willing, her Raffy—her lover of liberty—will see that no one is free when some are denied dignity. Then the seahawk will find a place in his heart for this chocolate son Leviticus she has adopted. The babe she took to her breast when his mother drowned crossing the Delaware River last fall, died escaping slavery *and* Union soldiers.

But the river is deep and the river is wide. . . .

And the singing has stopped. There's an immense black man blocking the doorway to the cookhouse. Seven or eight other men standing behind him.

"Can y'all finish up here?" Minty's forehead wrinkles as she looks at the men, speaks to the other women cooks.

"What's going on?" Maude stops rolling out her circle of dough.

"I gots to go." Tubman's voice has an urgent, shrill note.

"With these men? Where?"

"You don't wanna know."

***

When the woman whom many blacks and whites call Moses has vanished from the cookhouse, Maude asks, "Who were those men?"

"That Walter Plowden and his scouts."

"Scouts?"

"They working for the army."

"Scouting what?"

"All those nooks and crannies up on the Combahee River."

"For what?"

A large black woman shrugs. "Maybe something big coming."

"A fight, a battle?"

"Could be."

"What's Minty got to do with that?"

"Don't you know, gal?"

"What?"

"Minty the big tomato."

"What?"

"She a regular soldier . . . and the chief spy."

Oh no, not again.

4

SANTO DOMINGO
Early February, 1863

This city's gone mad, thinks Semmes. The Dominican Carnival's in full rush. The pounding, pulsing beat of a thousand drums. The blaring call-and-response of five hundred horns.

Every street is full of costumed giants, humans plumed as tropical birds. Silvery specters in loincloths, devils with twisting horns. Dark women in red greasepaint, haltered breasts, loose dresses, dancing. Hips rocking. Soft flesh swaying. All of it moving in waves through the streets. The late-afternoon air smells of burnt sugar, coconut, frying pork rinds, *mofongo* stew. Everywhere the clatter of feet tapping out syncopated rhythms. The scent of *sofrito*, that unforgettable saucy blend of thyme, salt, mashed garlic, parsley, diced onion, green pepper, cilantro, tomatoes, tomato paste, vinegar.

He should have known, he tells himself. Maybe did know, deep in his soul, that if today he walked down a byway called Calle Las Damas—Street of Women—he was inviting trouble.

Now, he has surely found it.

He told his officers that *Alabama* was stopping in Santo Domingo to discharge the crews off their last two prizes. But the truth is more complicated and not fully visible to his mind. Something within has driven him here. And something has been calling him to come ashore alone. Earlier today he prayed for wisdom and peace in the Cathedral of Santa Maria. He considered the fleeting glory of world conquest that he witnessed at the crumbling palace that once belonged to Diego Colón, son of the great Columbus. And he prayed again. For humility, strength, perspective. But his spirit remains as riotous as the crowds. As dissonant and stinging as the music echoing in these narrow streets. He has a strange sense that God or—more like—the Devil has commanded that he be here. At this precise place, at this time . . . standing before this magnificent woman.

She's a dark-skinned mulatto, just ten-or-so years into womanhood. Maude's age. With broad, bare shoulders. The body of a siren. Shadows of long legs, well-muscled arms, slender waist, breasts showing through a gauzy white dress. Black eyes. Long, straight black hair. Fine features. A golden headband with three hawk feathers like the spikes on a crown. She has silver and gold lines painted on her high cheeks, forehead, chin. Indian war paint. Ruby lips. Perfect gleaming teeth.

The charmer is standing in the doorway of an ancient stone building of several stories. Looking at him askance, an eyebrow cocked. Arms just now folding across her chest as if she's enjoying a moment of satisfaction or triumph. There are iron balconies with their potted flowers overhead.

"*Mon Capitaine*, I've been waiting for you," she says in her Haitian Creole accent, her lips curling into the sweetest smile. "Watching . . . for the pirate king."

Lord God in Heaven, have mercy on my soul. "What do you want of me?"

"Save you life maybe."

***

"There a black cloud hanging over your ship, *Capitaine*."

She has drawn him into the stone building, closed the heavy wooden door behind her, led him into a small courtyard.

"What do you mean?"

"You want to live or die, *mon corsaire*?"

He looks around. Does not know what he was expecting before he stepped through the portal. A Jezebel den most like, given the look of this brash Haitian transplant to Santo Domingo. Certainly he wasn't expecting anything like what's taking shape before his eyes. This is surely what the blacks in New Orleans call a Hoodoo House.

God damn.

Evening's coming on. The shadows have grown thick here in the dirt courtyard, which is lit by a hundred candles. There's a thick pole in the center of the courtyard with a helix of snakes carved along its shaft. A crude model of a ship, baskets, calabashes hang from beams that support the upper floors of the building. In one corner of the courtyard he sees a caged chicken, an old cutlass. Stone dishes full of seeds, herbs, pastes. The sounds of drums and horns make a low, distant song beyond the walls, the door.

"What the hell . . . ?"

The woman gives him a sly smile, cocks her eye at him again. "I here to help you, but . . . but you ain't got lots of time, *Capitaine*."

"I don't understand how you . . ."

"I seen your ship come to harbor this morning. Seen the strange flag. Seen the blackness boiling all around it. Smelled the death."

"Who are you?"

"People dem here calls me Mam'bo Mona."

He tugs at the tip of his mustache. "You some kind of Hoodoo gal?"

"I talks to the saints dem, the *orisha*."

"And now, let me guess. You want to use sea shells or pieces of coconut or some such things to tell my fortune . . . for a price?"

"The saints dem always want their due, *Capitaine*. We can't deny when they ask."

"I'm a Christian, a white man . . . and I was hardly born yesterday. So . . . if you will kindly excuse me, my dear, I will be finding my way out." He spins on his heel, starts for the door.

"She a very pretty woman."

"What did you say?"

"I said 'very pretty woman.' She the one done sent you to me."

Something has started melting at the base of his brain, seeping into his throat. Hot, syrupy.

"What woman?"

She smiles. "The saints dem done told me when I ask dem 'bout that terrible dark cloud over your ship. Very pretty woman. Young like me. She white. White as a ghost."

"Maude?"

"She your lady, ain't she?"

His brain's boiling over, his throat's scalding.

"Got a baby. Maybe two. Running from the law . . . just like you?"

Jesus Lord of Mercy. He just stares at this Hoodoo vixen, this Mam'bo Mona. *How? How does she know?*

"She be writing you every day, trying to tell you something."

"Tell me what?"

"You gots to get clean. The *orisha* dem say you never sees her again 'less you cast off that black cloud."

Mam'bo Mona says that dead spirits stuck between the world of the living and the dead have laid claim to his soul. He must be cleansed by Erzulie, the goddess of the sea and moon.

"Drowned men," she says.

He sees the *Somers* awash in foaming seas. Men trying to cling to anything in the wreckage that will keep them afloat.

The air filling with the shouts of swimmers, calling the names of their shipmates for comfort. Begging their God for mercy. Cursing the navy and the captain as whoreson floggers. The ship a cold-hearted sea bitch. Goddamn the ship.

More than thirty men lost.

"What am I supposed to do?"

"Give me four dollars . . . and take off your clothes."

***

He has shed his uniform, washed himself thoroughly from a barrel of rain water, doused himself with jasmine perfume. Wears only the shorts of his small clothes. This may well be the craziest, most irrational thing he has ever done . . . *but, Jesus the Redeemer, she invokes Maude, speaks of dead spirits?* And if ever there were a man who lives with ghosts, he's . . .

"Now what?"

She tells him to lie down on a hemp mat, ties a white cloth under his chin and up over the top of his head as if he were a dead man. She tells him to close his eyes, adjusts his arms at his sides, palms up. Then she begins to sprinkle ashes over his entire body, chanting in a language that does not sound like Creole. African maybe. A light rain has begun to fall. The courtyard reeks of incense, feels suddenly black. Searing hot.

The next thing he knows, the woman is sprinkling a mix of grain and burnt peanuts over him. Releasing the chicken from the cage, she waves it over him three times . . . then lowers it to his chest where it pecks at the food.

As the chicken pecks around his neck and face, he feels its talons scratching his chest. He arches his back, tries to rise off the mat, but she holds him down with a hand pressing at his throat. He moans involuntarily through clamped jaws. His eyes pop open, dart madly around. Blinded by the prickly light of candles.

"The dark spirits fight." Her voice is low, tense.

She snatches up the chicken, launches into a chorus of moans as she waves the cutlass in fast circles right above every part of his body. Holds him down, one hand still on his throat. He feels his arms, legs twitching.

"Mama Erzulie." Her lips are right next to his ear.

She takes the cutlass with both hands, raises it over her head like an ax as if to hack him to pieces.

"No!" His voice shouts through the clenched teeth of his bound jaw.

But she swings the cutlass.

There's a flash of white cloth. He bellows, springs upright . . . as the cutlass slices across the top of his head. The bow of the chinstrap ripping wide apart, dangling from the side of his face. . . .

The woman plunges face down in the rain, the mud.

"*Finis.*" Her breath's panting. "Devils gone."

"What about Maude? What about my ship?"

"How many miracles you expecting for four dollars?" She's rolling on her side in the mud, hugging her belly as if she, too, has been purged.

He stands up. Tries to scrape off the rain-damp ashes, grain, burnt peanuts from his shoulders, chest, belly. Feels a pox of welts where the chicken scratched and pecked him, tore hairs from his chest.

I can't ever tell anybody this happened, he thinks.

5

DISTRICT OF COLUMBIA
Early March, 1863

"So . . . Semmes has been in Jamaica of late," says Secretary of State William Seward. A smug smile on his thin lips. "Landed the captured crew of the *Hatteras* . . . and disappeared again."

"Why am I the last to know these things?" asks Gideon Welles. He feels a sudden loss of pressure behind his eyes.

"That's what we want to know," says the secretary of war.

"When are you going to catch that pirate?" Ed Bates, the attorney general, glares across the table. "When?"

Another Tuesday morning cabinet meeting is about to begin . . . as soon as the president arrives. And already, things are starting to go to hell for the secretary of the navy. The same old accusations, questions. These demon colleagues seated around the cabinet table give him no quarter. They taunt him with their looks, their news, like this latest from Jamaica that comes to Seward through his consuls, his personal spy channels. News the secretary of state likes to drop like explosive shells into conversation to demonstrate his preeminence. Then the other secretaries turn on Welles as if to make him feel that he's indeed the incompetent St. Nick, the Old Man of the Sea, portrayed nearly weekly in newspaper cartoons across the Union.

He wonders what they would do if they were he . . . or if they knew how his day had started? *Or do they know? At least one of them? About the latest threat?* Is someone right in this room, or some cabal, even now numbering his days? How much time does he have? How much time does Lincoln have?

"My sources think Semmes was heading for Santo Domingo . . . or San Juan," says Seward.

"Where's that damn Wilkes and his Flying Squadron?" Bates wants to know.

Just the mention of Wilkes makes Welles cringe. Makes him think again about the letter in the red envelope that he found on his doorstep this morning. Makes him think of treason. Wilkes is allegedly in Puerto Rico right now. Probably right along Semmes's cruising path, but the bugger will never catch Semmes. This is all but certain. Wilkes would rather make a show with foreign dignitaries and line his pockets with prize money by seizing blockade runners. And maybe he has darker reasons for missing Semmes. Major Allen has been investigating again. Says Wilkes comes from an old clan of headstrong, fantasy-ridden English radicals. A journalist and political intriguer of a hundred years ago, John Wilkes, a prime example.

"I'm thinking I should recall Wilkes," says Welles.

"Did not Wilkes crow to all the world that he was the man to bag Semmes?" Lincoln has slipped into the room while everyone has been ganging up on Welles. The cabinet members scramble to their feet mumbling, "Good morning, Mr. President."

The president unknots the black bowtie at his throat. Yanks it free, lays it on the table. Sighs before taking his chair at the head of the table. Once seated, the tall man shakes his head as if to clear his mind after being harangued for the last hour by special interests trying to curry favor.

"Well, Gideon. What about Wilkes. Has he failed us?" Lincoln again. "Is that what you are trying to tell us?"

Welles takes a deep breath, feels his scalp sweating beneath his toupee.

Moans rise from the other cabinet members.

Lincoln's eyes flare. "My God, man. Then replace Wilkes, yes? But send somebody competent after Semmes. The country will not wait forever for us to put an end to the devastations of that madman. Do you comprehend that?"

Everyone in the room knows what Lincoln is talking about. Since the army's defeat at Fredericksburg, the Copperheads have been extremely vocal in calling for an end to the war. Presidential elections are just eighteen months away and even the Republicans are making noises about not renominating Lincoln.

Meanwhile, Captain DuPont hovers outside Charleston Harbor with his fleet of new ironclads . . . finding reasons not to attack the Rebs. The South is gaining strength in coastal Carolina again and in Florida. Lee's gathering his Army of Virginia for what will no doubt be hellish attacks as soon as mud season ends this spring. And the Rebs are building faster, sleeker blockade runners in Europe, more raiders like the *Alabama* and the *Florida*. Monstrous ironclad rams are taking shape in Liverpool. Unless the men in this room can find a way to turn the tide against the South very soon, they will all be out of power . . . and the South will likely be free to go its own slave-keeping way.

"How are we going to get some action soon in nailing Semmes?" Lincoln's voice is suddenly low, quiet. The very signature of his anger and impatience.

Seward clears his throat. "As I have been proposing for some months, Mr. President, I believe the time has come for us to issue letters of marque and arm a fleet of privateers to chase the likes of Semmes. The navy seems unpre . . . er . . . most needed in our coastal and river campaigns."

Welles purses his lips, stares at his clasped hands on the walnut table. He is sick of Seward and the others trying to tell him what the navy can and cannot do. He's especially sick of trying to argue against this proposal to arm privateers. It's just such an obvious plan for Seward, Stanton, and Ed Bates to parcel out patronage to their ship-owning friends in New York and New England. Undisciplined privateers would no doubt start a war with England by hounding English merchantmen, seizing every ship that might be attempting to run the blockade, in order to line their own Puritan pockets with prize money. *It's a bad idea. Keeping the reins tight on an officer like Charlie Wilkes is hard enough, imagine if there were hundreds of such independent buggers.*

But this is not the time, the place, the company for a rebuttal to Seward. Welles can't win in this arena. Won't take up the gauntlet. . . .

Nor will he explain even the slightest thing about his gamble with Winslow. He would rather endure the anger of his president, the contempt of his fellow secretaries, than unfold his actual plan for Winslow here, today. Someone might use it for personal gain or leak his plan accidentally or on purpose to the English and the South. Even Winslow doesn't know what Welles has in store for him. And the secretary has another private stratagem brewing as well. This one to stop the Rebel ironclad rams in Liverpool before they put to sea. It has taken him more than two years to learn this job, but now he sees that his navy works best, is safest, when it sails in darkness, when the world thinks him the fool. Expects nothing from him.

So . . . for the moment, let it be. Some information is for the president only, maybe not even the president until the time is right. He must wait until discussion has turned away from him and Semmes to other matters. Then he can slip the tiny note cupped in his hand to Lincoln who sits next to him. Just two words. He wrote them this morning after reading the threat in the red envelope. *Iago's back.*

6

FAIAL, AZORES
Early March, 1863

Winslow stands just within the iron gates of the hilltop mansion, trying to catch his breath from the ascent. Trying to shake the dizziness, the chills, the gushing sweat on his face. His malaria has returned. He should be in bed, but he has been sent for.

"Is it true?" His eyes dart between the vista—the red roofs of Horta, the harbor, the sea, the snow-capped volcano of Ilha Pico glowing in the afternoon sun—and the two men facing him with muskets.

"That blackguard Semmes is back," says the older armed man.

He's portly, mid- to late sixties. Prosperous-looking in his tweed knickers and jacket. Charles Dabney's the American consul on the island and Faial's most important businessman and benefactor. The second generation of Dabneys to fill this post. The trim rake-hell next to him is his son Sam. The men are Boston Brahmins to be sure, but their family has increased its fortune a hundredfold since setting up a trading business on Faial early in the century.

Once they exported oranges, pineapples, and Pico wine to America. For the last twenty years they have made Horta a major whaling station and the setting for their luxurious townhomes like Fredonia, The Cedars. And this villa they call Bagatelle. Their storehouses sit on the isthmus connecting Monte Queimado and Monte Guia at Porto Pim.

No Yankee family has felt the sting of Raphael Semmes more than the Dabneys. Semmes has turned their fortunes upside down since he seized and burned a score of whalers here in the Azores last September.

"Some fishermen say they saw the *Alabama* west of Ilha Flores three days ago." Sam Dabney turns downwind and spits tobacco juice.

"You're arming?" Winslow's chest is still heaving, face still leaking perspiration as he looks at the Dabneys' weapons.

"We've been hunting grouse . . . and waiting for you to turn up, Captain," says the older man. "Why don't we walk up to the house . . . and have a little port."

Winslow wipes sweat from his brow.

The younger Dabney shoots him a wily smile. "How would you like to squash that infernal pirate right here? Maybe as soon as tomorrow?"

***

"I'm offering you my ship, the bark *Azor*, Captain." Charles Dabney pours beakers of ruby port for Winslow, himself, his son as they stand at the sideboard in the parlor looking out on the pale sea.

The younger Dabney has now tossed off his hunting jacket, is rolling his shoulders as if to work out some kinks. He says that the last time Semmes passed through the Azores they refused to sell him coal and, in turn, he threatened to burn any ship that might even hint at being owned or associated with the Dabneys.

"This two-bit pirate does not know what he's up against if he thinks he can threaten me, wreck my business and get away with it," says the Dabney patriarch.

"We want his hide, Captain. Why wait for your ship? We will give you one today," the younger Dabney adds.

"With guns and shells and powder and a seasoned crew."

Winslow pictures the *Azor*. She's a fit ship alright. But she's like hundreds of trading and whaling barks sailing the seas. Heavy, sluggish, small by naval standards. A leftover from the age of sail. Not a warship.

"With all due respect, gentlemen . . . and gratitude for your offer. I do not think the law . . ."

Streaks of red are rising in the older Dabney's neck. "I have it in a dispatch from the secretary of state that by now Washington is issuing letters of marque to private vessels. As an agent of the government, I believe I can issue a letter to the *Azor.*"

"Be that as it may . . . a man cannot go against the likes of a heavily armed, modern steamer like the *Alabama* in a sailing vessel."

"No one is asking you to go yardarm-to-yardarm with that monster, man."

"Then I guess I don't understand. How . . . ?"

That crafty smile from Sam Dabney again. "You go out there disguised as a fat and happy whaler. A decoy."

"You send up a smoke plume from your try-works that Semmes can see and smell at forty miles. You fly the Stars and Stripes with pride."

"And when he comes for you, you play dead, close alongside him."

"You let him send over his boarding party," Charles Dabney's face is now flush with enthusiasm. "Then you and your men seize them. Hold them hostage. Semmes won't fire on his own men."

"But then what?"

"You say you want to negotiate."

"He will never yield."

"But he's proud. Arrogant and angry. He will stand his deck. He will make a spectacle of himself on the flying bridge of that hell ship. With his first mate and his officers."

"So . . . ?"

"So then some of my best Portagee huntsmen whom you've hidden in your tops with their long rifles will shoot Semmes and every other officer on deck."

Winslow feels the pain in his bad eye swelling, the vision going from blurry to black. *Or is it red.* He imagines his old friend and the other officers ambushed in a shower of blood.

"The *Alabama*'s crewed by mercenaries. You decapitate their leadership, they'll surrender faster than you can say, 'Blessed be the Lord.'"

"I . . . I don't know what to . . ." Winslow searches for words.

How can he tell the U.S. consul, the most powerful man in these islands, that this is not how he fights. Not how a proper navy man goes into battle. Killing by subterfuge and ambush. Murdering like a coward. Without giving his opponent a chance to defend himself. This stratagem defies the very traditions of military conduct, not to say the laws of God.

The younger Dabney sets down his port, squints at Winslow. "Are you trying to tell us you won't go, Captain?"

His ruined eye burns in its socket. "Yes, sir. I will. I'll hunt Raphael Semmes to the ends of the earth when my ship the *Kearsarge* gets here. . . . But no, I will not go, not now."

The Dabneys look at him with slack jaws as if they cannot believe what they've just heard, as if he's mad. "Why?"

Winslow says he will not take a noncommissioned ship and an irregular crew into combat. It would exceed his orders from Secretary Welles. He's not a privateer. He's an officer of the line. And besides . . . the fishermen who claim to have seen the *Alabama* near Flores are surely wrong. They have seen something else, possibly a blockade runner, not Semmes. The raider has no reason to come here in March. He would be wasting his time. He cannot buy coal, and there are no American ships to burn. This is the season of northeast gales in the Atlantic, the slow time for trans-Atlantic crossings. The whales and whalers do not arrive until the end of the summer.

If Semmes returns it will be then. For now, the *Alabama*'s hunting elsewhere.

"No, kind sirs. I thank you . . . but I do not want your ship."

Charles Dabney slams his half-full beaker of port down on the sideboard. Wine splashes. "I thought you were an officer and a gentleman, man!"

Winslow takes a deep breath, "That's exactly what I aim to be, sir."

He does not say what he feels in his heart. That he will not be party to treachery. He will not murder his brother. Not for the Dabneys, not for Gideon Welles, not for Abe Lincoln. Not for any man.

But, Lord willing, I will find him. And stop him.

7

ST. JOHNS RIVER, FLORIDA
March 10–11, 1863

"Please . . . hush that baby, Madame." Colonel Thomas Wentworth Higginson squats down before Maude, his voice a whisper. "We go to war."

She hears the creaking of the leather of his riding boots as he bends to eye level, stirs from her bed of quilts on the moonlit deck of the transport *John Adams*. Eyes the handsome man with a full, dark beard who commands this expedition of five ships, 900 soldiers, steaming upriver to seize Jacksonville from the Rebs.

The splash of the ship's side wheels and the songs of birds on the riverbanks making an eerie nocturne. It's not yet daybreak, but Fiona's fussing. Not bawling, but whimpering loud enough that Reb sentries ashore could hear. Maude gathers her daughter up from the crib made of an ammunition box, hugs her to her chest. Rocks the five-month-old infant, while baby Leviticus snores softly in his own crate.

"I'm sorry, Colonel. I believe my baby girl feels the battle coming." *Maybe feeling my fear of what's coming, too.*

The officer puts the back of his hand against the baby's cheek, strokes. Fiona's cries stop.

"We go into the jaws of death for our children. Is it not so?" he asks.

She nods. There was a time not long ago—all those months last fall—when she was pregnant and running from anything that even hinted of war. But Minty Tubman says you can't hide from death, injustice, war. Can't run from it, either. You must rise up and take arms against a sea of troubles. Maybe. She tells herself she has to be more like Minty, more like her dead friend Fiona for whom she named the baby girl. Less like her onetime friend in Richmond, Varina Howell Davis, who tried to shield her eyes from misery and human folly. If Maude does not rise up against this monstrous war, she knows there will be little chance of ever getting her Raffy back. That's why she's here. For all the Raffys . . . and their children. On both sides of the conflict, and those caught in the middle. But courage is a sore-won thing.

Maude's traveling with five other Gideonite women. Two white, three black, including Minty. Nurses to help Dr. Seth Rogers with the wounded. Higginson has organized and trained freed slaves in Port Royal and Beaufort during the last few months to be the first two black regiments of Federal troops, the First and Second South Carolina Volunteers. Now their expedition's sailing up the St. Johns River to seize Jacksonville from the Rebs.

She looks up from kissing the baby's forehead at the colonel, feels fidgety herself. Maybe she should wake Leviticus, too, for nursing. "How much longer until we disembark?"

"It depends," he says, staring upriver at the dark shapes of two naval picket ships leading the way. Six more miles to Jacksonville. "There's like to be trouble ahead."

***

She hears the crack of musket fire ashore to the west, the soft thunder of hundreds of galloping horses, the shrill yodeling that must be the legendary "Rebel yell." Knows that the battle for the city has begun.

"It's time," says Minty Tubman, "Dr. Rogers gone need us nurses directly."

The *John Adams* has been tied at Jacksonville's upper wharf since yesterday morning. Higginson's troops seized the town without a gunshot. Five hundred locals welcomed the bluecoats. There has not even been a hint of war . . . until minutes ago. But already the gray mist of gun smoke and the stench of sulfur hangs heavy in the mid-morning heat.

Maude feels a nervous twitching in her arms, legs. She splashes water on her face and hands from an open butt on the ship's deck to calm herself. Kisses her children sleeping in their crates in the shade of the awning on the boiler deck, leaves them in the care of a young black woman. As she turns away, she makes the sign of the cross on her chest, asks the Holy Mother for a stout heart.

"We gots to go." Minty has already started down the gangplank to the wharf where the doctor and three other nurses wait with canteens slung over their shoulders and carpetbags full of medicines, field dressings, surgeon's tools.

By the time they reach the burned-out depot of the Florida, Atlantic & Gulf Central Railroad on the western edge of town, Maude's heart is raging against her ribs. The gun smoke's so thick she has to cover her nose with a wet kerchief to breathe.

A young white officer appears out of the fog. "Get down! On your bellies."

At first, she doesn't understand the purpose of the command. Until she sees the man's hat knocked from his head in a flurry of blue felt. Then she realizes that the buzzing she has been hearing is not just the sound of the blood racing through her head. Musket balls are flying through the air.

She cannot tell how long she lies like this, trying to force her heart back down her throat, stop the throbbing in her head. Long enough to see a shadowy line of black soldiers surging forward past the depot, firing their weapons. Long enough to hear another ghostly chorus of the Rebel yell, smell the fear of a hundred men driven back almost to these railroad tracks again. Long enough to hear the pounding of cannons from the navy's picket ships and the field cannons set up on the *John Adams*. . . . Long enough to see an officer with a sword in one hand and a pistol in the other encourage his young recruits to move forward again into the fray. Long enough to fear that if this shooting goes on for much longer she may get up and run.

And out there in the cloud of battle these black soldiers are shouting at the Rebels—horrible things, vicious things—as they're firing their guns, reloading, firing again. Never before has she understood the hatred that lies at the bottom of this war for the blacks, never fully understood what violence slavery has bred. Never truly known how misguided, how wrong her dear Raffy is to fight for the other side. She's wondering how it is still possible for her to love him as she does . . . when Minty pokes her in the ribs.

"Let's go."

She truly hopes she's being rescued.

***

This is not like the battlefield she remembers on the edge of Antietam Creek when she had gone there as a nurse for the other side early last fall. There are no meadows spread with the bodies of dead boys. No stench of death. Only the oppressive Florida sun, the slowly clearing smoke, the humming of cicadas in nearby woods. The strange smell of a million plants in their cycle of growth and decay.

The shooting has stopped.

At the base of a shade tree, Dr. Rogers and two other nurses are tending to a burly young private with a musket ball buried deep in his right shoulder. She's standing there, wondering what she can do, when a soldier grabs her by the wrist.

"There be a fellow down on the tracks yonder." His mouth yawns as if to vomit. Tears are running down his dirt-stained cheeks. "He hurt some bad."

Before she can think, her legs are churning. Running like they have wanted to run for hours. As if they know where she must go before her eyes or her head can tell her.

She fully expects to be headed back to the ship and her babies. But instead she's face-to-face with a wounded soldier. He's lying between the steel rails on the wooden crossties shrieking. Howling. His pants are soaked with more blood than she has ever seen before, and he's pressing his hands between his legs trying to stop the flow.

But it keeps spurting through a bullet hole in his pants, between his fingers.

His eyes seize on her. The pupils wide, starting to cloud. The whites of his eyes are not white at all, but yellow with tiny threads of red. She wants to turn away, run faster. Already knows how this will end. . . .

But she feels his agony, his helplessness. Doesn't want him to see her fear. So she returns his gaze, tries to think of daffodils and skylarks so that she won't just turn around and bolt.

"I'm dying," he says.

Something dark and hot and spiky is rising in her chest, her head's throbbing again. The urge to run surges through her . . . but she bites her tongue, tells herself she has a job here. Then she bends down to him, tearing the kerchief off her face. Presses it between the man's legs. Holds it on top of his hands with both of hers.

"What's your name, soldier?"

"Private Bristol Walker . . . Company A."

"The doctor's coming. Just close your eyes and rest." His blood's soaking the kerchief, her hands.

"I don't want to die." His voice is weakening, eyes still wide open—flicking in five directions.

The thing filling her chest, her throat, her head is starting to shred her. For some reason she pictures Raffy, pictures her babies . . . and knows there is only one thing to do to stop from crumbling into pieces. She puts her face alongside this black warrior's. Inhales his rich earthiness, smells the peanuts he must have been eating before the shooting started. Kisses his eyelids shut. Her hands still on his hands. The flies already swarming around them both.

"Tell my mama . . ." His voice is almost gone.

"Shssssh."

"I didn't run."

"Me either."

8

CSS ALABAMA

Late March, 1863

Near the equator. The ship's jogging into a northeast gale. For the fourth day in a row. There's a heavy, confused sea running, and the *Alabama* is pitching and rolling in a most unnatural way. Semmes has been more or less on watch for the last forty-eight hours. Now he has come to the sickbay to check with the doctor on the condition of the crew. He pushes wads of cotton up his nose so that he might no longer smell the stench of shite and vomit that has begun to permeate the ship, especially here in the sickbay where two-score men are lined up for ginger root and lemon drop candy to fight the demon in their bellies.

But the cotton in the nose is no use. Semmes lurches toward a slop jar. Heaves. He half misses his mark, but it hardly matters. The only thing he's been putting in his belly the last two days is water and a little stale bread. And now the water from his belly is just mixing with the water sloshing across the cabin sole. While the dry spasms continue.

Lord have mercy!

The ship, his bride, is a wreck. After months in the tropical sun, her deck planks and topsides have become so shrunken that she's leaking from everywhere except her bottom. And that's next. Because the dried-out condition of her English oak cannot be remedied until she gets to higher, moister latitudes. The creaking of timbers has risen to the level of a mad violin concerto as the ship works herself loose with each plunge, each roll. Each twisting of the hull, the springing of the masts.

If someone would have told him five days ago that he would encounter such a sustained gale here on the Line at this time of the year, he would have laughed in the fellow's face. Told him that the pilot charts say such a thing is nearly unheard of. The equator at this time of year, at forty degrees west longitude, should be a mill pond for easy sailing. Except for occasional thunder squalls building where the northern hemisphere's trade winds and the southern trade winds collide. And March is not a very active month for these squalls. This should be the perfect time and place to intercept all manner of Yanks on their way to and from South America and the Far East. Indeed, the hunting has been most excellent. Eleven of the enemy's merchant fleet either burned or released on bond since the *Alabama* left Santo Domingo.

But now the ship has come afoul of the Devil. Even Kell, a cast-iron luff if ever there was one, has been driven to his berth from exhaustion and the heaves. Only the youngest officers like Armstrong, Sinclair, the midshipmen—and the youngest Jacks—have been able to avoid the *mal de mer* so far and keep the ship jogging ahead safely. The doctor says more than two-thirds of the men, the officers, the prisoners off the prizes have been confined to their hammocks or berths. No one has to tell the captain that if the prisoners were to rally, they could overwhelm. . . .

"This is unbelievable," says Semmes. "The whole damn thing is unbelievable." *I will not lose my ship like this.*

"You need to drink some ginger tea with lemon, sir," the young British doctor David Llewellyn says. "And lie down for a spell."

"I don't have time, Captain. *Alabama* does not have time for this. We must . . ." A warm dizziness sweeps over him. His eyes blur. The last thing he sees is the black boy, David White—the captured slave who has become the ship's sickbay attendant and doctor's pet—reaching out to catch him as he falls.

***

At first, waking from a dream of nuzzling his Irish selkie, he thinks he's gone blind. But when he feels for his face with his right hand, he finds his forehead, his eyes covered with a cool, damp cloth.

"How goes the ship?" His voice is raw, almost a shout, as he pulls the cloth from his face.

He sits up, looks around. The scene before him is little more than spikes of light in a field of shadows. He no longer smells the vomit. Some other smell floods his senses. Oranges, lemons. As his vision begins to clear, he hears the creaking, feels the pitch and roll of the ship. Realizes that he's in his gimbaled berth, in the great cabin. With citrus-scented oil lamps burning.

"How you feeling now, Captain?" The black boy David is sitting next to him in a chair, fingering rosary beads.

"What the hell . . . ?"

"You had us some worried," says David. "I gots to tell the doctor you back with us now."

Semmes grabs the boy's hand. "Wait. How long have I been down?"

The slender teen, a youngster with skin the color of cocoa, bright eyes, and a bushy nest of hair, flashes a shy, white smile. "It the second dog watch. Night coming on."

The captain doesn't know why, but he continues holding the lad's hand. It's warm, smooth like a woman's. Like that strange woman who accosted him back in Santo Domingo.

The boy slides his rosary into the chest pocket of his white blouse, pulls out a harmonica. "You want me to dance for you now, Captain?"

Semmes lets go of the hand, shakes his head. No. *No damn dancing.* He thinks how David here has been the darling of the ship's first doctor, now paymaster, Pills Galt, since taken prisoner off the *Towanda* back in early October of last year. Galt has often promoted

David's dancing fandangos for the Jacks on the main deck during the hour of tobacco and grog before the night watch. The boy's relationship with Galt is one that Semmes has chosen not to scrutinize too closely for fear of what he might find. If he's being truthful with himself, he worries that Galt may have an unspeakable attraction for the boy. Llewellyn, too. Another kind and gentle soul. The doctors and their loyal attendant. Three peas in a pod. *Jesus Lord Almighty.*

But maybe he has been wrong in his suspicions. Maybe he has been judging these three based on what he has seen of ship surgeons and their minions over more than thirty-five years of going to sea. It's no secret that navy physicians are often a peculiar breed of lonely men with no family or women ashore. Yet Galt and Llewellyn are fine fellows—loyal, hardworking, skilled, full of wit. Brave, too.

Maybe they see something in this young David White that transcends his youth and pleasing body. Lord knows the ship has a fo'castle full of such young men. Maybe it's not David's youth or beauty that's his attraction. Maybe it's his blackness. The allure of the "other." Or something even more mysterious. Spiritual. *Maybe—strange thought—blacks are closer to God and the other world, the saints. Is this why I let myself be drawn into that devil's den by Mam'bo Mona on Calle Las Damas? Was I searching for something more than a clean shirt for my soul?*

***

He's staring with far-away eyes at the flame of the oil lamp swaying overhead, wondering how a man of his age could be beset with such strange thoughts, when the door to his cabin opens and in walks the doctor.

Llewellyn lurches across the rolling deck, bounces off the desk before he reaches Semmes's bedside. "You're up, Captain. How do you feel?"

"Embarrassed, young man."

The doctor takes his wrist. Feels for his pulse. Looks into Semmes's eyes with a magnifying glass. "You're still weak."

"Let me have some of your fine tea."

"Of course, sir . . . but I'm afraid you need more than that. You're exhausted. We all are."

"What are you saying?"

"We have barely enough men standing to sail the ship."

Semmes says that surely these gales will pass. They always do.

Llewellyn motions for David White to leave the cabin. "May I speak freely, Captain?"

"Have at it."

"Then I need to tell you what I think." He says that these gales are not the problem. It's the relentless pace *Alabama* has set for her crew.

"You think I'm driving the men too hard?"

"I think the demands of war weigh heavily on us. For half a year this ship and everyone in her has been hell-bent . . ."

"And now we're at the breaking point?"

"Few of us have been ashore for more than a couple days since we shipped. . . . If we are to continue to do our duty, we . . ." The ship lurches. Llewellyn nearly loses his balance.

"Sit," says Semmes. He nods to the corner of his bed. His eyes are getting blurry. "I need to ask you something."

"Yes, sir?"

"Do you think these gales are God's punishment for our hubris? My hubris?"

Llewellyn takes a deep breath. "Punishment? No, sir . . . but quite possibly a sign to us that we must temporarily cease this endless wandering. That *Alabama* must care for her children."

"And how does she do that?"

"We are all sore in need of land . . . for more than a day or two."

"Mr. Kell would never dare to tell me such a thing."

"He's not your doctor."

"But he knows that time and tide wait for no man."

"Nor health, nor love . . . nor death's dark self."

Semmes closes his eyes, feels his heart wavering. "Maybe I know a place."

9

DISTRICT OF COLUMBIA
Late March, 1863

"So . . . Iago's back, Mr. Secretary?"

At the sound of the voice, the sight of the small man on the chestnut mare, Gideon Welles reins in his gelding. He has been cantering downhill on a trail along Rock Creek, tuning himself to the animal beneath him, posting. Taking some daily exercise as his doctor has counseled him to do to improve his health. Breathing deeply. Feeling a bit like a boy again on this spring morning. Until he turned this corner in the trail to find Major E. J. Allen. The one-time cooper turned detective and presidential weasel.

"Mr. Lincoln sent me to talk to you."

"You've learned something about the red envelopes, the threats? About Iago?"

The full-bearded Scot purses his lips and shakes his head. "Nothing very concrete."

"Then why are you here? What do you want from me?"

"Do you remember last December when you told me that Secretary of State Seward confided to you that he, too, was getting threats in red envelopes?"

"Of course."

"Well, what if he was lying?"

"To protect himself?"

"Or maybe a friend."

"Who?"

"How well do you know Senator John P. Hale of New Hampshire?"

"He's the chair of the Committee on Naval Affairs . . . and a self-serving bastard."

"Exactly."

***

They are grazing their horses. A small patch of grass, sun-dappled. Creekside. Robins pecking at the ground for earthworms. Songbirds calling to each other.

"You think Hale's our Iago?" Welles feels a sudden shakiness in his arms.

"Probably not."

"Then why are you asking about him?"

"I'm not at liberty to tell you that."

"How can I help you, if you keep me in the dark?" Welles feels the old urge he has often had in the presence of this crusty little man, the compulsion to throttle him by the throat.

"Don't take this personally. This is a matter of national security, Welles . . . and you know as well as I that if this mysterious Iago is still at work, the president's life may be in danger."

The secretary takes three deep breaths, pretends to adjust the cinch on his mount's saddle to give himself time to regain his sense of civility, summon his sense of duty. "What do you want to know about Hale?"

"Do you think he has the best interest of the navy and the country in mind?"

Welles can't help but laugh. Says that since the day he first met Hale in early 1861, the man has been trying to advance the interest of his cronies at the expense of the government. He tried to get Welles to buy two absolute wrecks of ships for the navy from his friends. When Welles refused, Hale leaked stories to journalists about the secretary of the navy's do-nothing attitude. And during the last two years Hale has continued trying to influence naval contracting . . . always using the press to bring heat on Welles, raise cries for his resignation.

"The secretary of state thinks a lot of Hale."

"Is Hale behind Seward's sudden interest in promoting this plan that we issue letters of marque to civilian seafarers? Is this another way for Hale to line the pockets of his constituents?"

Allen says that just like the president, Hale's up for re-election in '64. And he's not all that popular back in New Hampshire.

"You're saying Hale's a desperate man? Desperate men do desperate things."

"I'm saying you may want to find ways to shield sensitive plans in your office from Hale."

"Not to worry," says Welles. He has rarely felt such a dislike for a person as he feels for Hale. *Well, except Bill Seward and Ed Bates.*

"But I do worry," says Allen. "You think you have your secrets, your private plans known only to you and Mr. Lincoln. But they are not so bloody secret."

Welles squints. "What are you talking about?"

"I know you are sending John Murray Forbes of Massachusetts and another fellow to England on a covert assignment. You want them to try buying the ironclad rams that the Laird's are building in Liverpool for the Rebs. You hope to win this naval duel with the South by outspending them."

"Where? How did you . . . ?" Welles is astonished. This plan has been one of his most secret initiatives.

"You know I can't tell you that."

Bastard.

"But I can tell you that Seward knows . . . as do his agents overseas. Probably the English government knows, too."

"And the secretary of state's letting me think the plan's still a secret?"

"Until the moment it could be to his advantage to expose your little gambit."

"He's setting me up for failure."

"It appears he could be, indeed."

Welles thinks on his other most private plans. "Does Seward know about the *Kearsarge*? About John Winslow?"

"What's the *Kearsarge*? Who's Winslow?"

The secretary feels the shakiness in his hands vanish, the tables turn. *Checkmate, you smug little weasel.* "I can't tell you that."

Allen shoots him a dark look, kicks a piece of horse dung into the creek. "Let me remind you, again, that I'm not here to save you from threats in red envelopes. I'm trying to protect the president."

"Then don't play games with me, Major."

"I have no time for games."

"Nor I," says Welles. "Corruption and influence peddling are not treason. What do you know about Hale that you're not telling me?"

"Tell me about Winslow and the *Kearsarge* first."

"Do you think I'm a fool?"

"Let me ask you one thing then."

"What?"

"Do you know who Charles Wilkes went to visit the night that you refused to promote him to rear admiral?"

"The president."

"Wrong. Seward . . . and Hale."

"Then he got his promotion, his Flying Squadron. Has done nothing to catch Rafael Semmes since."

"Are you starting to get the picture?"

Welles most surely is. He's truly hoping the secret message he sent to Winslow in the Azores has finally reached its man.

10

FAIAL, AZORES
Late March, 1863

Winslow's skin feels on fire. He has been on the half-moon beach at Praia de Porto Pim for so long today that sun and salt air have cured his hide to the texture and color of the sand speckled over his bare feet.

It's his fifth day in a row working on this project. The fifth day since the cryptic note from Welles arrived by merchant ship in a small crate of medicaments for him. The note was tucked in a small ointment jar labeled Gideon's Eye Salve. There was a quote from the book of Matthew about the First Temptation of Christ.

Man shall not live on bread alone,
but on every word that proceeds from the mouth of God.

This followed by four words of Welles's own design.

Despair not. Manna cometh.

The message here would be lost on most readers. That is, of course, the secretary of the navy's intent. But Welles knows Winslow is a devout Christian and lay preacher given to holding shipboard services for his men. Knows Winslow will see the significance of his quote as it relates to his present circumstances here at Faial. After Jesus' baptism, his rebirth so to speak, God sent him to endure a retreat in the wilderness to find himself and to twice be tempted by Satan. The Devil's first temptation was to ask the starving Jesus to prove he was the son of God by magically producing bread so that he might not go hungry. But the Savior had recognized how the Devil was playing on his insecurities, loneliness, hunger . . . and responded with the quote that appears in the Book of Matthew.

Winslow's detachment from the Mississippi Campaign and orders to proceed overseas to take command of the *Kearsarge* has been nothing less than an enforced rebirth for him as an officer. His exile here on Faial like Jesus' forty days in the wilderness. A test of will, of loyalty, of strength, of faith. The message is clear. Welles aims to temper him with adversity. Aims to forge him into another lone wolf like Semmes. Aims for him to be a savior of sorts, to undertake nothing less than a holy pilgrimage, to die for the Federal cause and the glory of God, if necessary, when *manna*—his ship—comes at last. He must drive the infidel from the temple. Raphael Semmes is the infidel, the temple the deep blue sea.

He grits his teeth when he considers the implications of extending the parallels between his exile and Christ's. So . . . God is Welles. Satan would be Charles Dabney. *Scary thoughts.* Scarier, still, the idea that this exile in the Azores is nothing in comparison to what is to come.

So he's preparing. Really preparing. Hoping that when Welles chooses to call the *Kearsarge manna,* he picked his words carefully. He means that this ship will be a gift from God, a sustaining food. A thing that can be more than it seems.

For the last six hours he has been drawing a chart of the Gulf of Mexico, the Caribbean Sea, the Atlantic, the Indian Ocean by dragging his left foot in the sand. He has repeated this task each of the last five days. Taking stock of the world, so to speak. The scale of his chart: One stride equals ten degrees of latitude. Six hundred nautical miles. Three days of sailing more or less. Today, for the last two hours, he's been pushing shoe-size pieces of driftwood around his oceans. One for the *Alabama.* One for the *Kearsarge.*

As far as Winslow knows, Semmes's last known position put him off Galveston on January 12 of this year. From this point Winslow can guess where the *Alabama* is by now. Given the prevailing winds and weather in these wintery months, Semmes has surely charted a course south and east through the Caribbean toward the equator. No doubt the *Alabama* is trying to ride the trade winds, hunting under sail. Conserving her precious coal. And searching for a new place to re-coal now that Semmes has been nearly caught twice by Federal vessels at Martinique.

He has to know that Charles Wilkes's squadron will be looking for him in the eastern Caribbean and on the old Spanish Main. So he must be heading offshore where it will be hard for the Yanks to spot him. Where he can raid the shipping lanes, alive with a steady parade of merchant ships sailing through the Narrows between Brazil and West Africa. Maybe Semmes will try stopping at Trinidad to land prisoners, buy coal. Or maybe he's heading south of the Line.

Winslow paces off the *Alabama*'s imagined course from Galveston, about seventy days ago. Takes twenty-three paces on a southeasterly course on his sandy chart. Sees that Semmes must be south of the equator, somewhere near the horn of Brazil. Twenty-four hundred miles from Faial. That puts Semmes more than twelve days of sailing ahead of Winslow if *manna* fell from the sky today. If the *Kearsarge* actually appeared and is ready to go. But his ship's still not here. And every day it is not, Semmes's location becomes a bigger unknown.

At this time of year there are two distinct possibilities as to where the *Alabama* goes next. One, if she's sound, her crew fit, she would likely head for Africa, the Cape of Good Hope, the Indian Ocean to prey on fat Far East traders. If Semmes has problems with boat or crew, he will head back to Europe where he came from, passing through the Azores on her way.

Winslow stands on the equator drawn in the sand holding the model of the *Alabama* in his hand as he has done each of the last five afternoons, stares south at the deep blue water of the little half-moon bay off this beach. Today he's trying something different, something beyond his giant chart in the sand, his driftwood ships, his time/speed/distance calculations. He's trying to imagine life on the hunt, and on the run, for Semmes. His crew left England eight months ago . . . driving the *Alabama* hard since they burned a flock of whalers here in the Azores last September. Morale cannot be good on that ship. The Jacks are English mercenaries. They cannot be used to the naval discipline that Semmes and Kell bring to the running of the *Alabama*.

"The wolf will come home." He shouts so loud that seagulls farther down the beach startle, swarm into the air shrieking. *The wolf always circles home. It's just a question of whether it will be this spring or next.*

Winslow heaves his driftwood *Alabama* out into the bay. Watches it tumbling in the breakers.

"You're in trouble no matter which way you go, Captain Semmes." His voice is low, breathless. "In the end you'll come back here where your cruise began. And I'll be waiting. All I need is faith and patience . . . like Jesus in the wilderness."

Man shall not live by bread alone, but on every word that proceeds from the mouth of God.

11

COMBAHEE RIVER, SOUTH CAROLINA
Late March, 1863

Until she sees the alligator, Maude has been half-asleep beneath her parasol, staring at the back of the oarsman. She's been having a little dream that the man beneath the straw hat rowing this boat is her long-lost Raffy. That he's ferrying her through this land of long shadows. Of egrets and pelicans. Spanish moss hanging from the trees on the levees between the salt-water river and the rice fields. The water a copper sheet in the late-afternoon sun. The air ripe with the songs of bobolinks and the sweet, fetid odor of the marshland in heat.

But now the gator has slipped out of its nest in the salt hay of the riverbank and is surging toward the boat. Just the top of its head and blank, golden eyes pulling a V-shaped wake across the calm water.

"Not again," she says to the boatman. He's her age. A black man, slender except for broad, powerful shoulders.

"You know what to do, young lady."

She reaches into the sweet-grass basket at her feet, pulls out a small striped bass and tosses it to the reptile.

A snap of the jaws, a swish of the long black tail . . . then the boat and its passengers are alone again on the river.

"You're getting good at this, Missy." Minty Tubman wakens from her nap among the blankets spread on the floor of the boat next to the babies Fiona and Leviticus.

The black woman takes a sip of water from a canteen, squints upriver at the northern shore of the Combahee. "We almost there, Walter."

"'Bout time," says the oarsman. There's a breathless fatigue in his voice.

Their little crew set off on this spy mission from Ladies Island this morning at just about slack tide. They've been riding the flooding current all day up the river from St. Helena Sound, hoping to hit Rose Hill before supper time and the turn of the tide. And all along the way the three of them have been scouting every bend, every snag. Looking to see where there's deep water enough for the troop carrier *John Adams* and the boats to follow. Watching the shore for stands of trees where pickets from the Charleston Light Dragoons might be hiding. Counting the number of blacks working in the rice fields. Maude has already tallied 387. And they have not yet reached Rose Hill Plantation, which has many scores of slaves.

Tubman believes that a surprise raid on these Combahee River rice plantations might free as many as a thousand people from bondage, enough tough young men to double the soldiers in Colonel Higginson's black regiments, enough to someday seize Charleston or Savannah. The woman everyone now calls Moses has gotten over $100 from Higginson to support scouting missions like this for her and her oarsman, scout, and pilot Walter Plowden. Maude has volunteered to come along. She and Minty have found that when Maude masquerades as a gentlewoman, and Minty masquerades as Fiona's wet nurse with a babe of her own, nobody takes note of Tubman the way they would seeing a black woman traveling alone. Here in the Low Country plenty of gentry travel by boat among the islands. Maude with her yellow linen parasol, her pale white dress of crinoline and lace looks very much like a plantation mistress out by boat to a neighbor's on a social call.

"Landing up ahead." Tubman says.

"That be Rose Hill," says Plowden without turning to look. "Time to rest these oars."

"You ready to play the princess, Missy?" Tubman stares hard at her. "Ready for some first-class spy work?"

Maude brushes the hair away from her forehead. Dips her hands in the river, splashes water on her cheeks. Pats them to bring out the pink.

Rehearses her story in her head. She knows the mistress of Rose Hill, young Mary Kirkland, is not here. She fled to her mother's home in Camden after Port Royal fell to the Federals. But this afternoon Maude will pretend otherwise, pretend she's Mary's cousin Sophie Boykin arrived home to the Low Country after a year abroad . . . and eager to see the mistress of Rose Hill.

"I do so hope I have not missed finding my dear Cousin Mary." She winks at Minty.

***

It's after sunset, after a fine dinner of deviled crabs. Maude's pacing the length of the front porch of the great house. Listening to the crickets, the whip-poor-wills, a lone owl. Twenty paces to the north, twenty paces to the south. Back again. She walks Fiona to sleep. Minty's walking by her side, humming a low three-note melody, little Leviticus pressed against her shoulder.

This being the South, Maude and her party have been welcomed by the slaves and the white overseer's family alike to Rose Hill, given food and beds for the night as Minty had predicted. Even though Cousin Mary is not at Rose Hill . . . hasn't been here for a year because she's too afraid to live so close to a place where war could break out at any moment. Those who care for the plantation know that it would simply never do to be anything but welcoming to a gentlewoman, to mistress's kin, to her party who have come calling. Slaves have been whipped, overseers tarred and feathered for less egregious social *faux pas.* So the tan linen sheets that cover the furniture in the great house have been removed, rooms for the white lady and her servants assigned, dinner prepared and served with grace and energy. But now the plantation has settled down for sleep.

"What are you thinking?" Maude asks her friend quietly.

"Two things."

"Yes?"

"Them Negroes in the cookhouse done told me and Walter there be more than ninety slave folk here at Rose Hill just waiting on the Yankee colonel and his black soldiers to set them free."

"And what else?"

"This big old house make a fine fire. A right fine bonfire."

"So we're going to be back this way?"

"What you think?"

12

FERNANDO DE NORONHA
Early April, 1863

If ever there was an enchanted island, it is this, Semmes thinks. A place like Circe's isle in the *Odyssey* to snare mariners—turn them to swine, distract them from their voyage—with wine, ambrosia, the too-easy charms of women. Surely Llewellyn did not foresee this tender trap when he urged the *Alabama*'s captain to give his men more than a day ashore. *But what a sweet mistake.*

They have landed at an island like a painting of paradise. It's only the *Alabama*'s second day stopped at this volcanic nub 200 miles off Brazil's Cabo São Roque. Semmes had intended that his crew start coaling his ship today from the American collier *Louisa Hatch* he seized offshore and brought to port. But he knows that he cannot turn his own back on time and tide and war without giving his Jacks time ashore. For better or worse, *Alabama*'s boys are at liberty.

And, oh, what distractions there are. Most merciful God!

Semmes is completely enthralled this bright tropical morning. He's face-to-face with the very incarnation of a siren. Her name is Liezel. He has been invited to this social breakfast with the governor of the island and friends. And now he can't take his eyes off the seventeen-year-old girl. Nor can she take her deep blue gaze off him, as they sit facing each other across the platters of fresh fruits, pastries, breakfast meats. He knows already that against his better judgment he is doomed to record every detail of her appearance in his journal. Wonders what it is about her that reminds him of Maude.

The long, flaxen hair. The complexion of a lily, tinted with the least bit of rose. Eyes so melting and lovely that they look as though they might belong to one of the *houris* of whom Mohammed dreamt. The slender curves of her body set off by a robe of the purest white. A wreath of flowers in her hair. She's the daughter of a German who's Semmes's age, a prisoner here on this isle that has the improbable distinction of being a Brazilian penal colony. An aristocrat, allowed to roam the island like most of the other prisoners. Almost all of them are gentry who have come afoul of Brazil's emperor. Liezel's father, says the governor, is a forger.

But nothing seems forged about this nymph or the ingenuous way she smiles at the seahawk as if he were a man half his age . . . and a prince.

"Do you ride, Captain?" A smile spreads over her lips. She nods toward the window. At the forests and meadows, the dark valleys, the island's granite peak—a queer spur rising hundreds of feet above the surrounding uplands.

He has no idea how to respond. The question is either so innocent or so bold that to utter even a word could be moral suicide.

"I believe Liezel is proposing an outing," says the governor.

"This is the first day we have not had rain in a week. You have brought us good fortune and my daughter would like to show you around our fair island, Captain Semmes." Her father's grinning. Can it be that he's giving Semmes his consent?

"Let's all go," says the governor, a sprightly major. "Now what do you say, Captain?"

"It would be an honor to . . . ride."

And may wives, lovers, and the Good Lord forgive a sailor. Who has been too long at sea.

***

The officers and men are at last in a jolly mood . . . as if Semmes has stopped the clock for them, as if every liberty trip to the *tavernas* and brothels of this little island lasts a season if not a year. The crew of the *Alabama* has been almost two weeks at Fernando de Noronha. Between distractions they have found time for coaling their warship from their prize the *Louisa Hatch*. Semmes knows that transferring cargo from a foreign prize in a neutral harbor defies international law, but here the governor has given him his full blessing. Given his blessing as well to the seahawk's using the island like a pirate's den—as a base to snag two passing whalers, the *Kate Cory* and the *Lafayette.*

Semmes burned the *Lafayette* immediately. But he has saved the *Kate Cory* hoping to make her a cartel ship to sail his prisoners—almost a hundred of them—to the Spanish Main. But today a Brazilian schooner stopped at the island and agreed to take the prisoners to Pernambuco in exchange for barrels of salt pork and flour. So tonight, at the request of the divine Liezel, her father, and the governor, Semmes intends to make a spectacle and a ghost ship of the *Kate Cory.* Out here on the calm seas beyond the three-mile territorial limit.

The firing party has just abandoned the whaler, darkness has settled over the sea, the third round of champagne is passing among officers and guests on the bridge deck of the *Alabama.* Flames are starting from the hatches, into the thatch of rigging, up the masts when Semmes feels the girl pressing so close to him in the darkness that her minty breath makes his mustache jump. She lays her forearm on his forearm, her fingers wrap softly around his wrist.

"Take me away from here." Her voice is more air than sound. "I'll do anything."

It's the kind of thing Maude would have said—did say—back in the cherry-blossom days of their forbidden love before the war broke out in Washington. She was then not much older than this lass. Brimming, too, with this bold, self-assuredness of youth.

Great God Almighty, it is a drug to me!

He recoils—an instinct—as if from something deadly. Steps back, falls to one knee as he stumbles on the threshold of the ladder to the main deck.

Kell, the ever-ready luff, is there with a helping hand. "Are you all right, sir?"

"I will be, Mr. Kell . . . I *will* be." He gets to his feet, dusts off his hands, gives a little shrug to Liezel. Then turns his gaze out toward the specter of the *Kate Cory*, now a ball of fire fading away to the west.

The luff's eyes sweep between the captain and the siren, whose face is blank with confusion. He seems to feel the threat. Sense his commander's new resolve.

"I see a voyage in our near future."

"Old age hath yet his honor and his toil," says Semmes. It's a line from Tennyson's "Ulysses." One he tends to forget.

13

DISTRICT OF COLUMBIA
Early April, 1863

Things are falling apart. Gideon Welles sits at a back-corner table in the Ebbitt Grill, listening to the soft clatter of forks, fresh oyster shells, plates. He feels the heavy gloom of the rainy evening, the somberness of the mahogany-paneled dining room, gas lights. The dark beams of the ceiling seem to be pressing down on him. He really wishes he had not agreed to meet the secretary of state and the attorney general here for dinner. Really hates that they are half an hour late. Really wishes the president would get back from his trip to the Rappahannock to help him sort out today's mess.

First, there was news that DuPont's fleet of ironclads has failed to breach Charleston Harbor. Second, word that Charles Wilkes has precipitated another major confrontation with England—another *Trent* Affair—by seizing the British mail steamer *Peterhoff* off St. Thomas in the Danish Virgin Islands after an illegal chase. Third, while Wilkes was mucking up relations with the English and the Danes to a fare-thee-well, Raphael Semmes sailed right by St. Thomas—quite possibly in sight of Wilkes if he had been looking—and has now been burning New England's best Cape-Horners out at the Atlantic Narrows, sending their crews home in a bonded prize, the bark *Washington*. And if this wasn't enough, Welles has received yet another threat in a red envelope.

This one turned up in his leather document case this morning. *How does such a thing even happen?* The case was only out of his sight while he slept.

"Why are you looking so glum, Gideon?" Rat-face Bill Seward stands over him, flicking raindrops off his coat with the back of his hand, the water speckling the table cloth, Welles's shirt, his left cheek.

"Give us a smile, man," says Ed Bates, the attorney general. "We've come here to save your ass. Isn't that right, Senator?"

For the first time since the cabinet members had arrived, Welles realizes his dinner partners will be three men, not two. The third newcomer is Senator John P. Hale. Pig-bellied, self-satisfied, back-stabbing chair of the Senate Committee on Naval Affairs.

Lord of Mercy!

***

"We want you to change the president's mind about Sybert," says Seward.

Welles takes another bite of his crab cake, lets the peppery spices, the tender backfin meat linger on his tongue as he tries not to let his face show his anger.

Sybert's a Prussian-born ship owner, a citizen of South Carolina, who now claims he wants to go privateering for the U.S. Navy. A week ago the man, complete with a letter of introduction and support from Seward, pestered Welles and the president in separate suits for a letter of marque. Said he had a hundred-ton steam schooner he could turn into a privateer and do more than the whole navy to bring Raphael Semmes and other Reb commerce raiders to justice. The idea that this man of questionable national loyalty, with his little teapot of a ship, could stand up against the likes of the thousand-ton *Alabama*—and a crafty veteran like Semmes for more than about thirty seconds—is beyond absurd. More likely Sybert wants a letter of marque so that he can prey on blockade runners and get fat on the prize money from his seizures. No doubt some of that prize money would find its way into the pockets or campaign war chests for Seward, Gates, and Hale. Worse, Sybert could be a Southern agent capable of causing all sorts of mayhem if given opportunity and official sanction. Welles kicked the man out of his office, counseled the president to do the same.

"Can you explain to me how supporting this Prussian is truly in the best interest of the United States?"

The attorney general clears his throat. "I don't think you appreciate, Gideon, what precarious legal footing you are on right now."

"By dismissing this request by Sybert?"

"The secretary's talking about the Forbes mission." Hale pats his ample belly.

"The what?" Welles feels the words dying in his mouth, the crab starting to sour in his gut.

Yes, Major Allen has warned him that Seward might use his discovery of the secret plan to buy the Laird rams against Welles. But he had not imagined that Seward would have disclosed the plan to Bates or Hale. Especially not to Hale, who is constantly leaking information to the press to intrigue against the secretary of the navy.

"Gideon, as a friend, I must tell you this looks bad for you . . . and the president. If it were to come out that with no official approval you singlehandedly sent Forbes and Aspinwall to Liverpool with a Naval Department draft for one million pounds sterling to buy ships from a country with whom we are nearly at war, why I might be forced to indict you for . . ."

"There would certainly be very public Senate hearings on the matter," says Hale.

"Imagine what this kind of scandal could do to the president's chances for re-election next year. And as for the citizens' confidence in us and our prosecution of the war . . ." Seward throws up his hands. *All gone.*

"Sybert is a solid man, Mr. Secretary. Just give him a chance to do some good for the nation." Hale's smiling. Thinks he's got the bit in Welles's mouth now.

"There's still a chance that your little project with Forbes need not come to light." Seward again.

"It would tear me up inside to send you back to Connecticut in disgrace and destitution. The fines for misappropriation of government funds are . . ." Bates closes his eyes, shakes his head as if the idea of indicting his colleague is too much to bear.

Smarmy bastard.

The secretary of state sighs. "We're really trying to help you here, Gideon."

Right, he thinks, *which one of you rodents snuck that red envelope in among my documents? Or was it all of you? Is Iago not a single person at all, but a conspiracy?*

"What do you say, Welles?" Gates signals to a waiter to refill his glass of bourbon.

There's a strange flutter in Welles's chest such as he has never felt before. Then words rush from his mouth. Hot, sweet words.

"I've recalled Forbes and Aspinwall. Their mission . . . never happened."

He's lying about the recall. Some kind of instinctive urge toward self-preservation, to thumb his nose at these bullies, too. *And, Lord, it feels just right.* Welles knows that Seward has already betrayed his mission to England's foreign minister, Lord Russell. Russell, an arch supporter of the South, will never let the Lairds sell their rams to the Union. The mission's already dead. There are no teeth in these gentlemen's threats. And clearly they know nothing about what Winslow and the *Kearsarge* will soon be up to.

"Come again?" Seward's left cheek shakes with anger.

"I said I will never spend a penny of government money on the Lairds' ships . . . or Mr. Sybert's either."

Ed Bates gives another shake to his head. "I fear you are treading on eggs, old man."

"Aren't we all?"

14

USS KEARSARGE
April 8–10, 1863

Winslow leans over the bulwarks near the mizzen shrouds, hammers on the planking of his ship with a belaying pin. Hears the satisfying ring of wood against wood echo across the small harbor where she's anchored in Horta. The sun is full and high. This morning's weather has been everything he might have hoped for as the backdrop for the change of command ceremony on the main deck. A day as bright as the dress whites he wears. Now it's time to get down to business. To think about the hunt ahead.

"Manna finally cometh," he says to his executive officer, Lieutenant Commander James S. Thornton. "She's a fine ship."

"A beauty," says Thornton. He's the picture of a naval ship's luff—his fit physique, ready eyes, proud nose, trim dark hair, beard.

Winslow's new command is a Mohican-class screw-sloop, displacing 1,550 tons. Virtually new. Built at the Portsmouth Naval Shipyard in Kittery, Maine. Only commissioned fourteen months ago. She has a length of 201 feet, beam of 34 feet, draft of 14 feet and a crew of 163. From what Winslow and Thornton have heard via dispatches from Federal spies in Liverpool, and one who was until recently on the *Alabama*, *Kearsarge* is virtually the same size as the Rebel cruiser. But her masts are lower, smaller. She carries only topsail yards, depending more upon her engines for speed than the ship she will chase.

Two boilers and two horizontal, back-acting engines power a single screw to drive her at a maximum of eleven knots. Her battery has seven guns. Two eleven-inch Dahlgren pivot guns, one thirty-pounder Parrot rifle, four light thirty-two-pounders. This compares to the *Alabama*'s eight guns. One sixty-eight-pounder pivot gun, one Blakely hundred-pound pivot rifle, and six heavy thirty-two-pounders.

"A thoroughbred," says Thornton. "Nearly a twin of *Alabama.*"

"That's what we want Captain Semmes to think when he sees us."

"But we need to give our girl some advantages. Am I right?"

"I'm open to suggestions, Luff." Winslow knows on some basic level that Welles has banished him here in the Azores for these last three months not just to test his faith and loyalty and temper his resolve, but also to give him some dream time, to make his mind more plastic. To inspire him to fresh thinking and resourcefulness.

"Would that we could add a third Dahlgren, eh, sir?"

The captain nods. He knows exactly where he would mount one more eleven-inch swivel gun. But such cannons can only be had back in the States. "The kinds of guns we can get here in the Azores, Spain, or France are useless antiques."

Thornton says that it's too bad she's not an ironclad. Then *Kearsarge* could face Semmes with impunity.

"Only the rolling mills in England and France could provide such plate . . . I doubt they would sell it to us." Winslow need not add what both he and Thornton have heard daily from the Dabneys. The British and French sympathies lie with the Rebs.

"Maybe there's another way, sir."

"And what would that be?"

"I'll have to give it some thought."

15

BEAUFORT, SOUTH CAROLINA
Mid-April, 1863

Long after midnight Maude wakes to a scuffling sound, sees the silhouette of a man coming into her bedroom window at the Oaks. Outside, the haze on the river swirls in smoky, moonlit pillars.

Her first thought is for her babies. They're right in front of him, sleeping in their cribs beneath the mosquito netting. But before she can even raise her head off her pillow, or shout for the woman in the next room, the intruder bypasses the children and is on her. Pinning her to the mattress with his considerable weight, covering her mouth with an immense hand.

"Make a noise and I'll kill you." His breath reeks of chewing tobacco.

Just don't hurt my babies, she thinks.

"Slow, deep breaths. Get a hold of yourself, gal."

She pinches her eyelids closed, tries to think of the bright, green moors of home—of the Irish West Country, Galway.

"Open them peepers when you're ready to listen."

The man is huge, crushing. But she's not going to open her eyes or anything else if she can help it.

"You ever see a baby with a broke neck?"

Every muscle in her face, her body is tight as cable. Outside, somewhere down King Street, a hound's baying after a coon.

"Listen to me . . . if you love them children."

Her eyes open against her will.

"That's better."

She feels more than sees that he's a white man. Long hair, bushy beard. He has the heavily muscled body, the full belly, rangy limbs of a bear.

"I seen you back in Washington two years ago with Miss Rose Greenhow and her lot. Seen you in Richmond, too, with Mrs. Varina Davis."

His accent is not New England Yankee. A little Southern. But not like the slow drawl of the Beaufort natives who have sworn allegiance to the Union and remained here in this Yankee-occupied town to keep their shops. Maybe he's from Maryland. It doesn't feel as if he's wearing a uniform. Could he be one of scores of teamsters, sawyers, masons, carpenters come to aid in construction projects around town and at Colonel Higginson's regimental camp at Old Fort Plantation?

"You're Raphael Semmes's sweetie. You ain't forgot him 'cause of these Negroes, have you?"

She shakes her head. No, she has far from forgotten her gladiator. *It's just that he seems lost. . . .*

"Helping me is helping Captain Semmes. Understand? And helping Mrs. Davis, her husband, too."

She just stares at the dark bushy face hovering over hers.

"You help me. You and those babies going to be safe. Captain Semmes safe, too."

Bloody Hell! He's either a madman or a Confederate agent, maybe both.

"If I take my hand away, you promise not to scream?"

She nods.

His palm lifts off her mouth, fingers drag across her cheek.

Her lips feel numb from the force of his pressing hand, her voice little more than wind over fallen leaves. "What do you want from me?"

"Tell me what that Moses gal is up to."

***

When he's gone, she gathers her babies to her breasts, slips out onto the third-floor verandah. Watches the moon continuing to rise over Ladies Island, the river. It's an old gibbous moon, and the light makes everything—the lawn, the river, the moss dripping from the oaks—look blue and out of focus in the damp fog.

"What have I done?" She's talking to her children.

Little Leviticus coos.

I've promised myself to two masters.

What else could she do? The bearded bear had covered her nearly naked body with his own. Plowed his knee between her legs in a way that promised he would make a camp slut of her unless she played his game. He had threatened her life, her babies. Threatened to expose her as the consort of the Southern seahawk.

"I had to get clear of him."

Baby Fiona nuzzles. Her little mouth opening, closing. Searching for a breast.

"Should I tell Minty about this?"

Fiona's hands have started rooting in the folds of her mother's night clothes.

He said he would kill me if I say a word. . . .

She decides she has not really betrayed Minty. Not yet anyway. She did not tell the bearded bear about Tubman's scouting expeditions on the Combahee River. She claimed she knows nothing. Said she needed time to discover Tubman's secrets. "I'm giving you two weeks," the bear had said. "Raphael Semmes, the South, and I—we're all depending on you."

"Now what, babies?"

Leviticus starts to coo again.

She settles down into a rocking chair. Thinks of Raffy as she unbuttons her nightshirt to nurse. Imagines him under this moon, pacing his deck, wondering how his rapacious voyage will end.

Wondering if she still loves him. Then she thinks of Minty, how she is in so many ways a sister. But she has changed. She loves Minty the nurse. Minty the Moses. But Minty the spy, the soldier? Minty who dreams of setting fire to her enemy? It is beyond strange that she has bound herself to two souls, both Promethean, both aiming to change the world with flames. Both of whom are being kidnapped from her by this bloody war. Each wrenching a part of her from herself and her children.

She feels the pinches of the babies' strong little jaws as they take her breasts, gives a little cry. She bites her lower lip to hold back the tears, to push back the awful questions rising in her mind.

Must I choose between my white lover and my black sister? My white daughter and my black son, too? And will the bearded bear, or the war itself, kill us all anyway?

16

USS KEARSARGE
Early May, 1863

Back in Faial. After a fortnight prowling around the Azores, chasing rumors of the *Alabama*, coming up empty-handed. Winslow's thinking he's quite possibly unfit for command.

He's been bedridden for the last two days in his cabin with fever from the malaria he contracted on the Mississippi. His injured eye has developed a deep red and purple color around the iris to the point where he thinks he looks like a blind old horse. Just about the only thing that has kept him from handing over the ship to his luff Thornton is the thought that these infirmities are part of the ordeal that Gideon Welles and the Almighty have planned for him. That this ordeal is the only way to school him for finding and catching his brother Esau, catching Semmes. This time in bed must be given him for reflection, to remember something he nearly forgot during all of these days of staring into the springtime haze for a sleek black ship and a man with a mustache like a tomcat. To wit: Finding the *Alabama* is only half his problem. He must assure the *Kearsarge* victory when he and his brother tangle. Constantly drilling his gun crews and marines will not be enough.

There's a knock on his cabin door.

"You called for me, sir?" Luff Thornton looks energetic, dashing, obedient as he stands at attention on the threshold of the great cabin.

It's the end of the noon watch. Winslow's sitting up in his berth. He's wearing a pale-blue nightshirt, holding a cold compress to his eye and forehead.

"Have you put your mind to a plan to give us an advantage when we meet Semmes?"

"Yes, sir. There's something Captain Farragut did back on the Mississippi so that our ships could safely bypass the Reb forts when we took New Orleans."

"You mean draping anchor chain on the ship's topsides to protect the steam chest and the magazines?"

The luff nods, says the same thing could be done on the *Kearsarge.* Homespun ironcladding.

Winslow pictures it. His ship draped from deck to the waterline with a closely packed network of spare anchor cable. Ugly and obvious, but effective in a fight. Farragut had proven the concept.

"But if I were Semmes, I would never dare to fight us if I saw *Kearsarge*'s chain mail shirt. I would be outmatched and I would try to run."

"Right, and there's a good chance *Alabama* could outrun us because she can carry more sail. She'd get away again."

"Unless . . ." Something like a wave rolls through the captain's head. "Unless what Semmes sees is two evenly matched wooden ships. It would be a matter of honor. I know Raphael Semmes. He would fight us if he didn't know about the chain."

"So . . . we disguise it?"

***

Charles Dabney stands on the pier this misty morning and scratches the back of his head. "You want my wood to do what?"

Dabney has thousands of board-feet of New England oak and local hardwood stacked near his whale oil factory on the harbor isthmus. He keeps it handy for whale ship repair and making barrels.

"We aim to build a box," says Winslow, wiping the malarial sweat from his forehead with the back of his hand. Tries to stand erect, look imposing with the patch over his bad eye. "A very big box."

"On your ship?"

"More like *around* it," says Thornton.

Dabney rolls his eyes, clearly doesn't get it.

"Look there, sir." Winslow hands Dabney a long glass, points to the starboard side of the *Kearsarge* as she rides at anchor in the harbor. The topsides of the warship have been fitted with chain plating made of 120 fathoms of anchor cable. One and seven-tenths–inch iron links, covering a space amidships nearly fifty feet in length by six feet in height. The chain stopped up and down to eye-bolts with marlines, secured by iron dogs.

"What's all that chain for?"

"We've just ironcladded the ship's vitals," says Winslow.

"So what do you need my wood for?"

"To hide the chain. We can get the local ship carpenters to build a wall of fresh planking over the chain . . . paint it black like the rest of the ship."

"You want *Kearsarge* to look just like a wooden ship again?"

"The masquerade could prove useful if we find the *Alabama.*"

"So . . . now you're going to take a page from my script for the *Azor*?"

Winslow winces, tries not to think he's becoming just as devious as old Satan Dabney. But this stratagem may be the only way to save his brother Raphael from himself.

"You aim to snare Semmes with a wolf in lamb's clothing?"

"Something like that, Mr. Dabney."

The Yankee businessman rubs his chin. A scarlet blush rises in his neck, his cheeks. He knows he's got this sailor boy over a barrel.

"Can we have some of your wood, Mr. Dabney?"

"How much are you willing to pay?"

17

DISTRICT OF COLUMBIA
May 29, 1863

"The nation's bleeding to death," says the president.

The Battle of Chancellorsville is some three weeks past, but he can't stop thinking about it. Can't shake the specters of defeat and death. Hooker had Lee outnumbered five to two . . . and still went down in defeat. With 17,000 casualties. Lee had 13,000.

Lincoln, Welles, and Major Allen are on the White House roof. Again. This is where they've taken to having their most confidential meetings over the last year. Either up here or in the musty attic below. With the rocking horse belonging to the president's dead son Willie, half a dozen women's dresses thrown over chairs, and an old sofa, remnants from Tad and his friends Bud and Holly Taft playing dress-up. The makeshift fort the children have built with pillows, fire logs, condemned rifles. The place always reminds Welles of his own dead son Hubert, who played here, too, with Willie and Tad during the first days of the administration. *My flawless four-year-old . . .* sent home to Connecticut in a box for burial. Just half a year ago.

Lincoln stares out at the gray morning, the Capitol shrouded in hot mist, the scaffolding around the Washington monument looking skeletal. The Potomac almost black, a River Styx in this light.

"Sometimes the air seems filled with faces of the boys we've lost in this damned war," he says.

"It's a hard thing."

Lincoln waves his hand as if to dismiss the ghosts. "What new horror brings us up to this roost, Gideon?"

Welles says there's news about the *Alabama*. Semmes has picked off more than a score of ships along the equator. He has made something of a pirate's den for himself at the Brazilian island of Fernando de Noronha. The very spot Welles sent the *Vanderbilt* to patrol months ago. But it appears Charles Wilkes commandeered the *Vanderbilt* for his flagship in St. Thomas and diverted her from her search of the equatorial sea lanes and Brazil.

"You mean to say we could have bagged Semmes by now except for Wilkes's intervention with the *Vanderbilt*?"

"The man exceeded his orders."

Lincoln grits his teeth. "I thought you were going to fire him."

Welles says he's already sending Wilkes's replacement to command the West Indies Flying Squadron. Seward has had a change of heart, suddenly agrees with Welles's choice to relieve Wilkes.

"Strange, Wilkes was Secretary Seward's darling." The president has begun staring at the clouds again.

"Passing strange," says Major Allen.

The president looks at Allen as if he has forgotten that the chief spy was up here on the roof, too. "Are you going to tell me again that you think Wilkes and Seward are tied up in this Iago business?"

"Seward's sudden change of heart about supporting Wilkes certainly makes me wonder if the bloke ain't just a rat fleeing a sinking ship, so to speak, Mr. President."

"I think Seward and J. P. Hale are up to something," says Welles. "Ed Bates, too." He tells the president about how the three men tried to bully him over dinner back in April at the Ebbitt Grill. Tells him that he has received two more threats in red envelopes. The latest saying he'll be dead if he doesn't leave Washington by the Fourth of July.

"Maybe we should have them all arrested," says Lincoln.

Allen, with all due respect, disagrees. He says he understands Welles's need to recall Wilkes. The man has been wrecking any chance of the navy catching Semmes. But to come down hard on Seward, Bates, and Hale might just be pruning the tree, not killing the roots.

"I don't follow," says the president.

Allen puts his hands on his hips as if to swagger. Welles hates the weasel's posturing, the obvious joy he takes from being in control. He says that his agents have learned of something the Rebs call the Secret Line. At first the Federal agents thought it was just a clandestine communication network that the Confederacy is using to smuggle information back and forth from the North to the South. But now it seems to be something more. Something with nodes overseas in England, France, Spain. In Mexico and Canada, too, tied to a secret quasi-Masonic society of Southern sympathizers called the Knights of the Golden Circle.

"We think the Iago plot, those threats in the red envelopes that Gideon gets, General Hooker's problems communicating with his commanders at Chancellorsville, Raphael Semmes's uncanny ability to avoid an armada of our ships . . . we think all of these things are connected—all part of a shadowy, well-coordinated strategy by the Rebs to undermine our best efforts. Probably conceived by Jefferson Davis and Judah Benjamin, but managed by their surrogates."

"What are you saying?"

"I'm saying the Secret Line and the Knights of the Golden Circle are every bit as dangerous as General Lee's army."

"Lee is heading up the Shenandoah Valley for Pennsylvania as we speak."

"I know that, sir. We have intelligence . . . we know where Lee is."

Allen says that while Chancellorsville was a great victory for the South, it cost Lee men that he could not afford to lose. He's low on funds and supplies. Eventually, according to Secretary Stanton, the

Union can beat Lee on the field . . . but who knows where the *Alabama* or the other Confederate raiders are, or where they are going? They seem to be well supplied, well financed. And they are just the tip of the South's secret war against the Republic. Lee and his army are just for show. The South seems to have a web of financiers and spies that stretches far beyond Dixie. Probably into Maryland, New York, Canada, as well as England and France. If the South brings the Union to its knees, it will do it with its irregular forces like Semmes and all that stands secretly behind him.

Welles hasn't thought of the war like this before. Has to admit that this annoying weasel may well have a point. He has always seen Semmes as an isolated problem to deal with. A lone wolf. What if, in fact, the seahawk is just the most obvious of hundreds, thousands, of the South's phantom warriors?

"What do you want me to do, Major Allen?" The president is sucking on the inside of his cheeks.

"Give me some time and money."

Allen wants to build his own army of irregular warriors. Wants time to watch Seward, Bates, Hale . . . and watch Wilkes when he gets home. Watch their families, too. Ed Bates's son Fleming serves with the South, for God's sake. Wilkes's son John is in the Confederate Navy. The entire Wilkes family has had mining interests in North Carolina for more than a decade. And Allen reported months ago that Hale's daughter Lucy seems vulnerable to attention from all sorts of questionable men, especially theater types like the youngest rakehell of the Booth family—who has the notable middle name of Wilkes. So . . . there are a whole lot of suspicious folks to observe. The major says he needs money to recruit more agents, time to infiltrate the Secret Line and the Knights of the Golden Circle so that he can see how information flows. So that he can find the taproot.

"Cut that off, everything else is going to die on the vine. Iago and Semmes, too." End of speech. The weasel has that infuriating, smug smile on his face.

"What do you think, Gideon? Do you support a secret war?"

The Union's Old Man of the Sea tugs on the edges of his long beard. Thinks about Winslow and the *Kearsarge*, his own secret weapon against the *Alabama*. Wishes for a second that he could confide in these men about his peculiar grooming of Winslow for catching Semmes. But then he thinks again. Realizes the lesson Allen has taught him here this morning. Secret information is power . . . and right now he needs every bit he can hoard.

"Gideon?" asks the president.

"I think we have to beat the Rebs anywhere we find them, any way we can find them."

"I pray for Grant at Vicksburg."

"I pray for us all," Welles replies.

18

BEAUFORT, SOUTH CAROLINA
June 1, 1863

As soon as she sees Minty Tubman's face, Maude knows tonight's the night. The raid's on. The raid that has consumed her friend's thoughts day and night for at least a month. The raid on the Combahee River rice plantations to free hundreds of slaves. The raid that just now's bringing a fiery glint to Tubman's gaze, a reddish glow to her cheeks. The raid the bearded bear would kill to know about.

"The exodus coming directly, Missy." Tubman settles onto a cook's stool.

Maude puts down the pig intestine that she's been stuffing with spiced pork from a pot, looks around the little cookhouse behind the Baptist Church on King Street. Sees the morning sun cutting a wedge of light through the doorway, across the floor. Knows by the shape of the wedge that it's about eight o'clock in the morning. Knows that in another hour and a half her babies are going to wake in their baskets by the vegetable bins and demand to be fed again. Knows, too, that any minute now other evangels will be arriving to help her prepare food to feed the masses of black refugees flowing into Beaufort.

"It up to you whether you gone help old Moses lead the way."

Part of Maude just wants to cover her ears and not hear about the raid. Does not want the weight of its secret in her heart where the bearded bear might squeeze it out of her at any moment. She barely sleeps these days for fear he will turn up again in her room some night.

"My babies, Minty. I don't know . . . I'm not sure . . ." She wrings her hands.

The black woman sees. "You wants to tell me what bothering you?"

Maude bites her lip, picks up the intestine again and starts packing more spiced pork into it with a pewter spoon.

"Missy, you acting twitchy as a sparrow on a willow branch. Don't be hiding nothin' from me now. Not after all we been through with each other."

Something's starting to tear in her chest. "I can't know about . . ."

"What are you afraid of?"

"A man." *Holy Mary what have I just said?*

"A man?"

"It's nothing."

"It not nothing. You packing that sausage 'til it ready to bust."

Maude feels more ripping in her chest. Guesses it's the truth trying to let itself out, get itself free to breathe in the light of morning. She turns her back on her friend . . . as the words spew out. Words about the bearded bear who came into her bedroom, who crushed her with his body, who threatened to kill her babies unless she exposes Tubman's secret plans.

"That all? Some big, old, white bear of a fool?"

"Not quite." *What am I saying?*

"Good, 'cause I ain't worried yet. I spent my whole life outsmarting crackers like that."

Her heart feels sick, swollen. "There's another man."

"Who?"

"The one I love."

"The sailor?"

Her chest tears wide open. "I believe you may have heard of Raphael Semmes."

"The Reb pirate? You love. . . ?"
"I'm sorry, Minty. I've been so afraid to tell you . . ."
"I have to go."

19

CSS ALABAMA
June 2, 1863

"Fire a second gun at the scoundrel, Luff." Semmes eyes the ship he's been chasing for hours—still over six miles ahead. His voice has a shrill edge as he speaks to Lieutenant Kell. "And have Galt's boy wake the Yankee's concubine. Bring her to me."

The sun's high—0930 hours. A fresh southeast trade wind blowing. The *Alabama*, every bit of canvas set, pulses with the whir of wind in the sails, the hull close reaching after her prey. It's almost halfway into the forenoon watch, and Semmes has already been on the bridge for five hours. Pacing. Feeling the blood humming in his legs, his arms. His mustache flicking with the thrill of the chase, a defiant adversary. And something else—a smoldering anger that has been building in his soul for days.

Maybe it roots in this fallen woman who has come aboard, or maybe something deeper. A fear he tries to give no quarter, a nagging sense that the *Alabama* and the South might be coming to the end of their luck. A sense that the world is turning its back on the Southern cause. The newspapers found on recently seized ships tell an ugly tale of carnage and deprivation back home. So much blood spilled at Chancellorsville, so many Yankee ironclads swarming around Charleston. Grant and the Mississippi fleet closing in on Vicksburg. Meanwhile, overseas, the English and French support for Dixie seems tepid at best.

The time has come to be bold . . . because it may never come again.

Near the end of the mid watch last night the lookout sounded the bugle, called "sail-ho." Since then *Alabama* has been chasing this Yankee clipper, a graceful bark with fine white canvas. A ship that has been trying to give the heels to her pursuer, that has already ignored the thunder of one cannon call to stop.

The forward thirty-two-pound starboard gun barks. It recoils against its breeching tackle with a rumble of the carriage wheels. The heavy scent of sulfur from the gun smoke is wafting over the ship as the girl arrives on the bridge deck, accompanied by Galt's Negro Nancy-boy, David. Her name's Rita. She's not much to look at. Little more than a child, just David's age. Sixteen at the most. A skinny little thing with olive hide, a hooked nose, black hair to her waist. Pox scars on her left cheek, pale lips. The frayed blue sailor's blouse and togs she wears make her even more waif-like. But—still—she's a female. And every time Semmes looks at her, or hears the soft rustle of her voice, he thinks of his own daughters. Thinks how so many Yanks disrespect females just as they disrespect the sovereignty of the South. Just as this clipper he's chasing disrespects his flag, his guns.

Damn the Puritan whoremongers, he thinks. *They would sully angels for the sake of their own craven pursuit of material treasures.*

The girl came aboard four days ago when *Alabama* seized and burned the *Jabez Snow* out of Bucksport, Maine, bound for Montevideo with a load of Cardiff coal. Her captain claimed her as his chambermaid. But she has told Semmes in a mix of broken English and Spanish that she was kidnapped from a tavern by the Yank on his last trip to Uruguay, forced into this life of humiliation, of slavery. After hearing her tale, Semmes put the Snow's captain in irons, and gave over his junior lieutenant's stateroom to Rita.

"You wanted see me, *Capitan*?" She raises her black eyes to meet his, then looks down at her hands clasped before her.

"I know you hardly need another illustration of the Yankee's arrogance and his callous disregard for the rule of the law or the sanctity of womankind, my dear. But look there at that ship."

"*Sí.*"

"Like the man who stole you from yourself, there goes an impudent blackguard. Hiding behind the comely guise of that fine ship yonder. Should I let him have his way with us? Let the Yankee escape? Let his kind take over the world from good and gentle people?"

"*Mátalo,*" she juts out her lower lip. "Kill him . . . kill them all!"

***

"Mr. Kell, ready number 145, live ammunition."

It's twenty minutes since *Alabama* fired her second, blank, warning shot and the Yank clipper has not hove to. She's cracked on even more canvas. Main and mizzen staysails.

Blood of Jesus!

Kell tries not to blink, not to squint, not to furrow his brow as he receives this most unusual order. Just the slightest twitch at the corner of his right eye shows the first mate's humanity. Maybe not fear—never fear in Kell. But concern. In more than a hundred sea chases, the captain has rarely ordered live ammunition loaded. And never has he requested the gun they call "145," the rifled, seven-inch Blakely pivot gun mounted forward of the bridge. It's *Alabama*'s long-range weapon. Her destroyer. The one Semmes said he's saving for the day he goes broadsides with one of old Gideon Welles's men-of-war.

"The Blakely? Powder and shell?"

"If that Yank won't stop after we showed him our colors and fired twice with signal guns at him . . . I'll stop the bugger with metal." Semmes feels the blood pounding in his neck, wonders if Kell and the girl can see the anger rising. See his cheeks starting to burn.

The girl catches his eye with a fierce look as she tosses her windblown hair over her shoulder with one hand.

"*Mátalo?*" he asks her. *Should I kill the Yank?*

"*De puta madre*," she says. His mother's a whore. Her lips have a fresh red cast to their paleness.

"I hunt, therefore I am, young miss."

Kell's eye twitches again at his captain's declaration. He grits his teeth.

Semmes feels a strange blend of dismay and thrill to discover that just now the luff has little use for his skipper's zeal. Has perhaps lost passion for the mission. Is thinking—quite possibly—that the fo'castle scuttlebutt has a bit of truth to it. *Alabama*'s turned into a hell ship. Raphael Semmes an avenging angel of Satan.

The world has barely felt the heat of my fire nor the hail of my brimstone yet, good Kell.

***

The wind has freshened more. The whir of the trades now a low moan nearly drowning out the crashing of the hull into the head seas. *Alabama*'s heeling fifteen degrees to leeward as the gun crew adjusts the cannon toward the windward rail with pikes and tackle. The master gunner cranks on the elevation screw. Two powder monkeys are slinging pairs of charges and cartridges on deck through the magazine hatch when Kell stops shouting orders through his megaphone and turns back to the captain.

"I believe we are within range of him, sir. How shall I direct the fire?"

There. Put it there. Mid-ships. Put a fire in the very heart of the Yank's glorious wind ship, he wants to say. *Put fire down Abe Lincoln's throat. Let this one pay just as the other pays in his shackles down in our jail. Let them all pay, these sons of whores, for all the misery they have brought on the South and her women. Brought on my daughters, my wife. Brought on Maude, too, who may well be lost to me forever. . . .*

His gaze veers from his prey to the girl Rita who has perched herself on the extreme windward wing of the bridge and scowls into the wind. Her eyes are blank, glazed, fixed on the ship his young officers have now determined to be named *Amazonian*. Tears are streaming down her cheeks. Her jaw grinds slowly. Her lips have now turned a deep crimson. He looks closer. Sees that they are slick with blood. She's gnawing on the inside of her cheek, eating herself alive with torment and a lust for vengeance. *My God and my Redeemer!* How many women in his life are likewise afflicted? How many men? Is the blood rising on his lips, too? Has he in his loneliness and anger and frustration begun to feast on his own heart, his soul? Is this what Kell sees but cannot say?

"What shall I do, sir?" Kell's voice struggles for a flat note.

Semmes feels one of his molars dig into his lip, tastes the blood. Its salty heat. Its bitterness. "Fall off the wind, Luff. When you have a clear shot . . . buzz one just short of his transom. We want him scared and penitent. Not dead."

Kell shoots him the slightest smile, a look of understanding, brotherhood, validation.

Suddenly, the seahawk feels the urge to open his heart a little. "We must bring an end to all the misery."

20

COMBAHEE RIVER, SOUTH CAROLINA
June 2, 1863

The steam whistle of the gunboat *John Adams* is screeching and will not stop. And so are a hundred Negro men, women, and children gathering on the nearby shore in the noonday sun. The whistle is the signal to the slaves to drop their hoes, their laundry, their cooking and come running to the riverbank. The black Federal troops from this gunboat and two others have set fire to everything. The rice fields, the barns, the great house at Rose Hill Plantation . . . all are burning as the refugees flock to the shore. Minié balls from the Reb pickets are bees in the air over their heads. Meanwhile, Minty Tubman's standing on the foredeck of the *Adams,* watching as her exodus is about to become a massacre.

"Speak to your people, Moses," shouts James Montgomery, the colonel in charge from the wheelhouse. "Speak!"

Tubman seems frozen with dread, her mouth's open but no words are coming out.

And through a crack in the door to a rope locker where she has been hiding, Maude's watching it all.

"Speak!" the colonel again demands.

Ashore the blacks are terrified that they will not be among those carried to the *Adams* in the ship's longboats. They hang onto the boats and will not let them leave shore with the first refugees. The air is thick with metal. Flames are pressing toward their backs. The heat searing.

"Say something, Moses. Calm them folks afore this thing all goes to hell."

Sixty maybe seventy people are in the water now. Many with bundles of clothes, pots of food, small children held over their heads. They're surrounding the longboats, trying to toss possessions and babies aboard. Clutching at the gunwales 'til the boats look about to swamp. A tremendous ululation rising from the host. Individuals starting to lose their footing, tumbling in the water.

It's like the day last fall in Pennsylvania when Maude watched little Leviticus's mother drown crossing the Delaware River to freedom. When Maude volunteered to take Leviticus as her own. When she knew that her fate was now grafted to the Negro's quest for freedom, perhaps as much as it was to the heart of her long-lost seahawk.

Maybe it's the memory of that other drowning in the Delaware that has paralyzed Tubman. Or maybe she's beset by some other terror, perhaps the overwhelming realization that now the lives of hundreds upon hundreds of people are on her shoulders today. Whatever the cause, Tubman seems on the verge of melting as she watches more and more people come adrift in the slow current, sees the small boats beginning to ship water under the tremendous weight of frightened humanity.

The steam whistle suddenly switches to a shriller note. Then stops.

"Speak to them, Moses." Montgomery's out of the wheelhouse on the cabin roof shouting. "Speak!"

Tubman spreads her arms as if to gather the people to her bosom, but no sound rises from her mouth.

Never before has Maude seen her friend flustered. But suddenly she gets it, knows somewhere beneath her skin what's holding Minty back. Tubman is a doer not a talker. If you put her on that riverbank she would take those poor people by the hands and lead them one by one into the boats. But out here on the *Adams* she's stifled unless she can find some active way to engage her body, some way to extend those spreading arms to the shore. . . .

"Sing, Minty. Sing to them!" Maude hears her voice shouting. Sees her friend turn and recognize her as she steps out of the locker. "Sing!"

And Tubman does. Louder than any steam whistle. Louder than the crowing of the crowd. She smiles a great grin at Maude as she adapts her message to the melody of a popular gospel song.

Come from the East

Come from the West

'Mong all the glorious nations . . .

Her voice is bold, sweet, strong, assured. Calm. Deeply calm.

And on the banks of the river the people raise their arms to her, drag themselves out of the river, let the boats go freely with the first load of passengers.

***

It's an hour before more than 700 refugees and 300 Negro troops are back on the *Adams* and the two other Federal gunboats. Another hour before Minty finds her West Irish friend nursing her children in a nest made of three bales of cotton beneath the engine's walking beam.

"The Good Lord told me you gone stand by me . . . no matter who you love." Minty settles onto the deck next to Maude. Leans her head on her friend's shoulder, takes baby Fiona in her arms.

"The bearded bear came through my window again last night. Just after dark. He knew something was brewing. Saw the *Adams* getting ready to load men."

"I feared he bring the whole Reb army down on me today . . . but we gots the surprise on everybody. How we do that?"

"I told him the raid was on Edisto Island."

"That 'most twenty miles from here."

"I know."

"You gone have bad trouble now."

21

CSS ALABAMA
July 2–3, 1863

Twenty-eight degrees south latitude, twenty-eight degrees west longitude. The ship's bound for the Cape of Good Hope. It has been almost a year since her sailing from England. For a week, northwest gales have been torturing the *Alabama*. Straining every stitch in the sails. Loosening the caulking in her shrunken decking, her topside planking.

The ship plunges toward the austral winter. With every lurch in these confused seas, the deck timbers creak, the bulkheads moan, the cabinet work in the captain's cabin lets out strange, creaking noises. Now her bottom has begun to leak. The ship—too long at sea without time for essential rest to overhaul gear, paint, caulk—is tearing herself to pieces, just as the *Sumter* had before her. It is only a matter of months, maybe mere weeks, before rot sets into her vitals, worms get into her hull. Unless Semmes finds a shipyard soon to care for her, *Alabama* will run out of time. And it has been cold, bitter cold. Scarf and topcoat cold.

The evening mess is over, the mid watch started. Semmes sits at his desk, studying a chart of the South African coast, shivering beneath two quilts. He has no interest in watching the remains of the *Anna F. Schmidt* burning off to leeward. She was out of Boston for San Francisco with assorted merchandise, including sealed casks of bread that he dearly needed. Weevils have ruined his own supply.

The *Alabama* Jacks spent the last two days plundering the *Schmidt* for everything that will make their ocean crossing to Africa easier.

But now Semmes is done with her; can't watch her burn or face the sad face of her master. Too much on his mind. Misgivings. He's wondering if he has done the right thing by turning the Philadelphia brig *Conrad*, captured some days ago, into the raider he has named the *Tuscaloosa*. Done the right thing by sending twelve of his best young officers and seamen off to man her. Done the right thing by pressing his bride of a warship so hard.

"She's weary," he says aloud. "And so am I."

He's imagining that if Maude saw him now, she would hardly recognize him as the man she held so close last June in Nassau. He has become a grizzled old seadog. Aged ten years since taking this new command. His wrists, elbows, hips, knees, ankles are so swollen and aching that he has taken to walking with a cane. *Sic transit vita hominis, usque ad finum*, he wrote today in his journal.

Like his ship he may not have too many more days left. He's wondering whether *Alabama* and he will have the strength to do their duty when the Yanks finally come for them, when the call to battle sounds. He's hoping that the fight with his enemy will come sooner rather than later . . . when he hears footsteps at his door.

"Ship off to port, sir," says the bosun. "Mr. Kell said you might want to have a look. It could be a Yank frigate."

***

"What say you, sir? Is she not a dark, strange thing?" Kell's not so much alarmed as curious, alert.

Semmes is on the bridge deck with his luff, eyeing the stranger less than two miles off to windward through a pair of fine, new double-lens binoculars taken off a recent prize. Through the eyepieces—in the moon glow—he sees a large, taut ship with exceedingly square yards, making all speed beneath a cloud of canvas. Her royals and topgallant studding sails set. The skipper's pressing his luck that his ship can take the strain of so much canvas in this half-gale of wind. No running lights showing.

Forward on the work deck, most of the crew is looking at the ghostly ship off to windward. Usually the Jacks coming off the second dog watch would have gone quietly below to their hammocks by now. But they have remained on deck with the current watch gang and the prisoners off the recent prizes. All eyeing the dark form flying past the burning wreck of the *Schmidt* as if it's nothing at all. As if she's sailing in a different universe.

"Some of the boys think she's the *Flying Dutchman*, sir."

Semmes grunts. He hardly thinks so. Does not put much stock in such romantic fantasies, opera stories. He has his own ghosts. All those men lost on the *Somers*, the children and wife he has all but deserted, Maude. But he must admit this dark ship off to windward appears most like a phantom, seems to be riding a black cloud spread between her and the silvery sea. It is, indeed, passing strange the unnatural amount of sail she carries, the lack of running lights, her absolute disinterest in the burning *Schmidt.* Never has he seen a ship that would not heave to at the sight of a burning vessel and look to rescue her crew.

"Beat to quarters, Luff . . . and prepare the starboard battery. Maybe this is the moment we've been waiting for."

"Sir?"

"Let's see if the Yanks have finally found us out."

"She has the weather gauge on us." Kell means that the stranger has the battle advantage, being the windward vessel.

"Tell the engineer to light his fires. Have the steward bring me my dress coat, my cutlass, and pistol."

***

Just seconds after *Alabama* fires a blank charge to signal the dark ship to heave to, a bright orange flash erupts from the phantom's waist.

"Down!" a warrant officer shouts. A hundred men hit the deck. Almost everyone except Kell and Semmes are on their knees when the thunder of the ghost ship's gun rolls over the *Alabama.*

"I'll be damned," says Kell.

"After him." Old Beeswax feels a sharp coppery taste in his mouth. Blood. Like the concubine, he's started biting at the inside of his cheek, and at his lip again. "Have the master-at-arms and the marine captain pass out the muskets."

For a second he thinks about Rita, the waif of a girl sleeping below in one of the junior officer's cabins. Feels a fine glow rising at the base of his brain, tosses his cane over the side. *I hunt, therefore I am, young miss.*

***

It's nearly midnight before they overhaul the stranger, burning massive amounts of the precious coal—that Semmes has been hoarding—to take the windward gauge away from the phantom. The two big swivel guns, the Blakely rifle and the eight-inch Fawcett-Preston smooth bore, as well as the port thirty-two-pounders are manned and loaded. The captain has posted sharpshooters aloft, a platoon of musketeers in the bows. The glow from the funnel casts a reddish glow on the boarding pikes stacked on the quarterdeck. The whir of the furnaces belching coal fumes has all but overwhelmed the sound of the half-gale in the rig, the sails. The phantom's sailing at more than eleven knots. *Alabama*'s steam-sailing at over thirteen, the deck glistening with spray from the bow wake.

As the raider overtakes the mystery ship, her size in comparison to the Reb astonishes Semmes. The dark sailer is fully half again larger than *Alabama.* Her black hull bears a broad white streak around her waist in man-of-war fashion. The gun ports yawn open, five massive cannons are aiming at this most impertinent steamer.

"Jesus God," one of the warrant officers whispers.

Semmes draws the .44 caliber marine pistol Sam Colt gave him as a present at the outset of the war.

Seventy-five yards separate the ships, the seahawk rings for his engineer Miles Freeman to slow the pistons to half-ahead so as to keep an even pace with the prey.

Semmes steps front-and-center on the bridge deck. The crew turns to face him, waiting for his call to arms.

"Remember the *Hatteras*, men." The captain need give no plainer order. Need not quote *Hamlet* to the boys again. *Readiness is all.* They know, every man jack among them. Except that the wind is half a gale, except that the dark warship off to leeward is monstrous in its size, this moment is much like that night off Galveston back on January 11 of this year. The night when *Alabama* went yardarm-to-yardarm with the USS *Hatteras.* Sunk her.

Now in full dress uniform, saber at his side, he stands as erect as a man of iron. Tries not to move or fidget. His officers and men are looking for cool leadership. He makes a show of twirling the tips of his mustache.

Semmes feels the strange clarity of battle come over him. He can see both the *Alabama* and her adversary clearly in the light of the nearly full moon. Winged, black monsters. Knows his gunnery officers will give the signal to fire without hesitation . . . if the quarry declares herself a ship of the United States of America.

For seconds the only sounds are the rush of wind in the rigging and the fuming funnel. The crew—barebacked, bandanas on their heads, wax stuck in their ears against the roaring of the guns—stand by their weapons. Master gunners hold lock-strings in hand. Guns loaded, quoins fitted, elevation screws set to deliver fire at the stranger's waterline.

"What ship is that?" Kell's voice booms from his megaphone.

"Her Britannic Majesty's ship . . . *Diomede*."

"Hold your fire!" Semmes's voice cracks.

Kell announces through his megaphone that they are the Confederate States steamer *Alabama*. The Brits say they suspected as much when they saw the Reb making sail in the wake of the burning *Schmidt*.

"We thought you a Yank." Kell again, the tension now gone from his voice.

"Spoiling for a duel, are you, mate?"

Semmes holsters his pistol, finds Miguel Cervantes's deluded *Don Quixote* rising in his mind. "I fear we tilt at windmills, Luff."

"Our day will come."

22

USS KEARSARGE
July 9, 1863

Captain John Ancrum Winslow rips the navy blue service cap off his head and sends it flying. It hits the glass chimney of one of the gimbaled oil lamps on the wall of the great cabin, knocking the glass to the cabin sole where it shatters into a hundred pieces. The hat itself lies amid the wreckage, smoking, the bill singed as it passed through the lamp flame.

"This is too much, Gideon Welles. You ask too much of me!" He barks at the hat.

He has just arrived in Tenerife tonight after charging back and forth between here and Madeira, Madeira and Gibraltar, Gibraltar and the Azores more times than he can count in the last two months. Each time he arrives to find the American consul waiting for him with word that the *Alabama* or one of her sister raiders, the *Florida* or the *Georgia,* has been sighted "just two days sail from here." And every time he arrives at the enemy's supposed latest port of call, he finds no Reb has been there. He has been in Madeira three times and never even gotten himself or his men off the ship once. Meanwhile, the pain in his dead eye persists, surging with each new frustration.

With all this chasing about he has had to return numerous times to Faial to buy coal from the Dabneys who seem to lick their lips with anticipation of their profits each time they see him. The consul here in Teneriffe is a Dabney, too, and Winslow wonders if all these consuls are conspiring together to send him on one wild-goose chase after another. He wonders if they laugh at him behind his back, call him Cyclops or some such thing because of his eye. Wonders, too, if they really give a hoot about Raphael Semmes, Confederate raiders, or ending the war. War seems like a great boon to a few of these consular fat cats who may well have bought their post from the secretary of state. But war is purgatory for Winslow and his ship.

He gives the smoking hat a kick. "This is all wrong."

The latest newspapers from England and the States are full of wretched notices. DuPont's continuing failure to seize Charleston with his ironclads, Hooker's terrible loss at Chancellorsville. But no recent reports on the *Alabama.*

His eye burns. *How long must I wait for my brother to circle home?* "And where must I wait, Raphael? Are these Portuguese and Spanish islands mere snares, delusions?"

The pain in his ruined eye flares with each new question. It's as if the very act of thinking is driving nails through his head. Only prayer and laudanum can soothe. Tonight he thinks he prefers the drug to God. It has been the *genii* in the bottle for weeks now. Two teaspoons of the tincture mixed in a glass of water is enough to turn his pain and thoughts of the Southern seahawk into nothing but a golden haze.

At least until tomorrow. . . .

There's a British man-of-war just come into the harbor from the southwest he must speak with. Name of HMS *Demeter* or something. Maybe they've seen Semmes.

***

"I believe he's looking for you, as well, Captain." The master of *Diomede* pours Winslow a second cup of tea in the wardroom of the man-of-war.

The man has not been as standoffish as most of the English sailors whom Winslow has met. Welcomed Winslow aboard the frigate with a ready laugh this morning and an invitation to join him for his "tensies," a spot of darjeeling and a plate of biscuits to tide them over until the lunch mess. He's past sixty years of age with a nest of curly white hair, spectacles, grog blossoms on his cheeks. Homeward bound from the South Atlantic, heading for Portsmouth and retirement to a little farm in Surrey.

"Then . . . you spoke to him?" Winslow feels the pain spike behind his bad eye.

"Six days ago. Just south of the Tropic of Capricorn."

"How did he look?" The words are barely out of Winslow's mouth, and already he's wondering what has prompted such a strange question. Can it be that he hopes to hear that his brother has been as physically wrecked by all these years at sea as himself?

"Cannot say I actually saw Captain Semmes. It was midnight, you see."

"Oh . . ."

"The watch had roused me just half an hour before. Said we had passed a ship afire off to leeward and a steam-sailor, bark-rigged, was chasing after us. I'm a sound, sound sleeper, sir. Was still a bit foggy."

"But you spoke to him?"

"A thunderous voice." The old man shrugs, sips from his mug of tea. He says the moon was bright. The *Diomede*'s officers could see the steam bark had sharpshooters in the tops, his guns aimed and manned, flying a flag he had never seen before.

"The stars and bars of the Confederate States."

"So I gather. But I'll tell you. I did not like the way he ate up my stern and seized the weather gauge on me. Very bold. Most aggressive behavior."

"He threatened you?"

"Good sir, we came within seconds of annihilating each other. My gunners were ready for him. But thank God it did not come down to . . ."

"But the *Diomede* is a much larger ship. Surely . . ."

"You haven't been yard-to-yard with that *Alabama*. She's a sinister-looking thing, I'll tell you. Like a jungle cat. With her raked masts, the sleek black hull, that bridge deck amidships, like your own, where a man can look down on his ship and see what's happening with each of his men, each of his guns."

"Still, you can throw more metal than the *Alabama*."

"Aye. I would have hurt her."

"She was under sail . . . and steam?"

The Brit says that the Lairds who built this dark ship know their business. They must have put some brilliant engines in her because *Diomede* is no slouch for speed. Yet *Alabama* had better than a knot on the man-of-war.

"I got the feeling that if it came down to shooting, your man Semmes could have sailed rings around me firing continuously with those swivel guns of his. A ship like that, like your *Kearsarge*, too, will change everything they ever taught us about naval battle tactics."

Winslow thinks about the sheathing over his ship's chain-mail armor. Feels not delight but a hot poker of pain behind his eye. Wishes he had brought some laudanum to sneak into this tea.

"You said he's looking for me?"

"He was spoiling for a fight. Said he thought we were a Yank."

"Did he say where he was headed?"

"Didn't bother to ask. Knew he'd give out a lie."

"No doubt."

"Balls. Brass balls."

"Beg your pardon."

"Captain Semmes. Never seen anything like him. Acts like the world's his oyster . . . man has to have balls of brass."

"He's always had an arrogant streak."

"What are you going to do when you catch up with that wild-cat? Or he catches up with you?"

The pain rips through Winslow's head in a jagged bolt. But it yields light, too. He hears himself say something he did not even know he was thinking. "I will find my brother's weakness, Captain . . . before he finds mine."

23

DISTRICT OF COLUMBIA
July 14, 1863

Gideon Welles, who has been walking across the north lawn of the executive mansion toward the gate with the president at his side, sees Lincoln suddenly falter . . . and stop. His face convulsing, eyes starting to tear in the summer heat and haze. The president has just summarily canceled the morning's cabinet meeting, five minutes after it started, and burst out of the White House asking Welles to follow. To Welles, his boss has never looked so distressed. Not even at Willie's funeral.

"I should be happy," Lincoln says. "In the last ten days we have taken Vicksburg. Meade has defeated Lee at Gettysburg, driven him back to Virginia."

"But . . . you wish Meade would have cut Lee off before he crossed the Potomac, captured him."

"I urged it. Lord, how I urged it. Talked day and night with Ed Stanton at the War Department, virtually begged the man to light a fire under his generals. Meade could have ended this war, right there, right then."

"I don't know what to say, Mr. President. Your disappointment is my own."

"Give me some good news."

Welles knows Lincoln refers to the joy the two of them felt so recently when David Porter's wire had come in about Grant capturing

Vicksburg. The president and secretary of the navy had celebrated with a party, rousing music.

"Charles Wilkes has been relieved at last. He's back."

"Another slacker."

"Cut off from the gravy train now . . . and under the careful watch of Major Allen."

"I hate this secret war. Allen does not have enough men to watch all the scoundrels who connive against us. I fear dark evil in our midst, Gideon."

"The Rebs' Secret Line and the Knights of the Golden Circle seem to have sunk their roots in many places—the army as well as the navy."

He does not add "and in half the branches of government" as it now seems. Does not raise the specter of the mysterious Iago, nor Senator Hale and his prodigal daughter who is dazzled by that South-leaning actor Booth. Does not mention the Copperheads and their sympathizers who have incited days of rioting against the draft in New York City. Does not mention Attorney General Bates with his son, the Confederate officer. Does not mention that Major Allen has proof that when Edwin Stanton was in the Buchanan cabinet he passed all manner of secret information on to Bill Seward . . . or that Stanton openly spoke of the virtues of the South seceding. Does not speak of Seward's endless intriguing with the British. Welles knows all these things are already boiling in his president's mind. Knows, too, that to name all the places where he suspects Rebel rats would quite possibly extinguish the sun, destroy all hope.

Lincoln chokes. "What does it mean? Great God, what does it mean?" He's asking if he, Welles, and the Republic are doomed.

"To think that we were once made anxious by the mere likes of Mistress Rose Greenhow and Raphael Semmes's tart . . ."

"And those threats you've been getting in the red envelopes."

"More thunder than lightning."

"Sir?"

"Do you remember that the last threat I got said I would be dead by the Fourth of July?"

"But you're still alive."

"Exactly. The Reb's bark is worse than his bite." Welles is trying to be optimistic here.

"Unless they have decided it's in their best interest to keep you and me alive for a little longer." Lincoln rubs his eyes, swipes at the tears on his cheeks with the palms of his huge, bony hands.

"You mean they consider us inept?"

"Or . . . at least they believe they've found a way to stifle all of our best intentions."

Welles suddenly thinks of his secret plan for Winslow and the *Kearsarge* . . . and a morsel of good news that he *can* share with the president. "I've dispatched the *Vanderbilt* again to find Semmes."

Welles says that the president might recall that Wilkes had commandeered the *Vanderbilt* for his Flying Squadron and his own personal prestige last spring in St. Thomas. But with Wilkes now recalled in disgrace, Welles has restored the able Charles Baldwin as captain on the USS *Vanderbilt* and ordered Baldwin after the *Alabama* with all haste and deliberation. The *Vanderbilt,* a converted high-speed, side-wheel passenger liner is the largest and speediest ship in the U.S. Navy. She's faster than *Alabama,* three times the Reb's size, and capable of throwing twice the Confederate's metal with her fifteen guns. The *Vanderbilt*'s two eleven-inch cannons fire 135-pound projectiles.

"A hungry monster of our own . . . to catch the seahawk," says the president, clapping his hands together. "Won't our friends in the press be impressed when they get a hold of this story?"

More impressed if they knew that our monster side-wheeler's just the show piece in my plan, Welles nearly says. But then he remembers that his plan's main advantage is its secrecy. Remembers that the spies of the Confederate's Line seem everywhere, that no one knows who or what Iago really is. So . . . let the press shine their lights on

Baldwin and the *Vanderbilt*, while Winslow and the *Kearsarge* hunt in the dark.

"I'm going to catch Raphael Semmes, Mr. President . . . on my honor."

"Could it please be soon?"

24

FOLLY AND MORRIS ISLANDS, SOUTH CAROLINA
July 18–19, 1863

It's just after dark when Maude hears a new and heavier note to the thunder, sees the first flashes of lightning. She shudders, knows that this storm comes from guns, not the clouds overhead.

All day the Union fleet with its ironclad monitors has been bombarding Fort Wagner on Morris Island at the entrance to Charleston Harbor. Now thousands of Union soldiers are on the move. The battle to wrench Fort Wagner from the South has begun in earnest. And the Rebs are fighting back. Right now it seems to Maude that all the world is trembling with dread of this beast that rends men limb from limb in the night. This insane war from which there seems no deliverance for America, for Maude, for her children. She wonders if this is how it has been, or will be, for the sailor she still loves beyond all reason—the deafening explosions, the blinding light, the terror in the dark—when the Yanks come calling on him.

Maude's camped with Minty Tubman, other nurses, doctors, the army's afterguard, teamsters, and bargemen on the beach at the north end of Folly Island across the ocean inlet dividing the shore here from Morris Island and the battle. Their tents are ringed around smoky campfires of driftwood and sea grass. Despite the July heat, they huddle close to the fires. Maybe, just maybe, the flames and the fumes may drive off the mosquitoes and the sand fleas. Since arriving here two days ago to support the young colonel, Robert Gould Shaw, and his Fifty-Fourth Massachusetts Volunteer

Infantry regiment of black soldiers, insect bites have raised scores of irritating welts on Maude's bare skin, everyone else's, too.

"I gots a bad feeling," says Tubman.

"The men are so tired." Another nurse's voice is faint, ragged. "They've been marching through the swamps and the sand without proper food since yesterday."

White flashes erupt nearly overhead. There's a cascading rumble of cannons . . . followed by the shrill wail of an infant.

"That's my little Levi!" Maude rises from the log where she has been sitting next to Minty by the campfire and rushes to her tent and her babies bundled into their beds of carpetbags.

She's ducking down to enter the wall tent, just two steps inside, when someone grabs her right wrist with one hand and covers her mouth with another.

"You went and lied to me about the last raid on the Combahee River." It's the bearded bear. She can smell the whiskey and tobacco on his breath.

She flings his hand off her face. "Leave me alone!"

He grabs her free wrist. His hands are vises as he pulls her against him. "You can't fool me no more."

"Go to hell."

"I've been watching your every move for a month."

"Bugger off."

"Dixie's going to feast on black meat tonight, darlin'. Thanks to you."

"Let me go."

He frees her wrists . . . is suddenly just a voice in the dark. "You know how I knowed this here raid was coming? You know why Brigadier General Taliaferro and the Charleston Battalion going to turn the beach red with Yankee blood?" He gives the general's name its local pronunciation—"Tolliver."

She feels something foul rising in her throat.

"I watched you, and I seed that when something big's coming for you and the black Moses, you start to take them babies of yours to your breasts two a time.

"So when I seen you nursing double this last week, I just followed you. And I passed word on up the Line. Now here we are. And Dixie's going to have her day."

She pictures the blood-soaked, mangled faces of all the boys she could not save. In the hospital in Richmond. Alongside the banks of Antietam Creek. On the railway tracks outside of Jacksonville. A terrible guilt's taking shape in her mind. "Why are you telling me this?"

"You're part of the Line now, gal. Just like before when you was in Washington. And when Mrs. Davis and Old Jeff had you carry dispatches to Nassau and Raphael Semmes."

"Bloody hell!" She can't believe this bastard knows her secret past. How could this be unless someone in Richmond is feeding him information. Someone high in the government, perhaps the secretary of war, that twinkly-eyed Jew Judah Benjamin. Or maybe someone in the executive mansion itself. But damn it all, she's never going back to those days of spying for Rose Greenhow or sneaking military messages through the blockade. She'll not sink to such treachery, not even to claim her pound of flesh for her abuse at the hands of Lincoln's Major E. J. Allen, not even to avenge the murder of her friend Fiona. Not even for her Raffy.

He snatches her, his hands claw against her shoulder blades. Pulls her hard against his immense body. "Lift up that dress. Slow and easy."

***

Sunrise. Maude stands barefoot in the sand, hugging Minty Tubman. Feels her tears coming. She wants to say that the bearded bear is here. She wants to say, "He raped me, and I want to kill him." She wants to say that this legion of dead boys spread the length of the Morris Island beach by the ebbing tide sprawl here in part because of her. She wants to say that she's started carrying a very sharp paring knife tucked in her corset to protect herself. But what comes from her mouth is a question. "Has God abandoned us?"

The battle for Fort Wagner raged much of the night. But now all is quiet . . . except for the moans of the wounded, the dying. The Federal commanders, those who have survived, have sent couriers, urgent pleas for doctors and nurses to come and help. And now they are here. The barge landed Maude, Minty Tubman, the other evangel nurses, the doctors on the beach at Morris Island half an hour ago. Hundreds of dead bodies are scattered at the ocean's edge, leaking blood into the sand and the sea. Hundreds of others lie or sit crippled where they fell, waiting for the miracles of morphine, a bandage, a gentle touch, a sip of coffee, whiskey, death.

Casualties to the Federal force of 5,000 men number more than 1,500. Twenty-five-year-old Colonel Shaw of the Fifty-Fourth Massachusetts Volunteers has died charging the ramparts of the fort, died with more than a hundred of his black soldiers. Fort Wagner has held. The Rebs, with the advance notice that came up the Line from the bearded bear, had time to prepare for the siege. Now Dixie is indeed having its day. Sand fleas, flies, mosquitoes are already swarming. Already the smell of this place—the torn flesh, blood, and shite steaming in the Carolina heat—is worse than Antietam. The locals call this place Coffin Island. This morning the name seems more than apt to Maude.

"I'm no good here anymore." She squeezes her friend Minty tightly. Thinks how all she has ever wanted to do in life is to love a sailor, love these babies, help make the world a free and peaceful place. But now look how she has been used by the fiends of war. *Look at all the blood of these boys on my hands.*

Convulsive sobs roll through her chest. "I thought I could help. But . . . now I take a knife with me everywhere I go . . . and I'll bloody well kill somebody before they hurt me or my babies. I've got to get away from this country."

"Ssssh, Missy." Tubman wipes the tears from Maude's eyes with a finger, wipes her own, too. "This here be the Armageddon. Maybe the advent of end times. But the glory coming. It coming one way or the other. We gone find you and you babies a ship to take you clear away . . . before anybody else get hurt."

25

CSS ALABAMA

Early August, 1863

The Rebel cruiser has been nearly a month under constant sail crossing the South Atlantic, sixteen days without even the sighting of another ship. Locked in a gray and stormy world unto itself, with no news of the war or loved ones. Now this. Death in Africa. At such a heartbreakingly beautiful place.

Alabama swings to her anchor in Saldanha Bay tonight, sixty miles north of Cape Town, a land-locked harbor ringed with palisades, rolling farms, forests, boulders that look like they have been dropped on the landscape by giants. And third engineer Simeon Cummings lies dead on the quarterdeck, wrapped in the Stars and Bars, attended by an honor guard of sailors with loaded muskets. As if manmade weapons can keep death's demons at bay.

From shore come riffs of lively, syncopated dance music played on concertinas, guitars, and fiddles. It's a soft, warm night and things are heating up in the taverns of the small Boer community ashore. The Afrikaners are in a festive mood. Their music reminds the captain of the *Alabama* of the Cajun songs he used to dance to as a younger man on the shores of Mobile Bay . . . reminds Semmes of a time when the touch of a woman's hand and the lingering taste of cane liquor on the tongue could make the night seem a spell that would never break. Nights like those, too, that he spent with Maude in Washington and Nassau.

But now the cheery music, memories of youth, women, love, magical nights—thoughts of a fine young life cut short—are too much for Raphael Semmes. All the *Alabama* seems in mourning. He's wandering this dark and solemn ship searching for some place to escape. A place where he can stop thinking about poor Cummings, who shot himself accidentally while returning from a hunting outing this evening. A load of buckshot shattering his chest when his loaded gun struck a gunwale while he was boarding the cutter to return to the ship. When Semmes closes his eyes to drive off images of the dead youth's ribs and heart blown all to pieces, he sees the faces of his sons Oliver and Spencer, who are now soldiering for the South. *What if they are among the tens of thousands of boys cut down by the Yanks at home?* His wife Anne would be shattered. Cummings's mother will be devastated. He must write her, has started.

Dear Madame,

As the captain of the CSS *Alabama*, it is my sad duty to inform you. . . .

But he has given up, left the letter unfinished on his desk. His hands are too shaky to write. And now he's wandering deep in the bowels of his ship. A lone man, a faint shadow, passing beneath the dim light of an oil lamp hung in the dark gallery between the *Alabama*'s four towering boilers. No flames in the fire boxes now, just damp, sooty gusts sighing through the open flues.

"Who goes there?" A thick Welsh accent. It's Chief Engineer Miles Freeman.

"A fellow in sore need of comfort." Semmes hears his voice confess before he can bridle it. He's relieved to hear Freeman, the man whose quick thinking and intuition have delivered the *Sumter* and *Alabama* from dozens of mechanical near disasters. The ship's wizard. A fellow who "knows things" sometimes.

"That you, Captain?"

"Afraid so."

Semmes can see the engineer now. He's back aft of the boilers, a silhouette perched on one of the engines' cylinders like some immense crow. His flowing black curls and full beard obscure almost all of his face except the soot and grease–stained nose, the huge wet eyes.

"I'm just having me a private wake for our young lad, sir."

"You're drinking?"

Freeman pauses before he answers, seems to consider whether he should admit to breaking the ship's prohibition against consuming alcohol from private stocks. Then he rolls his eyes like to hell with it.

"I just started on me second bottle of the local swill. Got another. A fair wine they make in these parts, if you ask me, sir. Goes down easy. You like a nip?"

"Are we alone?"

"Except for that rat yonder." Freeman nods at a furry shape scuttling away into the propeller shaft tunnel.

Semmes holds out his hand for the wine bottle, takes it. "If ever there was a night to drink, Mr. Freeman, tonight would be that night."

"Aye. Damned glad, I am, you come along, sir. I fear I was about to start to have me a cry."

"How this death does wound us, Mr. Freeman." Semmes takes another long sip.

"Cummings was much loved in your wardroom . . . and among me black gang down here, too."

"Jolly fellow."

"Lord, he was. I seen times that boy could make two dozen tired and pissed-off stokers laugh their bellies sick with the way he talked. Right vulgar he could be. But bloody hilarious. One time I heard him call old Abe Lincoln 'that flute-snooted, monkey-eared, mother-fucking giraffe that done hijacked America.'"

A little snort of laughter bursts from Semmes's mouth. He quells it with another drink, savors the crisp white wine on his tongue.

"Aye, that lad will be missed, sir."

"The superstitious men among the crew might take this as a dark omen."

Freeman reaches for the wine bottle, tilts it to his lips, takes a long gulp. "I'm afraid I might suffer a bit in that regard, Captain."

"Come again?"

"Our water maker, the condenser, it's just about to shite the bed, sir . . . and I heard a rumor when I was ashore today."

"Rumor?"

"Some New York bark just come into Cape Town with news that that fellow Gideon Welles has sent Beelzebub and his minions out to hunt us down."

26

SAINT HELENA ISLAND
August 16, 1863

Commander Charles Baldwin, master of the USS *Vanderbilt,* would like to hang someone right now, possibly himself.

He has had definite word today from a Danish schooner that she sighted the *Alabama* in Cape Town just two weeks ago. This is the freshest news of his quarry that he has had in months of searching . . . and the closest he has ever been to Semmes. So close he can smell the filthy pirate.

But there's no coal to fill his ship here at this little English island halfway between Brazil and Africa. The *Vanderbilt*'s bunkers are down to only 600 tons of fuel. Steaming hard, she can burn in excess of seventy-five tons a day. And with these nearly constant mid-winter gales blowing out of the southeast, expecting much help from the sails is foolhardy. The wind is right on the nose. The immense side wheels act as a drag in the water when they are not churning, and their shrouds create windage to slow the ship's progress even more. The *Vanderbilt* is at least twelve days of steaming from southern Africa, and there simply is not enough coal for the passage. *The goddamn numbers don't add up.*

"Yet I must leave for Cape Town *posthaste*. I must stop Semmes." Baldwin's voice is a bark in the direction of the U.S. consul who has just arrived on board this massive warship swinging to her anchor in the bight known as Jamestown Bay. The consul has come to confirm that other vessels, too, have passed this way of late from the east claiming to have seen both the *Alabama* and another Confederate raider, *Georgia*, off the African capes.

"Surely, another collier with a new load of fuel will arrive any time, Commander," says the portly young consul. "Why not relax for a few days? Give your men a taste of shore leave and the many delights of the taverns of Upper Jamestown, of which you have most surely heard. Let me take you into the hills to show you Longwood House where the great Napoleon spent his last years."

Napoleon Bonaparte. Until now Baldwin had forgotten that the self-made emperor of France had been banished to Saint Helena in 1815 following his defeat at Waterloo, abdication, and imprisonment by the British. Here Napoleon's kingdom, once almost all of Western Europe, had shrunken to a garden. He was no longer remembered for what he had accomplished, but for what he had lost. *Good God, will I, too, be so doomed?*

Baldwin feels a nasty twitch starting at the corner of his right eye. "I have ambiguous orders."

"Commander?"

Baldwin's a bantam cock of an officer with a tendency to pace restlessly when he's nervous or irritated. His red-haired and clean-shaven cheeks make him look younger than his forty-one years. Right now he's stomping around the quarterdeck of his ship so randomly, so quickly, that the consul can barely keep up.

"Look at this, sir." He seizes a dispatch from his pocket—a letter from Gustavus Fox, Gideon Welles's assistant secretary of the navy—passes it to the consul. It orders him to chart a course in pursuit of the Rebel raider according to his best judgment "be it to the uttermost parts of the earth."

"Do such words leave any room for doubt what Mr. Fox and Mr. Welles would do to me should I not take up the hunt for Raphael Semmes this very moment?"

"I'm afraid you have a problem."

Baldwin stops pacing, stares ashore at the tidy—but apparently saucy—little port of Jamestown stretching away from the harbor, up a long, deep, and narrow valley. Beyond this outpost, the interior of the island is a quilt of hills, their tops a thatch of green forests and what seem to be spiky groves of dead and fallen trees. His mind begins to drift toward those forests, the groves.

"What was that you said?"

"I fear you have a problem, commander."

Something seems to pinch him behind the eyes, and he hears himself saying words his father once told him. "There are no problems, good sir. Just solutions."

"How's that, now?"

The bantam cock stiffens, almost comes to military attention. Wonders how much of that dead timber on yonder hills his men could collect in the next day. Wonders how many extra hours or days of steaming he could buy with that wood. *And what about all the bagged coal on deck he has been using to bunker the guns and machinery from enemy fire?* There might be as much as 4,000 fifty-pound bags. A hundred tons. It might just be enough to get the *Vanderbilt* to Cape Town.

"Commander?"

"Where there's a will, there's a way, sir!"

27

USS KEARSARGE

Early September, 1863

Bay of Biscay. Course north. Wind northeast at force eight, the fifth day in a row. Seas running twenty feet, steep, sweeping the deck. Ship riding hard under storm jib and double-reefed fore-and-aft sails. Standing orders: All hands on deck must be lashed to the jack lines; keep the vessel full-and-by.

Three bells into the forenoon watch. On this gray morning two teaspoons of laudanum mixed with a mug of coffee is not enough to stop the pain that's burning behind the captain's blind eye, shooting down his neck, piercing his gut. Not enough to bring on the golden haze that will drown out the sounds of the storm. The waves slamming into the bows of the ship, rumbling and hissing over the deck. The moaning of the rigging, the shudder and creaking of masts in their partners, the working of bulkheads against frames. Worst of all, the heavy clanking as the *Kearsarge*'s new chain-mail armor shifts on its lashings with each lurch of the hull, threatens to come adrift.

Several days ago Winslow abandoned Madeira and the Azores as his hunting ground, wrote them off as distractions. He has reliable news that the Rebs' *Florida* was spotted in the Irish Sea, and—more than that—he has a strong intuition that his long-lost brother Raphael Semmes, his Esau, must soon bring *Alabama* home to the waters that gave birth to her. He has been hoping to cross the Bay of Biscay before the autumn storms begin to rage here, hoping to find shelter somewhere to the north of the bay, possibly at Brest, from where he can most easily patrol the southern entrances to the English Channel and the Irish Sea. But the weather gods have gotten to this dreadful bay first.

"And now they test me, torture me. As Gideon Welles has tested me. Why?" He's grumbling to himself, pawing through his sea chest in the great cabin for another bottle of tincture of laudanum to quell his pain. Tossing neatly folded small clothes, socks, packs of letters from his wife all over the cabin floor.

He has another bottle somewhere, could swear he hid it here in his chest. But right now it seems to be missing. Possibly it rolled off into some corner during all of this unpacking, this searching, this tossing of his ship. *Lord Almighty.* He's crawling around the sole on his hands and knees. Every bone in his body aches, every muscle. And with only one good eye and this jagged pain twisting inside his head, he can barely see in the dim light. If anyone were to come into the cabin and spy him like this. . . .

"They would bind me in a straitjacket and lock me in sickbay."

The *Kearsarge* gives a hard lurch to starboard, falls off the wind a point. Takes a wave nearly abeam and rolls viciously. Men shout from the berthing deck in the fo'castle. Everything in the great cabin that is not anchored to the sole or bulkheads—chairs, charts, books, bedding, Winslow's chest, its scattered contents, the captain himself—they all tumble to leeward.

He does not know how long it takes the ship to right herself. Now not even his good eye can see. His face is pressed hard against some sharp wooden edge. Perhaps the leg of the sideboard. Something heavy like the weight of a man pins him down.

And then it *is* a man . . . wrestling with him in the darkness. Crushing him, bending him. Blasting hot breath on his neck.

This is it. It's happening. Again. The same story he has been intending to read and discuss at Sunday's Bible study with his officers in the wardroom, the story that has been eating at him since he was first ordered to find his brother. The story of Jacob, son of Isaac and Rebecca, returning to Canaan to find his twin, find Esau.

During his journey Jacob had learned that Esau was approaching to meet him, and the news struck Jacob with fear, according to the Book of Genesis. Then Jacob was alone in the dark, "and there wrestled a man with him until the breaking of the day . . ."

"Who are you?" Winslow calls to the thing on his back.

A voice like burning wind. "Jacob says he saw God face to face. So who do you think . . ."

"How's it possible that you, the Lord God Almighty, could not overpower Jacob, do not annihilate me here and now? Is God then bound by man?"

Something like a claw tears at Winslow's hip. It feels suddenly detached, dislocated as Jacob's was at the end of the fight.

"Tell me when you've had enough."

"What?"

"Tell me when you no longer wish to fight with me."

"Is it time for me to die?"

"Is it time for you to let go, stop your whining . . . and trust me?"

He feels the pain in his hip flare until the agony of his ruined eye is nothing at all. A strange music is filling the space. Not a song exactly, more like the rippling rise and fall of ten thousand birds taking flight. And he can see again. The tumbled cabin contents, the mattress and quilt from his berth that have fallen on top of him. The heap of wool winter socks piled up at the foot of a settee. And nesting among them, the small amber bottle of laudanum he's been missing.

"Mercy," he says.

He's already squirming out from under the mattress, already has his hand on the laudanum when an odd memory strikes. There was a time back when he and Semmes were awaiting their fates aboard the *Raritan* off Veracruz, awaiting their courts martial during the

Mexican War. Winslow had been so anxious to make certain that the logic of his case for exoneration was built on the soundest models of reason. He had been driving himself crazy with sleepless nights of worry when Semmes put a hand on his friend's shoulder and asked him if he had ever read *Hamlet.* Asked if at times like this would it not help to remember Hamlet's final epiphany? "There's a divinity that shapes our ends, rough-hew them how we will."

Mercy.

The time has come to stop fighting this storm, to let the wind steer his ship. Let it blow *Kearsarge* back to the southeast. There's shelter in the river at Ferrol on the Galician coast . . . and, no doubt, a peaceful place to pray and consider Isaac's injunction to his son Jacob.

Genesis 27:40: By your sword you shall live, but your brother you shall serve; yet it shall be that when you are aggrieved, you may cast off his yoke from upon your neck.

28

BEAUFORT, SOUTH CAROLINA
Early September, 1863

Six weeks and I'm still bloody here. That's what Maude's thinking as she carts yet another chamber pot full of a wounded soldier's night soil down the back stairs. *Where's my ship? Where's my escape?*

Every morning she and the black women who help her lug more than forty pots to the outhouse behind this confiscated mansion for emptying into the pit. From the outside, the Berners Barnwell Sams House still looks elegant with its four Corinthian columns and balconies. But since being turned into a hospital for the wounded brought back from the assault on Fort Wagner, it reeks of butchery and death.

Maude and her babies have been living in this bedlam of filth and misery and moans since they got back here from Morris and Folly Islands. What else could she do to keep her mind off the killing—to keep her hand away from the knife tucked in her corset—when Minty and the young volunteer doctor from Massachusetts, Esther Hill Hawks, implored her to make this mansion into a hospital? Somebody had to help these poor men. And she had thought that it would only be for a week or two . . . before Minty could get her on a ship. But no vessel has yet left Beaufort willing to carry a woman and two babies, and now 201 Lauren Street seems Maude's own personal cage. Now the worst of the battle-wounded have died. The soldiers remaining suffer, dying slowly from the twin plagues of dysentery and malaria. It seems only a matter of time to Maude that either she or her babies will contract the diseases.

"Maybe we're going to die here," she says aloud to herself as she steps into the outhouse with the chamber pot.

"Maybe you are," says a rough voice from the shadows inside, "unless you put down that stinking thing and bend over, slut." It's the bearded bear. She hears a pistol cock as he slams the door closed behind her, locks the toggle.

Her first thought is *Oh no, not again!* But fast on its heels comes a reflexive action that is so swift and so mindless that the bearded bear is blinded by a pot-load of shite before she can even exhale.

And when she does, she's got her knife in her hand. The first slash catches him with a slanting blow across the right eye, nose, and left cheek.

He falls backward on the bench seat, dropping the pistol. His hands are just beginning to rise to his shite-soaked bleeding face when she goes for him again.

***

The sun has not fully heated the morning air when Minty Tubman takes Maude by the arm. She leads her to the landing in front of the Oaks mansion on the Beaufort River, while four other black women follow with bundles of clothes, the babies Levi and Fiona in their carpetbags. Maude's still weeping, her face so tortured that the freckles on the bridge of her nose are lost in a field of blotches.

"We ain't got time to explain to Colonels Higginson and Montgomery that filthy bear been working for the Rebs," says Minty Tubman. "It all too messy and complicated. You got to go with Walter right now before folks find out what happened, Missy."

Maude wipes her eyes and sees Minty's loyal scout Walter Plowden seated in the stern of a large canoe.

Tubman presses a wad of gold coins wrapped in a kerchief into Maude's hand. "Get in now. Go. He gone take you to Hilton Head."

"But I can't take . . . I . . ."

"Go now."

Maude feels more than sees the women around her lifting her into the canoe, settling her bags, her babies. She looks at her friend standing on the landing, wants to tell her that she loves her, that she's the best friend a mixed-up Irish lass from the West Country could ever . . . but when she opens her mouth nothing comes out.

"This ain't no time for sentiment," says Tubman.

"But I . . ."

"You been saying you had to get out of here. Don't be looking back."

Plowden dips his paddle, strokes.

Maude reaches out toward the shore, grabs for Tubman's hand. But the canoe is already pulling away, sliding away into the ebbing tide. Moving fast now.

"Take care of them childrens. . . . Maybe you finally gone find that sailorman of yours."

"Come with me."

Tubman clasps her hands together, presses them to her lips. Maybe she's praying, maybe trying to stifle tears. "We from different worlds, Missy."

"You're a saint," Maude hears herself shout, to the fading figure on the shore.

"So are you," says her friend.

Then the canoe rounds a bend and there is only the river ahead . . . with the sun turning the water into a sheet of hammered gold.

"Tonight you gots to follow the stars in the sky that make the drinking gourd," says Plowden.

Maude hugs her babies to her chest, nuzzles them. Speaks to them.

"We're going to Hilton Head, then Canada." Her voice is choked, faltering. "How . . . ? I haven't a bloody clue."

29

THE CAPE OF GOOD HOPE
September 14, 1863

"Something really big's sitting out there, Captain." Lieutenant Sinclair's whispering. "We were just about to sound the middle of the watch, when we heard a bell off to seaward ringing the watch, and the splash of side wheels starting for a minute or so, then stopping again."

Semmes feels something tighten in his guts. He has just been called to the deck. Had been asleep, lost in a strange dream about nuzzling Maude in a Cape Town graveyard when his steward, Bartelli, rapped on his door at about ten o'clock. The deck watch had spied something suspicious.

"Where away?" The captain and Sinclair, the officer of the deck, are on the port wing of *Alabama*'s bridge.

"Three points off the port bow." It's still winter here, and Sinclair has on his great coat and a muffler. The muffler falls away from his neck, nearly blows overboard as he swings his arm eastward toward the Indian Ocean.

The *Alabama* has been loafing along under reduced canvas, no lights showing. Hunting on this moonless, misty night. Hoping to surprise a fat Yank merchantman homing in on the lighthouse winking from Cape Agulhas twelve miles to the northwest, trying to steer clear of Point Danger while rounding the African capes. But merchantmen rarely have side wheels. And they certainly don't stop and start while rounding these capes during the stormy winter months.

"The enemy?"

"Perhaps. Yes, sir."

Semmes reaches for the night binoculars hanging round his neck. He confiscated these off a prize. *What a marvelous invention!* He scans the dark waves off the port bow moving his binoculars from left to right, sees nothing but mist tending toward fog. Scans back again from the bows—right to left. Something catches his eye for a second, a greenish shadow against the black night, then disappears into the mist. He scans back. This time he sees the towering round stern of an immense, high-sided warship three times the size of the *Alabama*, the faint glow from two stacks. In Cape Town he had read newspapers about the Confederate Army's devastating losses in Pennsylvania and on the Mississippi . . . and cringed. Now he wonders if this is how Lee felt at Gettysburg, Pemberton felt at Vicksburg. Outclassed, overwhelmed. *Jesus Christ Almighty*!

"Should I clear the ship for action, sir?"

"Not yet. Nobody makes a sound."

***

"He's out here somewhere, Luff." Captain Charles Baldwin's pacing his quarterdeck with his executive officer at his heel on this black night. "I can almost taste his blood."

The captain of the *Vanderbilt* has barely slept for the last three days since leaving Simon's Bay just east of Cape Town. His usually clean cheeks have become a snarl of red whiskers. His crisp blue uniform and cap wrinkled, sweat-soiled. He thinks that he smells combat like a pit dog before its fight when it's starving, can think of nothing but chewing on an enemy's neck.

No sooner had his ship limped into the British naval port at Simon's Bay under sails and the very last of the coal dust in his bunkers, than he heard that he had missed the Rebs' *Georgia* here by only eighteen hours. Missed the *Alabama* by fewer than three weeks.

Semmes, by all accounts, was treated like royalty during his visit. The gentry of Cape Town and British high command had wined and dined the seahawk. The press pursued him endlessly for interviews and photographs. Women from the countryside traveled for days just to gaze into his gray eyes and have him linger as he took their offered hands, their arms for escorting. Hordes followed him through the streets begging autographs. Never before had South Africa seen such idol worship. The locals have even come up with a rousing song called "Daar kom die Alibama."

The news was enough to make Baldwin nearly sick to his stomach. He liked it better when Rear Admiral Walker told him that more than fifteen Jacks had deserted Semmes while his cruiser undertook re-coaling and myriad repairs at Simon's Bay. Liked it better, too, when British officers gossiped that Semmes seemed to have lost his sense of maritime law and was slipping into acts of hubris and piratical knavery.

According to the cape wags, the seahawk had seized the Yankee bark *Seabride* just beyond the three-mile limit of South Africa. Now the *Alabama* was heading up the east coast of Africa to find some remote place to rendezvous with his prize and a collection of businessmen from Cape Town. Semmes aimed to sell the ship and its contents without ever seeking the blessing of a prize court. Some of the locals believed that after Semmes brokered his deal for the *Seabride*, he intended to come back to the capes, to hunt and bask in the glory granted him by an enthralled populous. Others claimed Semmes was heading for the island of Mauritius.

Baldwin felt a surge of battle fever. He hired every coal porter he could find, took on more than 900 tons of English anthracite to fill his empty bunkers and headed east beyond Point Danger to wait in ambush for *Alabama*.

Now here he is. Still waiting after three days and three nights. But tonight feels different somehow. Maybe because the gale that has been battering his ship almost since the *Vanderbilt* left Simon's Bay has finally abated. The glass has begun to rise again. The wind has backed to the westward.

"Confound this damned mist," Baldwin says to his luff.

"I believe dry wind off the land will burn it off shortly."

"If Semmes is under sail, he could sneak right by us within a mile and we might never see him tonight. He could be right there yonder in that fog bank."

Both men stare off to starboard into the swirling miasma, squint. See nothing.

"Have you heard anything suspicious?"

The luff waits some seconds before answering. "No, sir. Not a peep."

"That's what scares me."

30

DISTRICT OF COLUMBIA
Late September, 1863

Gideon Welles is reading a dispatch from the consul in Liverpool about the Rebs' current shipbuilding in England . . . when a shadow falls across the dispatch and someone clears his throat. Looking up, Welles sees the president standing in the doorway with a cockeyed grin on his face.

"Don't this beat all, Gideon?"

Welles unconsciously adjusts his wig, starts to rise out of respect. . . .

"Sit, man."

The secretary of the navy settles back in the chair, feels distinctly small and childlike with the president towering over him in a stovepipe hat. Feels clueless as well, has not the faintest idea what on earth the president is talking about or why he has shown up this cool, fall afternoon at the Navy Department. The president has only been here about three times in his life.

And this odd grin. Strange. Lincoln has been gloomy for more than a week since he got the casualty reports from the battle at Chickamauga Creek on the Tennessee-Georgia border. The Union losses were over 16,170—about 1,600 killed, 10,000 wounded, and 4,500 captured or missing. Even though the Confederates won the battle, they seem to have lost even more men.

"I've just been talking to Major Allen," says the president. "That man is a wonder."

Welles doesn't know what to say. E. J. Allen is a lot of things, mostly disagreeable things. The word *wonder* is hardly the first word the secretary would use to describe Lincoln's pet weasel.

"Do you know what he told me?"

"I'm sorry, Mr. President, I. . . ."

"He told me that Raphael Semmes's whore is not dead as we thought. She has resurfaced, Gideon."

Welles recalls the day two years ago when that red-haired Irish tart hit him with a tin of beans. They were at a stable in the Murder Bay section of the District where he and Allen held her captive.

"She has been working in one of our hospitals for Negro soldiers in Beaufort, South Carolina. She was nursing those boys. Working for us, mind you."

"You mean she switched sides?"

"So it seems."

"More like that Jezebel was spying on us for the Secret Line."

"Allen doesn't think so."

"Really, Mr. President?"

Lincoln nods, the odd grin back on his face.

"I can't believe it. That woman was a terror for the Southern cause. She . . ."

"Allen says she's got herself two babies now. One vanilla and one chocolate."

Welles feels himself squirm in his seat, his small clothes knotting between his legs.

"Have you ever heard anything as plumb crazy as this?"

The secretary says he can't believe it. Maybe Allen's sources have the wrong woman.

"She killed a fellow a few weeks back in Beaufort. He appears to have been a Reb agent."

"What?"

"Cut up his face. Ripped open his jugular and windpipe. Then drove a paring knife up to the hilt into his chest."

Welles remembers the night she hit him with the beans in Murder Bay, clocked E. J. Allen with a horseshoe. "Then she got away, right?"

"How did you know?"

"She always does."

Lincoln drops into a chair, rubs his chin. "Allen thinks we should find her."

Welles gives the president a look that asks what he has in mind.

"Something's changed that girl. Allen says maybe she's ready to turn against Raphael Semmes."

"But where has she gone now?"

"That's what I want you to follow up. Talk to Allen."

Welles can't help the sigh escaping his chest. *Why me again?*

"I trust you, Gideon. It would not do for me to have any hand in the Major's . . ." Lincoln pauses to choose his words carefully. "In his activities."

The secretary understands. The national elections are just a little more than a year away and already popular national figures like General George McClellan have made it known that they may well challenge Lincoln in the 1864 election. If he wants to have even a prayer of a chance at re-election, the president cannot risk being linked to one of Allen's dirty little witch-hunts.

31

USS VANDERBILT
Late September, 1863

The Indian Ocean. Eighty-four miles east of Cape St. Marie, Madagascar. Westerly gale blowing. Ship rolling in confused seas, steaming. On course for Port Louis, Mauritius.

Commander Charles Baldwin has just finished serving himself two lamb chops when he feels a peculiar shuddering rising through the *Vanderbilt.* Growing. Sees the faces go pale on the officers seated around the wardroom table for evening mess. Hears the china and silverware start to rattle. Then two muffled bangs.

He rises from his chair, heads for the quarterdeck, thinking the goddamn deck watch has run his ship on a reef, or Raphael Semmes has ambushed him, when the chief engineer, his eyes wide as oysters, shouts.

"Everybody down!"

A searing, white wind bursts through the cabin tumbling everybody and dinner to the floor. Somewhere up forward, deeper in the ship, men are screaming.

"Boiler rivets letting go, sir." The engineer has found his feet. "We have to . . ."

The ship's whistle starts screaming and doesn't stop.

But it's nearly drowned out by the increased thumping of the walking beams and side wheels, the roar of vapor blasting from steam relief valves. The men in the engine room curse, scalded skin sliding off their arms and chests and faces, trying everything to head off a full-blown explosion.

"Beat to quarters." Baldwin's yelling. "All hands on deck."

The best he can hope for is to get as many men as he can as far from the engine room, and as close to the boats as possible, before more rivets fail and boiler plates start tearing the *Vanderbilt* and everybody aboard to shreds in a tornado of metal, wood, steam, blood. Even with the engines running as they are at a mere ten pounds of pressure to conserve coal and nurse the aging boilers and tubes, an all-out explosion could sink this ship.

The commander grabs his engineer by the arm. "Now what?"

"Hope the crown sheet doesn't go dry before we've blown off steam . . . and pray God owes us a fucking favor, sir."

***

"I thought I better see this for myself," says Baldwin to his luff and the chief engineer as he leads them down the ladder.

It has been twelve hours since the number two aft boiler blew five rivets and came within a minute of completely self-destructing. The engine room still feels and looks like the very furnace of Hades.

Even in the dim light of the oil lanterns everything has a white, baked look. The steam has blasted the paint from the bulkheads and ceiling on the inside of the hull, and spread a white film onto every surface and into every crevice of the vast boiler room. The air stinks of vaporized grease and something akin to rotting chicken.

Glancing around, Baldwin imagines the terror the firemen and assistant engineer must have felt as they desperately tried to blow off steam, shut down the failing boiler, escape the killing heat. Four men did not make it. Six others are in sickbay, their blistering skin plastered with a mix of pork tallow, arnica, and causticum. Four of these men are unconscious and running high fevers. All have been dosed with morphine. None will probably survive.

"This is awful," says the commander.

No one responds. *Awful* is too weak a word.

"How bad is it, Engineer?"

"We've got steam up in the number one and number two forward boilers. Just six pounds pressure to be safe."

"They're that bad?" Baldwin asks.

The engineer nods his head. Says the tubes in the forward boilers are corroded all to hell. Same with the number one aft boiler. The boiler that came apart, the number two aft, was the best of the lot.

"Can we repair them at sea?" asks the luff.

"Not a chance . . . and then there's the starboard side-wheel shaft. One of my oilers thinks he's spotted a crack about two feet inboard of the bearing."

Baldwin claws at his left cheek unconsciously. "Is there any good news?"

"Those men that were down here when she let go, they saved the ship." The engineer's voice struggles not to crack.

"We owe them our lives," says the luff.

"And so does Raphael Semmes and his bunch of pirates." Baldwin's words burn in his throat. "For the moment."

Nobody speaks for half a minute. The pistons chug . . . slowly. The twin Allaire engines' ninety-inch cylinders hissing with each exhaust stroke as the piston rods pound.

"We're going to turn back for home aren't we, sir?" Only the engineer could have the brass to ask the skipper this question.

Baldwin claws his cheek again, leaves red marks with his nails. "If we can get to Mauritius, we will make what repairs we can. Then we must take stock."

"Surely the Brits at the capes have warned Semmes that we are hard on his heels, sir."

Baldwin has a faraway look in his eyes, seems to be staring into one of the open fireboxes as a stoker lays in some coal. "We've been playing at chess, Luff."

"Yes, sir."

"Then let's hope that our sacrifices may have some value, that Semmes fears us still."

"So that his fear may yet drive him to a fatal mistake?"

"Check."

"Except for these machinery problems, we would have had Semmes by now, sir."

The captain of the *Vanderbilt* flashes his executive officer a withering look. "Tell that to the history books."

32

HILTON HEAD, SOUTH CAROLINA
Mid-October, 1863

"You gone be safe now," says a voice. It sounds as sweet and smooth as molasses to Maude. She inhales deeply, hugs her babies to her chest. Then she heaves a sigh as a strong female hand guides her into a dark building, closes the door behind her.

For the last month she has been moving from house to house among the Negroes in Port Royal and on several islands in the Low Country, hiding from Federal soldiers and men in plain clothes with dogs who seem to want her for much more than killing the bearded bear. Tonight a boatman has landed her and her babies here at a place called Mitchellville on the northern end of Hilton Head Island. It is a newly built, planned village of black freemen where Port Royal Sound meets the ocean.

Her nose catches the heavy scent of men's sweat. She hears the low rumble of drums. There is something else in the air. Wet and smelling like a malt of crushed mint, cloves, something sharp and musty. She begins to shiver with exhaustion . . . and worry that tonight's odyssey is just beginning.

"Fear not," says the voice of the female who has been leading her by the hand. Suddenly, her arms clasp Maude from behind. She tries to cast them off. Can feel tears starting to run down her cheeks.

"Shsssh, honey, shsssh. Don't be crying. Things dem gone be fine."

It's too dark, and Maude's eyes are too full of tears to see. But she feels one of the other person's hands loose itself from her waist and takes the hem of a skirt or apron and wipes the tears from her eyes.

"Those soldier boys and the mens dem with the dogs never gone be crossing this threshold. They be righteously afraid of what's in here. Can't touch you or babies dem."

Maude hears the heavy beat of drums again. "Where am I?"

"We calls it the Blackfish."

***

At first, Maude sees only the play of shadows against candlelight on a low ceiling. But little by little the shadows begin to settle into shapes. She's reminded of a place called the Spouter Inn that she read about in Mr. Melville's novel about the white whale. This must be some kind of tavern. The tobacco smoke is choking.

The wall nearest her and the door to the street are festooned with rusting chains, sprung leg irons, broken iron wrist cuffs, dried out bullwhips, and a crudely painted sign in letters like lightning bolts.

NEVER AGAIN

On the opposite wall hang wooden masks, spears adorned with red feathers, and a pair of intertwined snake skins stretching from floor to ceiling. A bar spans the length of the room in front of this wall. Before the bar stand the silhouettes of more than half a dozen men whose woolly heads almost touch the ceiling. Behind the bar an old Negro woman with a head scarf sparkling like fish scales pours potions into goblets from earthen jars, serves up hogs' feet from a wooden pickle barrel. In the distant corner of the room two men mounted on stools rap drums the size of tree trunks with their palms. This place feels like another world to Maude. Like the world of those old African chants when the black women back in Pennsylvania helped her birth Fiona. But here they stare at her as if she's some sort of ghost.

"I must go." Her words are loud.

The drums stop.

"Not yet. You can't." The owner of the molasses voice releases Maude from behind.

She spins to meet her captor, her arms hugging her sleeping children tight to her chest.

The men at the bar turn to look. A wooden crutch falls from where someone left it propped on the bar, raps the floor.

"What you fools be looking at? This ain't none of your business. Can't you see she scared to melting?"

For the first time Maude sees the face behind that smooth voice, those strong arms that held her. It's a girl, not more than eighteen years old. She's several inches smaller than Maude. Thin as a reed, with an explosion of frizzy, orangish hair tied behind her head with a purple ribbon. She's wearing a boy's white cotton shirt unbuttoned at the neck and a pair of blue pants cut off above her calves. Her feet are bare. She has a knotted rope for a belt.

The girl's face totally arrests Maude with its broad forehead and high cheekbones. Her skin is the light reddish brown of cinnamon, eyes like black stars set above a fine nose and full lips . . . just now spreading into a smile. Her left ear looks like a slice of fresh plum with the earlobe missing.

Just as Maude feels as if she might faint right here on the floor of the Blackfish, the girl pushes her through a curtain of wooden beads and points to steep stairs.

"Beds for you and the babies dem up there," she says. "And I left you a little jar of lemonade."

"Who are . . . ?"

"Everybody call me Cally."

***

It's morning when Levi's crying wakes her, and Maude sees that this is not the cramped garret she imagined last night. The attic has one wall and a section of the roof cut away, opening the room to sunlight, cooling breezes, a vista looking out on the Atlantic. On the remaining walls are large turtle shells, a red and orange quilt, fans woven from sweet grass to look like giant scalloped shells. Scattered around on the floors and tables are large whelk shells painted bright blue, pink, yellow, purple.

"If you put them to your ear, sometimes you can hear things and people from far away," says Cally, who's standing at the top of the stairs with a plate of steaming grits.

Across the room from Maude's straw mattress and the babies' crib fashioned from crab traps, there's a shady corner with a hammock strung from the rafters, a small bookcase and a hooked rug to match the colors of the shells. Perched on the back of a rickety chair sits the largest, blackest raven Maude has ever seen.

"What you called, pretty?" The bird cackles at Cally's question.

Maude says her name as if she's in a trance while she lifts Levi and raises her blouse to feed him.

"You feeling any better?" asks Cally.

Maude can't answer, can't take her eyes off the raven.

"This be Obi." She scoops the bird off the back of the chair, cradles him into her arms. He does not even try to find his footing, just rocks there like a baby. "You safe as sugar now."

"Are you an angel?" That's what terribly wounded men used to ask Maude when she was nursing them. Now she finds herself asking the same question. Everything and everyone has been so strange and dreamlike since she entered the Blackfish.

"I be thinking you the angel, honey."

"Not according to all those men chasing me."

The girl seems unsure what to say next, looks away. Finally she asks, "You like Cally's nest?"

Maude looks around. For some reason she thinks of a little hut in Nassau, the one where she loved her Raffy for a few days. The cottage like the one he said he would find for the two of them in Brazil after the war, after he made his peace with his wife. Just one room, but clean, freshly painted in pinks and blues. Windows wide open to the trade winds. Scents of acacia, bougainvillea drifting in. Hummingbirds darting among the blossoms outside.

"I want to live here," says Maude as she nuzzles the top of little Levi's head with her nose.

"You already are."

"I mean forever."

"That not possible."

"Because the soldiers are after me?"

"Mens dem chasing me from both the North and the South."

Bloody tell me about it, lass, she almost says. But what comes from her mouth is something different.

"We're on our own." Maude looks out at the indigo sea, wonders if this persecution, this isolation is how her Raffy feels, too.

"Amen," says Cally. "But I gots us a plan."

33

CSS ALABAMA
Late October, 1863

Semmes: in his berth . . . tonight it feels like a coffin.

He fears that he has made a terrible error by heading *Alabama* to the Far East in hopes of running down a pack of Yankee clippers. His ship has been more than thirty days at sea battling the ceaseless storms of the southern Indian Ocean without once finding a Yank to prey on, nineteen days without seeing another ship. Every day the wind and seas take their toll on his ship and men. *Alabama* has made a run of 4,410 miles due east on the thirty-ninth parallel. In twenty-four days under sail, she has averaged 178 miles a day. Perhaps a record for vessels at this latitude. But the copper plates on the bottom have begun to corrode and curl, slowing the ship more every day. Leaving her seams open and leaking.

The constant abrasion from mountainous seas has opened topside leaks as well. Semmes's bookshelf, his volumes of Shakespeare, his bedding are damp from dripping salt water. The cordage is chafing so fast the bosun can scarcely keep up with the necessary splicing. Pills Galt, the paymaster, has reported that the ship is running very low on butter, coffee, beans, tobacco. And there has been little music since the Irish fiddler Michael Mahoney jumped ship in Cape Town, no dancing from Galt's Negro Nancy-boy, David. The young doctor Llewellyn says he suspects the onset of scurvy in a number of the crew. Not four watches pass without Mr. Kell having to discipline the Jacks for fighting in the fo'castle.

At Simons Bay the English told Semmes that the *Vanderbilt* was hovering around the African capes hoping to get close enough to ram and sink the *Alabama*. He coaled, shipped some scallywags to replace the fifteen men who had deserted and put to sea on September 24, sailing south into the Roaring Forties where he hoped to avoid Captain Baldwin's monster. Since then he has been sleeping little, constantly imagining that at any moment the *Vanderbilt* will come swooping down on the *Alabama* with fifteen guns manned and loaded.

When he thinks of Maude and home, if he has the energy to think of them at all, he sees the people and things he loves as phantoms on the far side of the planet. There is no other place on earth that is farther from home than this spot. Perhaps the crew's apprehension that the *Alabama* has become the *Flying Dutchman* is coming true.

Was there a moment when those on that ghostly ship knew that they had sailed into oblivion, or do they sail as we do from watch to watch, imagining that at any time these constant storms will stop, that home and loved ones will stand waiting and wreathed in gold on the horizon?

Some days ago Semmes turned his ship north toward the Straits of Sunda between Java and Sumatra, the gateway to the South China Sea and the East Indies. Since then, *Alabama* has crossed the Tropic of Capricorn and is now approaching the twelfth parallel of south latitude. The winds have turned gentler. But sticky and *hot*. It's the monsoon season.

Semmes cannot sleep. He tosses off his sheet, jumps to his feet.

What if Cape Town and all the fuss they made over us back there was our high note? What if we now go swiftly toward our own wretched and mortal ends . . . just as all those men at Gettysburg and Vicksburg?

The sweat soaks his brow, his chest. He feels the torment of boils beginning beneath his skin. They have come so often to him in the hot, humid weather on this cruise. A veritable pox at times. He tears off his nightshirt, soaks a cloth in his water pitcher and bathes his skin as he paces the sole of the great cabin. How he wishes that the Lairds had built this cabin fully in the stern of the ship, built it with opening ports for ventilation. Opening ports through which he could watch and wait for the light of day. Opening ports through which he might gaze upon the wonders of the Creator and pray for deliverance. Pray that someday soon he might be with his red-haired Irish selkie again.

"How disgusted I am with you," he says aloud.

He's addressing the sea, telling the rolling waves what he has already written in his journal. He is past the age when men ought to be subjected to such hardships and discomforts of deep-ocean cruising. The roar of the wind through the rigging, the rolling, the tumbling, the overcast skies give him melancholy feelings. *How strange seems the drama of human life when one looks back upon it . . . how transient, how unsatisfying.*

But when the captain of the *Alabama* is being honest with himself, he knows that his harsh words are aimed at himself as well. He is disgusted with what he has become. A scourge, a figure of the night. A name. A curse. There was a time before the war broke out when he had felt this way. Disgusted with his own behavior, his pathetic attraction to Maude, a woman less than half his age. Appalled by his disloyalty to his family, his utter failure to do anything of greatness with his life. He had knelt and prayed and bashed his forehead with his fists. This old revulsion creeps over him now, too, despite his having made a whole nation fear him.

So . . . he is slipping onto his knees before the crucifix mounted on the wall, folding his hands together into a battering ram, taking aim on his forehead when he hears through the open skylight a voice from aloft.

"Sail ho!"

***

It's about 0730 by Semmes's pocket watch when his second lieutenant, the strapping and handsome Richard Armstrong, reports to his captain on the bridge. He's just back from leading a boarding party to the English bark hove-to off to port.

"The master claims he has seen our enemy, sir."

Semmes runs his hands through his hair then twists the tips of his mustache slowly, hoping to gather some poise and chase off the jitters, the aches in his knees and elbows, of another sleepless night. "Come again, mister?"

"The British captain—didn't quite catch his name, sir—says he's bound southwest from the Sunda Straits to Cape Town. He saw the USS *Wyoming*, not two days ago patrolling the straits. She anchors nightly in the lee of Krakatau right at the southerly entrance."

Semmes twirls his mustache again. "*Wyoming*? Built at the Philadelphia Navy Yard just before the war."

"You know her, sir?"

Semmes thinks back on how he outran the *Wyoming*'s near sister, the *Iroquois*, when she had the *Sumter* penned into the harbor at Fort de France, Martinique, nearly two years ago.

"I saw her before she sailed off to California," says Armstrong. "The *Wyoming*'s a bit shorter and fatter than the *Alabama*."

"But heavier by four hundred tons, with guns much like ours."

"Yes, sir."

"She's anchored in the strait at night?" asks Semmes. He's too weary to concentrate.

"Along with a schooner she's using as a coal tender."

"Gideon Welles has decided he can stop me by plugging up the great passes of the world's oceans."

"Yes, sir, so it would seem."

"My God, man, it would have taken any fox hunter worth his salt about five minutes to come up with such a plan."

"People say that old man Welles is right slow to meet the challenges of his job."

"But it seems he's at last catching on to how he might lay a trap for us." Once again Semmes runs his hands through his gray hair, feels its oiliness, those wretched boils rising on his scalp, too. He wonders how many of the world's straits Welles has already blocked, whether *Alabama*'s crew will ever get home.

"Do you want me to fetch you the Englishman?"

Lord Almighty, no. I'm a tired, filthy, pimply mess, unfit for company, he thinks, shaking his head no.

"Let him be on his way, Mr. Armstrong. Give him our mail . . . and a case of Bartelli's best South African vintage as a token of my gratitude."

"Yes, sir."

"And tell the man . . ." Semmes feels a black, swirling anger rising in him.

"Sir?"

"Tell the English yonder that the captain of the *Alabama* is no wandering, toothless vagabond from a dying nation . . . though some might wish it so."

He imagines slipping into the harbor at Krakatau by night and surprising the *Wyoming* with a taste of fire from his guns. Pictures a good fight.

34

DISTRICT OF COLUMBIA
Early November, 1863

"As we speak, I believe my boys may be putting the pinch on a boatman who can help us," Major E. J. Allen says.

He and Welles are meeting at their usual spot, the grove in the woods along Rock Creek where Welles takes his exercise on horseback each morning. The morning dew is still on the tall grass where the men's horses are grazing. The weather has finally turned coolish in Washington. This morning is downright chilly beneath the canopy of trees. The secretary and the detective are dressed in heavy tweed riding jackets, but to keep warm they are skipping stones across the creek like a couple of boys.

"What boatman?"

"A Negro named Plowdon. He's an army scout in Carolina for us."

"I don't understand what . . ."

"It seems this Plowdon helped Semmes's flame-haired hussy escape."

"To where?"

"That's what I aim to find out."

"Do you truly think she could be any use to the nation's cause?" Welles winds up, tosses a small, flat stone. It skips twice on the water then sinks short of the far bank.

"Wouldn't you like to get your hands on that bleeding wench again after all the trouble she caused you and me back in . . ."

"Don't tell me this is about settling an old debt?"

Allen asks if Welles remembers that a year ago the major was interrogating Maude Galway in a barracks outside Frederick, Maryland. For weeks. It was shortly after the battle of Antietam. Federal troops caught Maude and her tomboy girlfriend Fiona O'Hare posing as nurses for the South. O'Hare had a page from Shakespeare's *Julius Caesar* secreted in her corset, folded over and addressed to someone with the initials "J.W.B."

"Those initials didn't mean anything to me then," says Allen as he reaches down for a throwing stone of his own. "But now I believe the script was meant for the actor."

"What actor?"

"Booth. John Wilkes Booth."

"The fellow you once said you thought was involved with Senator Hale's daughter?"

"Exactly."

"And Booth you say was named for an ancestor of our old friend Rear Admiral Charles Wilkes."

"Booth, Hale, Wilkes, Seward. I believe they are all peas in a pod. All arms of the Secret Line or the Knights of the Golden Circle and Iago."

If Allen is so sure, Welles asks, then why bother trying to track down Semmes's strumpet? She and her girlfriend were at most lowly spies and couriers for the Rebs. Besides, hasn't Allen had his men watching Hale, Wilkes, and Seward for months?

"These are clever people we are dealing with. They know how to cover themselves, Welles."

"I think tracking down the tart is wasting our time and resources, if you want to know the truth. I think you would be better off putting your energy into developing a better network overseas."

Allen gives him a glaring look.

Welles says that from what he hears from the consuls and his private sources, England, France, and Ireland are all thick with

Confederate agents up to no end of mischief. The Rebs have become virtual street gangs in Liverpool . . . and possibly the ports of southern Ireland. So, really, why worry about someone as insignificant as Semmes's misguided ex-mistress?

"Is it so you can rub her nose in her betrayals? You want to show her you're the boss, Major?"

The spy master picks up another stone, throws it so hard it sails right over the creek into a blackberry thicket. "Have you forgotten that it is the president himself who wants her found?"

Welles shakes his head. Sometimes he thinks the poor president lets himself get distracted by the most insignificant things.

"That woman could prove the truth in my suspicions, and yours, about Washington's most vile traitors. Might unfold for us an insider's look at how the Secret Line works. She could probably give us Raphael Semmes . . . and maybe Iago. End game. War over."

Welles sees where this all is heading.

Then Abe Lincoln gets re-elected. Allen gets a Cabinet post and his own secret army, sets himself up for life. I will be able to bring home Baldwin, Winslow, and the wolves I've sent hunting for Semmes and his brethren raiders in the Far East.

Welles skips another stone. This one reaches the other side of Rock Creek on its last bounce.

"I think Maude Galway may have gotten off in a ship somewhere."

"What? A ship? You mean she's heading back to Ireland? Good riddance."

"If she's fled to sea, I'm going to need help from the navy in finding her. Are you with me, man, or not?"

"What are you going to do about these threats I've been getting? My wife wants me to leave Washington."

"Someone sent you another red envelope?"

"Two days ago."

35

USS KEARSARGE

November 7, 1863

Winslow's all but sure that it's not the will of his God, but rather some darker force that has stirred up this current kettle of fish.

The ship's two days out of Queenstown Harbor on the River Lee, County Cork, Ireland. Repeating her search pattern of crisscrossing the entrances to the Irish Sea and the English Channel, hunting for Rebs. Just now she's running for Brest before a half-gale out of the west. Winslow's hoping to intercept the raider *Florida* while she's repairing in the French port . . . before he turns his full attention back to snaring the *Alabama*.

But today it's not the weather, or even catching the *Florida* or the *Alabama,* that concerns the captain of the *Kearsarge*. It's the fifteen Irish stowaways his luff, Lieutenant Commander Thornton, discovered aboard yesterday afternoon begging to be hired on as crew.

"I've thought all night on this gang of Mickey Finns, Luff." Winslow sits at his desk in the great cabin, staring with his good eye at Thornton seated opposite. It's one bell into the forenoon watch and already this morning's dose of laudanum has ceased to cut the pain in his destroyed eye. *Lord have mercy.*

"You think it's a problem?"

"I think what we have here, is all the marks of a major international embarrassment for our government."

Not only are the men destitute, in virtual rags and in no way, shape, or form able-bodied seamen, but their mere presence here puts Winslow, the *Kearsarge*, and the United States of America in direct violation of England's Foreign Enlistment Act. This is the very act that Secretaries Welles and Seward, as well as the U.S. minister to London Charles Adams and the U.S. consul in Liverpool, have been nagging Britain's leaders to enforce against the Rebs. The law that bars foreign navies from enlisting English sailors in crown territory. The act that the Yanks claim Raphael Semmes and his fellow raiders violated by shipping English crews aboard the *Alabama*, *Florida*, and *Georgia*. Now, it will appear that Winslow has done the same thing. That the Irishmen's presence on the *Kearsarge* is ample evidence of the hypocrisy and cavalier tactics of the Lincoln government.

Winslow can imagine it. No doubt the Irish and the English papers already have the news that he has these Irishmen illegally on board. Probably some snitch or spy has supplied the journalists with the names of the men, brought forth affidavits from folks on shore who saw the men dragooned into servitude under the Yanks.

"Our careers—and much more—hang in the balance, Mr. Thornton." Winslow grits his teeth, lets a wave of pain from his eye sweep through the base of his skull and down into his shoulders. He shivers.

"Sir?"

"I think someone back there in Ireland would like to snarl this ship, you, and me in such a public debate that neither we nor our government will be able keep focused on our hunt for the seahawk."

"Are you saying you think the Rebs are behind this?"

"I'm saying things are not exactly as they seem in this matter, Luff."

"So what do we do, sir?"

"Bring me those Mickey Finns. One at a time. Clapped in irons."

"You want them to sing for their supper, for their freedom, Captain?"

"I want to know who put them up to this misguided adventure . . . who helped them hide on board. And I want to know if anyone connected to Richmond, Virginia; Jefferson Davis; or Raphael Semmes lies behind this mess."

***

It's now nearing the end of the noon watch. Winslow has just finished interviewing his ninth stowaway, and he's still no closer to knowing who orchestrated the men's migration aboard his ship or why.

He has not eaten anything except porridge and a sliced apple at breakfast, nor taken any laudanum. For the last hour he has had to lace the fingers of his hands together to stop them shaking from pain, had to wear a patch over his bad eye to keep the daylight from touching off an explosion in his head. So . . . he's thinking he's got to eat something and crawl into his bed, let Thornton take a turn at trying to squeeze some information from his unwanted guests. But then he sees the marine sergeant at arms standing in his doorway with another stowaway.

His name is Dennis Leary. The young man has the body of a broken boxer—muscled but hunched and twisted—and a ruined face to make even Winslow's look relatively healthy and presentable. Something long ago has burned the left side of Leary's face into a pulpy, purple mass of scar tissue.

"Heavenly Jesus." Winslow's too exhausted to swallow his horror, his instant and overwhelming sense of kinship to this poor fellow.

Leary gives the captain a sad, little grin. "Aye, Captain sir. Do you believe the Heavenly Jesus has special plans for the afflicted?"

"Let's get you out of those irons, man . . . and have the steward bring some food. Could you fancy a bottle from the Bordeaux country?"

***

Winslow and Leary have finished the goat stew and are halfway into a second bottle of five-year-old French *rouge*. Leary has just finished his story about being burned in a terrible fire as a boy at his parents' home in Ringaskiddy, when Winslow drops his question.

"Do you really think the Good Lord meant for you to slip secretly onto this vessel, for the two of us, afflicted as we are, to meet?"

"Aye sir, God works in mysterious ways, he does."

Winslow doesn't know why—maybe out of some primal sense of affinity with this damaged man, maybe out of some urge to charge this meeting with shock and revelation—but he pulls the patch from his red, swollen, sightless eye.

"I believe we were meant to find each other. That we understand each other's troubles. Our Holy Father wants me to help you. Wants you to help me."

Leary nods. He hasn't taken his gaze off Winslow's ruined eye.

"I believe that you and I are different from the other men who sail on this ship and the other men who came aboard her with you."

"They think life is a lark, sir."

"They do not understand the burdens we carry. And I don't just mean the burdens of our faces."

"It's the bleeding truth, sir."

"I can help you with your burdens. What do you need, Dennis Leary?"

"Can you get me to America, Captain?"

Winslow sighs. "Yes, I promise you. I can get you to America with thirty dollars in your pocket. On a better ship than this one. . . . But I need you to help me, too. I have a brother . . ."

He tells Leary his fairy tale. Says his heart aches from an old feud with his brother, and he needs to find his kin and make peace. He believes his missing brother has been involved for some years as a crimp, an agent who gets paid to gather seamen to sail on American ships, mostly Confederate vessels. Ships sailing out of Liverpool and Cork. He says his brother's a Southern patriot. Could it be that Leary or any of the other men who stowed away aboard the *Kearsarge* back in Cork were recruited by a man of the South, perhaps his brother.

"I got a few shillings for coming aboard. . . . There was two Americans . . . if that's what you're asking."

"Two?"

"Yessir. One of them was from the South, I could tell by his accent. Come over from Liverpool some weeks back. Said he was looking for seamen for a lot of ships. He give me the shillings."

Winslow needs to manufacture and toss out a name. "His name wasn't Esau . . . Winslow was it?"

"No, sorry, sir. Last name of Bulloch. Could have been James Bulloch."

Why does that name sound familiar?

Leary takes a quick, deep swallow from his glass of wine.

"You said there was another American, too?"

"One of your own petty officers, sir."

"Who?"

"Mr. Haley it was, Captain."

"Haley?" Winslow thinks on the petty officer who's captain of the fo'castle. He leads the crews on the eleven-inch forward Dahlgren pivot gun and the Parrot rifle. The chief's a salt with twenty years of service. A great gunner. The best of the best. *In league with a Reb? It doesn't square.* "James Haley?"

"Don't know his first name, sir. But he said he come from Ringaskiddy a long time ago."

"He was the one who invited you aboard my ship?"

"He asked me how I would like to end the war between the states, how I'd fancy meeting up with the pirate Semmes."

36

SCHOONER JACQUELINE B
November 8, 1863

It's sometime before sunrise, and Maude has a problem. The bucket that she has been using for washing her babies' napkins and as a chamber pot is nearly overflowing. But right now, right here, emptying that bucket seems beyond difficult.

She and her new friend Cally have hidden themselves aboard the schooner *Jacqueline B* bound on a fall whaling trip from New Bedford, Massachusetts, to the coast of Nova Scotia. Cally's plan to escape from Hilton Head, flee the United States, has led the women and Maude's children here. This schooner marks the final leg of their journey. Last week they arrived in New Bedford aboard a packet from Hilton Head. For a pretty price the packet's Negro captain, an acquaintance of Cally's from the Blackfish, carried the refugees to New Bedford. He hid them for the whole voyage in his private cabin so that the soldiers and other men looking for these runaways would not find them.

But New Bedford was not a safe place for a pair of wanted females and two toddling infants. It was teaming with soldiers, rough sailors, low women, and bounty hunters in search of fugitives who seem to congregate in that port. And it was clear to Maude and Cally that they would not be safe for long ashore in New England. They really must get to Canada without delay. Cally hit on the idea of sneaking aboard a whaler sailing that way, and her friend the packet captain searched the wharfs and found this schooner.

Two nights ago—just before the vessel dropped her lines and headed offshore—Cally with her pet raven Obi, and Maude with her children, sneaked aboard the *Jacqueline B*, and for the last thirty-six hours they have secreted themselves in a corner of the ship's cargo hold. Behind a wall of water casks, hogsheads of salt beef, tubs of potatoes, and about a hundred empty barrels for whale oil, the women have built a little nest for themselves and the babies with old packing blankets. They have had all that they've needed to eat and drink by raiding the ship's stores. They've even had fresh air. The weather has been fair, and the crew has kept one of the hatch covers cracked open to let the hold breathe.

But now Maude must empty the filthy bucket before the babies stir. *It can't wait. An empty bucket is an absolute necessity for meeting the needs of their bodies.*

There will be no more lazing about, no more sleeping unless that wretched bucket can be emptied. No more easy playing with the children as they practice their walking. No more reading aloud—actually whispering—to each other by the light of a tallow candle.

And this would be a loss. Their catechism has been a book that Cally calls her bible, *Uncle Tom's Cabin.* A Negro preacher back in Port Royal who taught Cally to read in Sunday School gave her the book. He said she might find it an inspiration, after she shot a Yankee sergeant with his own gun when he tried to molest her little sister. After it became clear that she had to flee Carolina before the blue coats jailed her or did something worse. She has to follow the drinking gourd north to Canada like Eliza in the novel. She and Maude have to live Harriet Beecher Stowe's story. At least for a while.

But the novel says nothing about how Eliza dealt with the natural functions of her body when she was in hiding. Dealt with her own waste in secret. And Eliza didn't have babies. Little Levi and Fiona will soon be awake and their napkins will need washing. The bucket must be cleaned out and filled with fresh water.

So now Maude scales the ladder to the deck.

She checks to make sure no one is moving about, then heads toward the leeward bow of the schooner to empty her bucket where the splash can't be heard over the rush of the bow wave. Since coming aboard, she and Cally have been dressed like boys in wool sweaters and canvas sailor's togs. They hide their curls under knit watch caps. So . . . right now she's hoping that if any of the crew on watch back aft by the wheel sees her shadow moving about on the foredeck, they will see her as just one of the boys from the fo'castle come on deck to take care of his necessaries.

Still, she moves quickly and softly in her bare feet toward her goal. When she reaches the bows, she's starting to spill the contents of her bucket when she spies a bench tucked between the bowsprit and the bulwarks. There's a privy hole cut in it. The head. This is where the sailors take their relief with the waves rushing beneath their bare fannies. The wind is light and fish fresh. Carolina warm. A crescent moon hangs overhead, and the morning star winks on the horizon.

She wonders if even now her Raffy is under this same sky, smelling this same fragrant and warm air, loving the rolling of his ship beneath his feet. Hoping that somehow, some way, it will carry him back to her. Carry them both off to that little seaside cottage in Brazil that he pictured for her.

The next thing she knows, she's sitting on the privy bench, stargazing with her pants down around her knees. Her eyes search the sky for the North Star. Her ears tune themselves to the lullaby of the ship rushing through the sea. A line from Shakespeare comes to her.

"Look you, this brave o'erhanging firmament, this magical roof fretted with golden fire," she says softly to herself.

"Hamlet is it?! Do ye quote the bonnie prince for us . . . young lady?"

The voice from the dark hits her like a cyclone. She tries to will herself to dissolve and wither small enough to just disappear into the waves beneath the privy bench. But here she sits, fanny to the wind, pants slipping down around her ankles. And the silhouette of a man, standing just a dozen feet away. He looks as large as a giant against the stars.

"I was just . . ." She has never felt so vulnerable, not even when collared by the bearded bear.

"My back is turned," says the man.

She hears the lilt of Ireland's West Country in his voice as she leaps to her feet and clothes herself.

When she's dressed, she sees that the man, his face still turned away, is holding out a mug of steaming coffee to her.

"So ye run off to sea, have ye, lass?"

"Please don't hurt me."

The man turns to face her, still offering her the steaming mug. In the light of false dawn, she can see he's Raffy's age, but taller, rawboned with a thin face. Strong brow, soft eyes and mouth.

"They call me the mate, hereabouts. Noah Howell at your service." He actually tips his cap. Dips a little from the waist the way men do back home in Ballyheigue.

Suddenly she finds herself thinking of her father. She misses how safe he made her feel, and how she would do almost anything to please him. "I'm so sorry. I'm sooo very sorry that . . ."

"The past cannot be helped, lass. Ye will have to live with the weight of what ye have done. Whatever it is that has brought ye on this vessel, must be a mighty burden. But what will we do with ye now?"

She pictures her babies and Cally still sleeping down in the hold. "I'm not alone."

The mate remains silent for a long while, stares off at the first streaks of dawn cresting the horizon. He takes a deep breath and releases a heavy sigh. Sips from the mug that she has still not dared to touch.

"We better go see Captain Jacobs."

37

CSS ALABAMA
November 11–13, 1863

A heavy dread is starting to creep through Semmes's chest. He has been on the bridge since the watch called "sail ho" fifteen minutes ago. Now he eyes the black ship in the mist four miles off to leeward, examines its every detail through his binoculars. Watches as its crew hauls the Stars and Stripes aloft in response to his own ship's raising the Federal jack, the false colors.

The *Alabama*'s in the Java Sea, heading north. Bound for the Straits of Gaspar. Two bells into the forenoon watch. Fresh westerly breeze.

"What is she, sir?" Lieutenant Sinclair has the watch this morning. He's asking about the strange ship the lookouts have raised.

"Not the *Wyoming*, nor the damned *Vanderbilt*, I'll tell you that, mister." He feels a thick lump growing in his throat.

The last two weeks have been ones of constant vigilance. He still sails with an uneasy glance cast over his shoulder for fear that the *Vanderbilt* has trailed him all the way across the Indian Ocean. And some ten days back he sailed into Krakatau by night hoping to launch a surprise attack on the *Wyoming* . . . only to find the Yank had departed to re-coal in Batavia. Since then Semmes has made a spectacle of seizing two Yank freighters, the *Amanda* and the *Winged Racer*. He burned them at either end of the Sunda Straits in plain sight of Java and Sumatra so that legions ashore might see that the

Alabama is here, is hunting. Is daring the Yanks to come out and fight. But he has seen nothing resembling the enemy . . . until now.

But would you look at this thing?!

Never before has he seen a more magnificent ship . . . never one so fast under sail. So powerful. So ripe. The size of the *Alabama,* but with much taller masts, twice the sails.

She's riding high on her lines. Flying north. A full-rigged China clipper, a greyhound, with the unmistakable raked masts, fine bows, and sweet lines of a vessel designed by America's most noted naval architect, Donald McKay. A ship such as this one might well have been enlisted like the *Vanderbilt* into the Federal service. She may be armed and patrolling out here, hoping to lure a Confederate cruiser into an ambush with herself and a naval steamer lurking farther off in the mist. More than once Semmes has used a prize, a sailing ship, as a decoy to lure the enemy into his snare.

Do I take the bait?

He thinks on his crew. Kell says they have been uncommonly restless since the *Alabama* failed to engage the *Wyoming* back at Krakatau. They have been spoiling for a fight for weeks, maybe months, and since the enemy has given them no satisfaction, they have turned on each other. Just yesterday a stoker took a swing at one of the petty officers.

Right this minute more than three dozen men are gathered along the leeward rail. They're watching the Yank clipper . . . and they are also watching Semmes. They know he has already waited uncommonly long before ordering the gun crew to fire a signal round from the bow chaser to stop the clipper. They seem to sense Old Beeswax's uneasiness, his uncertainty. And they have begun to grumble.

What's holding me back?

Semmes raises the binoculars back to his eyes so that no one sees he has closed them. That he is praying to the Heavenly Father for a sign.

"The Yank's setting studding sails," says Sinclair.

Semmes opens his eyes. Sees men on the clipper's yards, setting their stunsails at the ends of the yards, from high up on the royals right down low to the courses.

It's the sign. If she were baiting him, she would not be so anxious to set extra sails, to add speed. All these men on *Alabama* can see. It's time to fire the chaser, to go for the kill. And yet the captain hesitates.

What do I fear?

"She aims to run." Sinclair again.

Semmes feels something thick and hard at the back of his throat, doesn't understand his hesitation. But he knows what his men expect him to do, what he must do whether he doubts his choice or not.

"Fire the bow chaser. Show them our true colors."

He squints into his binoculars, makes out the Yank's name painted in gold leaf on the transom. "Damn."

"Sorry, sir?"

"Her name. *Contest.*"

Sinclair says nothing. Doesn't need to. The Yank's name says it all. She's one of that small class of ships like the English *Cutty Sark*, built to race for prize money and hefty wagers all the way to the Orient and back with loads of tea. Built to outrun anything under sail.

***

"She's getting away from us, Kell." Semmes bites off the end of his cigar and spits it over the side of the bridge. He tunes his ear to the oddly uneven hiss of his ship's bow wave. There was a time when she seemed like a good hunting pony to leap forward into each oncoming sea. Not now. Her head dips into the swells.

Damn.

There's only one thing worse for the morale of the crew aboard this cruiser than not chasing the *Contest*—not catching her . . . and right now the fox is giving the heels to the hound. The Yank's only response to the *Alabama*'s cannon signal to stop has been to crowd on more sail and fall off the wind a point or two for even more speed. In the last hour the clipper has put a half-mile more between herself and the cruiser.

"This is a pretty pickle, Luff."

"Yes, sir."

"My bride has grown slow."

"The clipper is very, very fast, Captain."

True enough, thinks Semmes. But once *Alabama* could give even a clipper ship a run for her money under sail. Not now. *The vessel like the captain has been too long at sea, grown weary of the constant chase. We no longer love the wind.*

"Mr. Kell."

"Yes, sir."

"Ask the engineer to lower the screw, get on a full head of steam."

Kell seems to feel his captain's disappointment in not being able to go this chase under sail, feels Old Beeswax's worries about how he will appear to the crew. Feels Semmes's anger at having no choice but to pursue this sea witch of a ship.

"There's no shame in steaming, sir," says Kell.

Semmes jerks his gaze back from the enemy toward his luff, a black look on his face. "I really don't give a damn if there is. Beat to quarters. I want every man at a gun. Every gun pointed at that slippery bitch."

***

It has taken the fortuitous dying of the breeze, almost all of the *Alabama*'s remaining coal and throwing a live round from the Blakely pivot gun right between the *Contest*'s foremast and mainmast, but the Yank has finally heaved to. The clipper has been plundered for sugar, tea, tobacco, navigation instruments. Her crew has been brought aboard *Alabama*.

It's dark now. As the firing party rows back from the Reb cruiser, Semmes hears the laughter, the singing, the too-loud voices. His men have obviously helped themselves to the *Contest*'s liquor stock before putting their torches to the lovely craft. He ought to have the whole gang thrown in the brig for their damned rascality. But his control of the Jacks has grown most tenuous. His officers barely keep order, even though they carry cutlasses and pistols at all times these days. To punish the Jacks for a little joviality at the expense of the Yank's rum could cause a mutiny.

"Your men are drunk as lords, sir," says Captain Lucas of the *Contest.* He stands on the quarterdeck alongside Semmes, watching the first flames rising into the clipper's rigging, sheets and braces turning to whipping, golden snakes.

Who can judge another for his desperate clutching after a few moments' illusion of peace and plenty, even when that illusion comes from a bottle?

Sparks are whirling high over the *Contest.* The ship has begun her death groans. Her fiery image shimmers on the water.

"This is a most unholy night," says Lucas.

The seahawk barely hears his Yankee captive. Semmes is nearly lost between thoughts of his duty to his men, his ship, and his government on one hand . . . and, on the other, memories of a white-washed cottage by the sea, the lavender scent of a red-haired selkie waiting within.

"If you let me have my small boats, sir, I would most like to gather my crew and start for home," says Lucas.

"So wished the great Ulysses." Semmes's voice is nearly a whisper. *So will we all when our final end is nigh.*

38

DISTRICT OF COLUMBIA
December 21, 1863

"This is a bloody bonanza for us, Welles. Don't you see that?" Major E. J. Allen's face looks even darker—more intense, more vicious than usual.

It's almost midnight, and Gideon Welles has begun checking his pocket watch every five minutes. He has this odd sense that every minute more that Allen keeps him awake tonight is a minute his muscles and organs are withering beneath his skin, a minute less he has to truly serve his president or love his family.

Welles, Allen, and the president are in the place they've started calling the "roost." The White House attic. It's just about the only place where Lincoln will discuss the secret war with Jefferson Davis. And he will only do it when he feels a compelling urgency. Otherwise he wishes to remain above the fray. But right now remaining aloof is not possible for the president. Today, Welles told him about Reb letters seized on the captured blockade runner *Ceres* at Cape Fear. Letters that, among other things, expose a scheme by Confederate spies in England, Bermuda, and Nassau to use New Yorkers and New York financial houses to purchase previously seized blockade runners and put them back to work carrying contraband to the South.

Welles and Lincoln have decided to release the letters to the *New York Times*, hoping that the letters will rally the national will against the South. But earlier this evening three cabinet members—Seward,

Stanton, and Chase—got wind of the letters and the plan to publish them. These men have most strongly urged Welles to stop the publication of the letters.

After a few days of almost summery temperatures that belied the holiday season, Washington has been struck with a wintry blast of north winds that rattle the windows, whir around the cornices of the executive mansion. All three men are in topcoats, pacing the length of the attic to keep warm. They walk in their stocking feet so as not to call attention to themselves or disturb sleepers downstairs. Against the moonlight playing through the windows, Welles can see fine crystals of snow filtering into the attic through cracks in the eaves. The snow's settling on poor dead Willie's rocking horse and the forgotten fort the Lincoln children built with pillows, fire logs.

Lincoln blows into his hands. His breath seems a cloud of steam that fills the room. "You really think these letters can help us, Major?"

"Mr. President. We stand at a confluence of important and, I think, interconnected events," says Allen.

He claims that Welles and Lincoln are right to want to publish these letters from the *Ceres.* The public exposure of treasonous plotting is likely to make associates of the named traitors do all sorts of hasty things to cover themselves. And, therefore, mark themselves as complicit, shining new light on the way the South's Secret Line is woven together. There's a fair chance that these letters may lead Allen to finding out who it is that's still sending those threats to Welles. And who the rats are in Washington, who Iago is.

"So . . . the question is why do Seward, Stanton, and Chase not want us to publish these letters," says Lincoln.

Allen stops pacing, picks up one of the broken army muskets in the children's fort. "Why do you think, Mr. President?"

Lincoln turns to Welles. "Is there something incriminating in those letters that might bollix this administration's capacity to govern or to prosecute the war?"

"One of the treasonous buggers is a nephew of Mr. Seward."

Lincoln rolls his eyes. "That may cast some public doubt on Seward, but I don't see how it can really cut us to the core."

"Exactly, Mr. President," says Allen. "But I believe that Seward, Stanton, and Chase fear further revelations once we arrest the named traitors in New York."

"Revelations of what?"

Welles clears his throat, checks his watch—11:53—feels it's past time to bring the president into the intrigue that has plagued the secretary of the navy of late. He explains that during the last several weeks he has been besieged by senators complaining to him about the underhanded, self-serving, and illegal activities of Senator Hale, the chair of the Senate Committee on Naval Affairs. Hale has been quietly accused of extortion and bribery. His fellow senators go so far as to question Hale's loyalty.

Lincoln blows into his hands again, inhales slowly. "Have we not heard all of this before?"

"Yes, Mr. President, but there are new flies in the ointment," says Allen, who has been investigating Hale for months. "First, Hale has suddenly changed his tack most abruptly with Gideon."

"The scoundrel came to me on December fifteen offering to be my new ally and claiming that some of my most trusted friends are dealing double with me," says Welles. *11:58.*

"What?!" Lincoln can't believe it. He knows all too well what a thorn Hale has been in the side of his government and the navy in particular. For the past two years Hale has been leaking to the press all manner of fictional scandals and criticism related to the navy with the clear intent of driving Gideon Welles from office unless Welles passes out lucrative contracts to Hale's cronies.

"I believe that some of these bloody traitors in New York named in the seized letters, particularly a financier named N. C. Trowbridge, will eventually prove to be part of Hale's circle," says Allen.

"What in tarnation?"

"That's not all, Mr. President," says Allen. "You know that Rear Admiral Wilkes has leaked to the *Philadelphia Inquirer* and other papers a most salacious letter of indictment against Secretary Welles for replacing him as the officer in charge of the squadron chasing the pirate Semmes."

"And now Wilkes must present himself before a court of inquiry . . . for violating regulations against public criticism of his superiors." Lincoln's voice sounds as if all this personal drama is becoming tiresome. "Come to your point, Major."

"My point is that Charles Wilkes has met for three evenings in the last two weeks with Senator Hale at a road house in Clinton, Maryland, run by some people named Surratt."

"Really?" These meetings are news to Welles. He checks his watch—*12:04.*

"That's not all. On one occasion there was another personage at the meeting. The attorney general."

"Bates?!" Both Lincoln and Welles speak at once.

Allen gives the self-important smile that Welles so detests, the smile of a magician pulling the ace of spades from behind a fellow's ear.

"You see why I say these letters can be a bonanza for us?" asks Allen. "You see why I say that we have here a bloody confluence of interconnected, singular events?"

Lincoln settles onto one of the sofas that had been integrated into his son Tad's forgotten fort. He clears his throat and speaks softly. "Then I must tell you of some other things."

The president says that he has heard from sources in the Republican Party that Sal Chase aims to run against him next year for the party's presidential nomination . . . with Stanton's and Seward's support.

Welles drops onto the sofa, his legs feel weak, muscles all but vanished. *12:08.*

"And Ed Bates, I suspect . . ." says the president, "will soon tender his resignation to me. He's scheming about something."

"Bates, Wilkes, Hale, Seward, Stanton, Chase. There's a rogue's gallery for you, certain." Allen's Scotch accent sounds thicker than ever.

"You think one of them's Iago?" Lincoln asks.

"Or all of them," says Allen.

"What do I do about publishing the letters off the *Ceres*?" Welles still feels dizzy. It's 12:10 and he needs to get home to his wife and family, needs to salvage his body to fight another day.

"Publish them," says Lincoln, springing to his feet as if to meet an opponent. "Tell the rogues it was too late to stop the presses . . . then let's see how and when and where they start to squirm. Maybe we'll catch one of them sending a threat in a red envelope."

***

The three men are halfway down the stairs from the roost when Allen stops.

"We can't forget about Raphael Semmes's tart . . . " he says.

"Her, yet again?" Lincoln.

Allen remains stopped on the stairs. "I believe she may have gotten off to Canada."

"Well, then we're shut of her."

"I bloody hope not, Mr. President."

Welles clears his throat, checks his watch yet again. *12:12.* "I have a ship on its way to Halifax. Pair of Major Allen's men are aboard."

"If they can find her," says Allen, "she might tie the whole gang to Jeff Davis."

"How?" Lincoln's confused.

"My people in Richmond tell me that two years ago Maude Galway was right intimate with Varina Howell Davis. . . . At least on one occasion, Semmes's dolly acted as a courier for the Rebs. Took dispatches from Richmond to Raphael Semmes in Nassau."

"So why would she kill a Reb agent?"

Allen shrugs. "Maybe it was self-defense—maybe he was trying to kill her. Maybe the Rebs think she knows too much for her own good."

"Then they may still be after her," says Lincoln.

"That's what I'm trying to find out, Mr. President."

"How?"

"I have a woman working right inside Old Jeff's kitchen."

12:13. And I have my wolf Winslow sniffing for Semmes around Old Jeff's back door.

39

HALIFAX, NOVA SCOTIA
December 23, 1863

Blood and fish gurry are more than half an inch deep on the floor.

"We gots to get out of this place," says Cally. She has been grumbling quietly to herself and Maude, at her side, for hours.

It's six o'clock in the evening, and they've been cutting cod fillets since seven this morning, each with one of Maude's babies strapped to her back in a canvas sling. Like Cally and fifty other women, mostly black, Maude stands in a wooden barrel to keep her feet out of the mess on the floor of the McMillan Fish & Bait Company. The backs of the barrels have been cut away so the women can get in and out for their fifteen-minute "supper breaks" every three hours. They have a work bench in front of them for trimming the fillets from dead fish with very sharp knives.

"They ought call this place HELLifax." Cally again.

Maude nods. *Bloody right.* It has been a month since Captain Jacobs of the whaling schooner *Jacqueline B* put Maude, Cally, babies, and pet raven ashore here. And so far, Atlantic Canada has been no paradise. More like the other place all together.

When Minty Tubman had talked about following the drinking gourd to Canada, Maude pictured a wilderness of pine and maple trees surrounding crystal lakes. Indians and settlers moving around in birch-bark canoes in the summer and sleds pulled by dogs in the winter. Moose, wolves, and bears roaming the forest. Beavers and huge silver fish called muskies filling the lakes. Flocks of geese crossing the pale blue sky like slow arrows. Everyone living in log cabins and wearing clothes made of deerskin and fur.

"This is just like Hilton Head and New Bedford," says Cally. "Stink of fish, lots of boats, plenty of drunk sailors, mischief afoot. Negroes dem all herded into a crusty shanty town and the white man ruling over everything like King Herod and his cousins. We still in the purgatory place, sure. Nowhere on the road to the Promised Land."

Maude says nothing but thinks Cally may well be right. Life has been such a scramble here. They arrived in Nova Scotia thinking they would be met by a Negro relief society. But there was no such thing even though there are hundreds of fugitive blacks here. The fish houses look after them. They give the blacks and the poor work cutting, packing, icing fresh cod and haddock off the fishing boats. And they have set up the workers with local Negro families to house them until they can get a place of their own in the north end of Halifax. A warren of rickety slums with a store and church called Africville.

"AfricKILL, that be the proper name for dark town." Cally's voice has grown louder as she grumbles about the rats, two-legged wolves as well.

"Hush up, gal." A black man the size of the biblical Samson jabs his long wooden walking stick into Cally's lower back, just beneath the sling holding little Levi. "You falling behind with that pile of fish."

Maude swings her knife, strips another fillet off a cod. Swings again. She has felt the bite of the overseer's stick already twice today. Not only does it hurt, but each time he hits one of the women, he charges what he calls a "tribute." It's a deduction from her wages. And Maude can't afford any more tributes. She's already in debt to the McMillan's company store for clothing and necessities for her babies.

"I can't stand much more of this." Callie whispers.

"We are indentured servants."

"It just slavery by another name."

Maude hears the whack of the overseer's stick as it raps Cally across the buttocks, then feels a fierce sting across her own.

"Tribute!"

Maude wheels on the immense black man, knife in hand.

He steps away, sneers at her. "You know . . . they not one but *two* bunches of fellas going round town saying they pay gold to anyone know where at they can find a red-headed hussy with one light and one dark baby. What you want me to tell them?"

40

CSS ALABAMA
December 24, 1863

Straits of Malacca. Five hours out of Singapore bound for the Bay of Bengal. Hove-to under steam. Three bells into the noon watch. Breezes light and variable. Boarding party returning from a suspicious English vessel.

"The captain's refusing to leave her, sir." The boarding officer Master's Mate George Townley Fullam has just come back aboard the *Alabama* from the clipper calling herself the *Martaban*, hailing from Moulmein, Burma. She's bound from India to Singapore with a load of rice.

"Did you tell him he is required here aboard our ship to present me his papers?" asks Semmes.

He's back aft on the quarterdeck keeping company with himself. One foot propped up on the flag locker as he smokes his cigar, watches the low, marshy shore of Palau Rupat change from bright green to a deepening black while the sun sets in swirls of gold, orange, violet over Sumatra to the west. The peacefulness of this vista puts him in mind of a cottage by the sea in Nassau, and the one he dreams of in Brazil, the red-haired selkie he cannot banish from his dreams.

There was a time, most of the last three years really, when he felt his blood racing in his veins every time he stopped a suspected enemy. But now he feels something different. Hollowness and anger. During his brief stop in Singapore he saw over twenty American ships laid up and resting at anchor, unwilling or unable to get a cargo for fear of the depredations of the *Alabama* and her sister raiders. He has done his job so well he has all but eliminated the need for it. A bittersweet notion. More bitter than sweet in light of the news he heard while re-coaling at the P&O Line dock in Singapore. News that the Confederacy's money is worthless, that his government is nearly bankrupt, that the Yanks control the Mississippi and are pressing in on the South from all sides.

His mind shudders with bloody thoughts. Unless he and those patriots like him—not the army, but those fighting in the shadows, the Secret Line, the Knights of the Golden Circle and the ghost warriors—can do something monumental soon, the glorious cause may be lost. In Singapore the local people called the *Alabama* the *kappal hantu*—ghost ship. Would that he could sail this phantom right through Abe Lincoln's bedroom with all guns blazing. Surely other ghost soldiers are planning such a strike. Without some stealthy and bold move against the Yankees, it may well be that all his predations—that this endless war, this slaughter of innocents—has meant nothing, stood for nothing, changed nothing.

And another thing . . . after nearly being outrun by the *Contest*, after having caught her only because the wind failed her at a critical moment, he feels the incipient frailty of his ship. Feels it more after a meeting yesterday with his chief engineer who says the boilers' tubes are so pitted and scaled and leaking that they are nearing the point where they will lose steam as fast as they make it if the engines are run at more than half speed.

Semmes eyes Fullam, who remains at attention before him, probably hoping his captain will not shoot the messenger. Twenty-three-year-old Fullam with his boyish English face, his clean chin framed by outlandish lamb chops of reddish brown beard to hide his youth.

"Did you tell the captain, Master's Mate, that if he refuses to come aboard the *Alabama*, I must assume he's a Yank hiding behind the Queen's flag . . . and condemn his vessel?"

"Yes, yessir, I . . ." Fullam is visibly pale with anxiety as he searches for the right words. "He says that he stands on his rights as a royal subject, that you cannot force a master of an English vessel to leave his ship."

"Damn his rights!"

"Exactly, sir."

"Do you think he's trying to dodge us? Is he a Yank?"

Fullam, a born-and-bred son of Britain, says this is most assuredly the case. The master of the *Martaban* is pure American, doesn't even try to fake an English accent. And the gold paint for the name on the ship's transom is most fresh. One can see the outline of another name beneath.

Semmes pitches his cigar into the sea. "Tell Bartelli to fetch my pistol, my dress jacket, and my best cutlass. If Mohammed will not come to the mountain, the mountain will go to Mohammed."

***

Captain Samuel Pike of the state of Maine, master of the *Martaban,* sits opposite Semmes and Kell across the table in the main saloon of the clipper. His tongue's pushing the large chaw of tobacco around between his lower lip and teeth. He's rawboned, tall, middle-aged, clean-shaven. Blue eyes glare at Semmes.

"What do you think you're doing stopping and searching one of Her Majesty's ships? You got no business interfering with the Queen's commerce."

Semmes takes a deep breath. "Let me say again, Captain. As Lieutenant Kell here is my witness, there are irregularities in your ship's papers."

Pike thumps his index finger on the thick stack of papers that lay on the table before Semmes. "Lookee here, Captain. That there is the very stamp of Her Majesty's chief of customs in Calcutta."

"It just says that as of ten days ago your ship was registered as English, that you were cleared from that port with British cargo."

"Exactly."

"But look at this crew manifest, claiming English citizenship for your crew," says Kell. "All the names are written in the same hand with the same ink."

"Does it not bear the stamp of the custom house as well, and the name of the inspector?"

"It bears the look of a forgery."

"That stamp says otherwise."

"Anyone can get a document stamped . . . for a price."

The merchant captain spits some of the tobacco into his brass spittoon. "I'll thankee to get your miserable arse off my ship, sir."

Semmes feels his cheeks starting to warm. "I'll thankee to show right much respect, sir."

"Go to hell!"

The captain of the *Alabama* draws his revolver and sets it on top of the stack of ship's papers. "I do believe that I've lost my patience with the likes of you and your kind, Pike."

"Are you threatening me?"

"These papers say that as recently as three weeks ago when this ship arrived in Calcutta, she was named the *Texas Star* out of Boston. If you cannot produce a bill of sale, *prima facie* evidence that this vessel is *legally* transferred to British ownership, I am going to burn your ship."

"You hadn't ought to do such an evil thing, sir. She carries English cargo."

Semmes feels a jolt of hot needles pierce his chest, his arms. He grinds his back teeth together at this Yankee's bold pretense, his foolish threats. This arrogance, this audacity, so like that of the captain of the *Contest* who thought he could outrun his fate, outrun Raphael Semmes and the *Alabama.*

Are they born with such bravura? Can such boldness be brought on by a fear of war's imminent flames? Or do these Yanks sense some fateful weakness in my country and me?

Pike bolts from his chair, flails his arm toward the companionway and the British Union Jack fluttering overhead. "That flag won't stand it."

Like hell it won't, Semmes wants to shout. But he grinds his molars again to stifle the words. Swallows hot saliva.

"Keep cool, Captain," he says, speaking as much to himself as his enemy. "The weather is right warm." His eyes shift to the Colt .44 pistol lying on the papers, settle on the gun.

"It's Christmas Eve. You would burn my ship on Christmas Eve?"

Semmes looks at Kell for affirmation, thinks of his children and Maude's, stockings hung by the chimney tonight—so full of hopes, and—no doubt—dreams of peace. Then he says as softly as he can, "We will light her up for the glory of God."

"Only the Devil would delight in such outrage."

41

USS KEARSARGE
January 1, 1864

Winslow has spent half his life, he thinks, enduring wicked, wicked weather at sea. But never has he faced off with anything like this. Never in such close proximity to land. But he doesn't give a damn about risking his ship today, if being here means there's a chance that a Confederate Esau will come sailing into his arms.

His ship's off the island of Ushant, Finisterre, Brittany. The most western edge of France. Under full steam, *Kearsarge* is barely holding her head into the storm. She's struggling to find a little shelter from force ten winds in the lee of this small island to the west of Brest. But there's precious little relief from the land's shadow. Even within a mile of Ushant's shore, the seas roiling south out of the English Channel are running fifty feet and greater. They swirl in dark coils around the island as if it were nothing more than a pebble in a raging river. *Kearsarge* is pitching her bows into foaming, gray monsters, constantly awash in freezing seas, rolling on her beam ends as she tries to rise from the weight of water on her decks.

Not so long ago, Winslow would have been hiding in his cabin, nearly lost in a haze of laudanum, believing that this storm was yet another test set for him by God and Gideon Welles. But today he knows he has no one but himself to blame for this madness . . . and he doesn't care. Something is changing deep inside him. It started when he met the Irish stowaway Dennis Leary in early November. When he felt a kinship to that Irishman with the destroyed face.

When he felt that the torment of his own ruined eye and disfigurement was no longer handicapping him, but freeing him from the judgment of ordinary mortals. Maybe even marking him for greatness.

"Few people even remotely suspect what men like you and me are capable of," said Leary just before Winslow helped him find passage to America on a French steamer out of Brest. "You show them, sir. You find your brother. You crush your enemies."

That I will, he had thought then.

And so he thinks now. He wipes the salt spray away from his good eye, tightens the drawstring of his sou'wester cap and starts forward from the quarterdeck holding onto the windward jack line for balance, as waves surge over the deck one after the other. Even with all the gun ports slung open, *Kearsarge* can barely shed all the water coming aboard. But Winslow is bulling forward, sometimes in waist-deep water, as if his heavy and awkward oilskins are nothing at all. As if nothing can stop this man with a mission.

His object just now is Chief Captain of the Fo'castle James Haley. He's spied Haley in conference with the luff up forward. Haley, the master gunner who runs the crews on the eleven-inch forward Dahlgren pivot gun and the Parrot rifle. The man Leary fingered as instrumental in hiding the Irish stowaways on the *Kearsarge* back in November.

In Brest, Winslow learned from the U.S. consul that James Bulloch, who had recruited the stowaways, was no crimp at all, but a high-ranking officer in the Confederate Navy and the ringleader of a Reb spy network in Liverpool.

The question that has been festering in Winslow's mind is whether Haley is, in fact, a Reb agent, too. A Judas who aims to keep the *Kearsarge* from doing her duty, from ever finding Raphael Semmes. And right this minute Winslow means to put Haley's loyalty to the test. It's the perfect moment—the middle of a ship-killing storm—while the captain hones his crew for a fight with the Rebs that he's been craving for months.

Since mid-November the question of Haley's loyalty has been nagging at Winslow, while he lingered in Brest to see whether the Confederate raider *Florida* being repaired there would venture to sea again where he might engage her. Waiting, too, to see if two other Reb cruisers just up the coast, the *Georgia* in Cherbourg and the *Rappahannock* in Calais, would risk putting to sea. Waiting to see if his brother Esau would bring the *Alabama*, the queen of the Reb raiders, back to the safety of France to refit as well.

He has heard rumors that all four of the Reb cruisers plan to gather in the English Channel at once and challenge his ship together. "I welcome them," he has told the French newspapers. But as yet none of the Rebs has made a move. *Alabama* has not arrived. Winslow has decided to wait out here off Ushant where he can pounce if she does . . . or if one of her sisters comes spoiling for a fight.

He reaches the foremast and the fo'castle companionway where the luff and Haley are hunched over with their backs to the wind and seas, arms looped around halyards to steady themselves. The storm screams in the rigging.

"I'm sick of waiting," says Winslow.

"We were just planning how we might get some extra lashings on the anchors, sir," says the luff. He's clearly surprised by his captain's presence on the foredeck and uncertain of the meaning behind what the master has just said.

"Forget the anchors, Mr. Thornton. I want you to beat to quarters."

"Beat to quarters, sir." Thornton's tone of voice is as close to a question as it can be without being insubordinate.

"I want all guns manned. I want them firing on that little island yonder." Winslow points to a sea-scoured rock about the size of a packet schooner about six cables off to starboard.

The luff looks at Winslow as if he must be mad.

"Target practice, sir?" Haley gives a cockeyed look. Maybe he's picturing himself and his gun crew of the foredeck guns swept overboard and drowned in the next big wave to roll over the *Kearsarge.*

"Until each of our guns is firing every two minutes and we score fifteen hits in a row." *And here comes the first part of the loyalty test.* "You have a problem with that, Mr. Haley?"

The gunner, a thick-chested, black-bearded soul, shakes his wet head, grins. "No problem, sir. Sounds like the most bloody fun I've had in months!"

Winslow feels something like a string of bubbles starting to pop in his throat.

"Way I figure it, sir," says Haley, "we survive today, fighting Raphael Semmes and the Rebs will seem like a roll in the clover."

"You really want to clip the seahawk's wings?" asks Winslow.

"With a flurry of hot lead."

"You don't talk like a Judas," the master of the *Kearsarge* says before he can bite his tongue.

"What, sir?"

Winslow wants to ask Haley *why. Why did you collude with a Reb agent to bring those Mickey Finns aboard? It's not in your nature.* But this is the wrong place, the wrong time. So what he says is what he hopes, maybe all that he can hope. "Don't disappoint me, man. I need you with me."

"Let me at my guns, sir."

"Attaboy."

42

HALIFAX, NOVA SCOTIA
Early January, 1864

The worst thing about Canada is not working in the fish house, sleeping on a straw pallet on the dirt floor in the back room of the Widow Todd's . . . or even battling the rats. Maude has gotten pretty good at sticking the nasty creatures with her fish knife. The worst thing is the widow's gentlemen callers . . . and the fear that any night a caller may be one of those men who have been asking around town after a red-haired gal with one white and one black baby.

The Widow Todd's a young Negro woman with two young children of her own. She has taken in Cally and Maude as boarders at her three-room cottage on the edge of the reeking night-soil fields in Africville. Just about every evening the fishermen and sailors come calling for the widow about two hours after supper when the children, Cally, and Maude have bedded down. The men come one or two at a time, laughing, trailing the scent of raw tobacco and cheap liquor. They knock three times on the window, and when the widow answers the door, they stand there in the damp and cold, flirting. She laughs low and wild. Almost purring.

It's always the same.

"I'm tired," she says. Or "My children need me," or "My fish stew's gone burn on the fire."

It's then that the man or men offer her money, and she begins to whisper. In short order she invites the caller or callers into the house and latches both the front door and the door to Maude and Cally's room, closes the window shutters. Then Maude hears the sounds of shoes scuffing across the dirt floor into the widow's bedroom. Sometimes the lovers shout or sing with each other. Maude covers her ears with her hands until she sleeps.

So it is this Thursday night.

She's lost in dreamless sleep when she smells the stench of whiskey and tobacco blowing into her face, feels the weight of a man pinning her in her bed just four feet from the pallet where her babies sleep.

"Come on, gal. Give Daddy a kiss."

This can't be happening again, she thinks. She must be having a nightmare of the bearded bear in Beaufort. The rough lips and facial hair rubbing against her cheek. She's sure she must be dreaming until she feels his hands pinning her wrists to the floor, feels her nails dig into the clay floor.

"Let me go!"

"Just a little, kiss, sweet . . . I been looking a long time for you, Red."

She twists and squirms to break away, but his body has the weight of a plow horse and smells like one, too.

"Get off. I'll scream."

"That wouldn't be a smart thing to do, Red. Then I'll have to hurt you. And nobody's going to be happy about that. They want you alive and well . . . back in Washington."

They? Washington? Her eyes fly open. At first everything looks dark and spidery. But soon her eyes focus, and even though there is almost no light in the room, she can see the monster clearly as he grinds her into the dirt floor with his long, lean body. He has a fish-white face, a scraggly little beard around his mouth, and he wears a salt-crusted sailor's tunic. In one of his hands, he holds a set of nickel handcuffs.

She can hear the panting of a man and a woman coming from the widow's bedroom, the creaking of a bed. Realizes this monster must have broken into her room while his chum was having his way with the widow.

Maude tries to drive her knee up between his legs, but he locks a leg like a tree trunk over her knee.

"Be nice, love." He slobbers next to her ear. The heel of his right hand jams her mouth open for a kiss.

She bites. Hard. The meat between the thumb and the forefinger. She wants to devour his hand. Drive him off.

"Wench," he roars. And with his free hand, the one holding the metal cuffs, he belts her in the side of the head.

Her ears ring. Biting is not even something she can think of now—it's beside the point—because suddenly she knows he no longer gives two figs for whoever it is that wants her in Washington. She's maddened him past all reason. He's raging.

"You want to play rough, you saucy witch?"

He strikes her across the jaw with the cuffs cupped in his hand. She feels her lower lip split like a peach.

It's now, in the midst of her pain, that she darts her hand beneath the pallet in search of her fish knife, her rat sticker. She has killed one bastard; she can kill two.

"I'll show you rough!" He sits up, straddling her hips and rips her nightgown open from the neck to the waist. He's springing the cuffs open, looking around for her wrists . . . when she raises the knife to strike him.

"Nooooooooo!" Cally screams.

Her shrill voice stops Maude cold. A child cries.

The monster snaps his eyes around the room in search of the new voice. But he's looking in the wrong direction when Cally kicks him so hard under the jaw that Maude can hear his teeth crack. His hands drop the cuffs and fly to his head as he topples off her. He has barely fallen onto the floor before Cally kicks him in the jaw again.

Maude sees that Cally is already dressed in a sweater and canvas trousers. She's wearing her black fish-house brogans. And this time when she kicks the man, his teeth shatter around the room, hard little pieces of broken crockery.

Baby Fiona squeals.

Maude tries to cover her nakedness with a blanket. The monster has curled himself into a ball on the floor, whimpers.

Cally locks the handcuffs on the man's wrists. "We gots to go."

She hands Maude her shirt and trousers. In less than a minute the two women are tearing down the frozen roads of Africville with the babies in their arms and Cally's pet raven flying after them.

"That wasn't just a random bloke." Maude feels a cold fear spreading from her belly.

"Somebody dem want you bad, girl."

***

The next morning before dawn, she leaves a letter to Raphael Semmes with the captain of an English bark bound for England. The letter is addressed "care of Mr. James Bulloch, Liverpool." She gives four of her last ten dollars to a black teamster named Virgil Sykes. He's a young man she and Cally know because he hauls cod heads from their fish house to a fertilizer plant every day. He says he has heard of a place called Lincolnville where Negroes, mostly fugitive slaves, are clearing farmland and building a community of Negroes for Negroes.

"I'd like to see that," he says, "and taking you two and the babies is just the excuse I need. Could be the Promised Land after all."

"Gots to be better than Hellifax," says Cally, as the wagon rumbles out of town.

Slowly the sun rises. The fog lifts. They are traveling through a land of pines and rocky meadows, sugar coated in fresh snow. Obi the raven circles overhead. Maude huddles beneath a horse blanket and holds her children tight to her chest. She sucks on her split lower lip . . . can't say anything. Not now.

She still wants to scream and cry. Not just because of what the monster in the dark did to her, but because she realizes now that he doesn't work for the blue coats who were chasing her back in Carolina or for the South's Secret Line as the bearded bear did. He works for someone far more powerful and dangerous. Someone in Abraham Lincoln's government. An old enemy who must still be after her . . . probably because he has not yet found or stopped Raphael Semmes.

How she wanted to get on that bark for England this morning. Raffy had told her in Nassau nearly two years ago that she could always find help, find him, through James Bulloch in Liverpool. But she won't go. Not now. Not yet. Not with Yankee spies and warships lurking around the ports of Nova Scotia. She will not lead the Yanks to her gladiator. Not while this evil war still rages. Not if she can help it.

The Good Lord knows Raphael Semmes may be on the wrong side of the slavery question and will have to answer to his Maker for his error . . . but he has risked everything for the principle of liberty. A girl has to respect that, doesn't she?

43

DISTRICT OF COLUMBIA
February 5, 1864

Gideon Welles is smiling a bit drunkenly at the couples twirling to a Strauss waltz beneath the gas-lit chandeliers. He's thinking that this is one expensive, wicked party and it's time he starts for home before he gets into trouble . . . when a comely serving girl steps right into his line of vision and leans close. She presses her breast against his arm, whispers into his ear. "Will you please come with me, Mr. Secretary? Major Allen requests your presence."

Her chestnut tresses tumbling over the shoulders of her black dress and the straps of her snowy pinafore sway in a most provocative way as she spins away. Leads Welles through the clutches of drinkers, gossips, and flirts at the back of the ballroom. This is Green Hill estate on the northeast fringe of the District. It's Friday night in the depth of winter, and Washington is in a party mood. Black ties and ball gowns. Virtually all the city's debutantes are here with their gallant escorts. Top military men, congressmen, senators, and cabinet members are hobnobbing with each other, intriguing with other men's wives, maiden daughters.

His enemies are here, too. Charles Wilkes is chatting up Seward. Senator Hale and his bodacious daughter Lucy are locked in a tête-à-tête with Stanton. Chase and Bates are sucking up to the host, George Washington Riggs Jr., the founder of the rich and powerful Riggs private bank. He's the man who nearly single-handedly bailed the United States out of the debts of the Mexican War, the man who has volunteered to cover, out-of-pocket, the expense of maintaining the Mount Vernon plantation as a national historic site until peace is restored. From what Welles can gather, this party and the offer to pay Mount Vernon's bills are attempts by Riggs and his family to make peace with official Washington. Their way of re-entering Washington society after two years in seclusion because of their secessionist leanings. According to Postmaster General Montgomery Blair, who has brought Welles here, this party is an important sign that "America's money is now betting on Lincoln."

Who said politics makes strange bedfellows?

"This way," she says as she leads him down a narrow corridor away from the crowd, lights a candle, and starts up a dark staircase.

It has been years, really, since he has ventured into the District's rich and dangerous social scene. Years since he found himself entrapped and blackmailed by Raphael Semmes's Jezebel after one of those Friday *soirées* that the Reb spy Wild Rose Greenhow used to have. But those parties were nothing compared to this in terms of opulence, the depth and breadth of the guest list, the potential for all manner of shadowy liaisons. And now he's being led God knows where . . . by God knows whom, for God knows what Allen requires of him.

***

"It's alright, Welles," says Major E. J. Allen. "She's one of us."

Welles and the serving girl are standing in what is clearly an office. Not as baronial as the rest of the house, but well appointed with a large desk, floor-to-ceiling bookshelves, filing cabinets, and several wingback leather chairs, one of which has Lincoln's chief spy sitting in it. The heavy curtains are drawn. A candle on the desk adds to the light from the one the girl carries.

"Do you want to show the secretary what you found, Emma?" Allen nods to a closet door on the far wall.

She hands her candle to Welles, crosses the office, opens the closet door, and pulls out a carton of stationery. Lincoln's Old Man of the Sea cannot help but admire the curves of her shadow cast on the wall by the flickering flames.

"I came across this last night," she says. "Major Allen said you would want to see this for yourself."

Welles accepts the small box, sees it's divided, one side for note paper, the other for envelopes. Red note paper, red envelopes.

Jesus Lord!

Allen pulls a red envelope and note from his inside vest pocket. It's the last threat that Welles received before Christmas. He takes the threat and a clean sheet of note paper from the box and holds them both up to the candle light.

"You see, Welles?" Both sheets of paper have a trident watermark in the lower right-hand corner.

"It's the same paper." The secretary of the navy can hardly believe that after all this time Allen has possibly found the source of these unsettling threats.

"I told you I would get to the bottom of these threats." Allen can't suppress his smug grin.

"How did . . . ?"

"Emma's a rather fetching young lady, don't you think?"

Welles pretends he's still examining the fresh stationery, doesn't want to let on how much he has been taken by this female agent's looks.

"How could an old fellow like the senior Mr. Riggs not want to add such a vixen to his domestic staff?"

"You think that George Washington Riggs has been sending me these threats? The banker's part of the South's Secret Line, the Knights of the Golden Circle?"

Allen scratches at his bearded chin. "I don't know yet."

"I saw him talking with Secretaries Bates and Stanton. And Hale's daughter was hanging on his arm earlier."

"A lot of the usual rogues are indeed here."

"This is Mr. Riggs's secretary's office, Mr. Fillmore Spenser," says the agent Emma. "I have no evidence that Riggs knows anything about this."

"Now what?" Welles is still feeling lightheaded from his whiskey and water, the climb up the stairs, this surprising news about the source of all the threats he has received. He had suspected Charles Wilkes, his surrogates, or someone in the cabinet. Never suspected someone in business, a banker. Or this Mr. Fillmore Spenser. Never heard of the fellow.

Allen rises to his feet. "We need to keep looking for a link between that traitor Trowbridge in New York who was buying ships for the Rebs and this gang of mischief makers here in Washington."

"That's it? We just watch and wait?" Welles feels like time is getting away from him again.

"And follow the money," says Emma.

Allen nods. "Yes. And I need to trace this watermark, see where it bloody leads. Should have done it a year ago, but . . ."

Emma's eyes have started darting between the men and the door. "It's not safe here. We should get . . ."

"One thing more," says Allen as he blows out the candle on the desk and starts for the door. "I just got news from Halifax."

Welles thinks he knows what's coming, feels the urge to get to the point before someone catches him in this office. "Two of my ships have captured Raphael Semmes's brothers-in-arms on that makeshift raider *Chesapeake*."

"I'm talking about his wench, man."

"The Galway woman? You got her? Now?" For some reason Welles pictures John Ancrum Winslow, ruined eye and all, raining blood and thunder on Raphael Semmes.

"She's on the run again, and it seems like the Rebs are after her, too. But things are coming to a head."

"How's that?"

"She's headed down a dead-end road. In the snow."
"What if the Rebs find her first?"
"Somebody's going to have to adopt those babies."

44

CSS ALABAMA

Late February, 1864

Mozambique Channel. Southbound for the Cape of Good Hope. Six bells into the morning watch. Running before a fine topsail breeze.

Week after week of magnificent sailing in the clear fresh breezes. The seahawk has been riding the northeast monsoon—all the way from the Malabar Coast at the tip of India where he took the Maine freighter *Emma Jane*. *Alabama* has crossed the equator and is following summer south toward Cape Town . . . eventually north to England. Not home . . . but close. Semmes should be loving this ride.

Still, he can't shake the melancholy. Last night he sat in his chair on the bridge deck during the second dog watch, smoking a first-rate manila, twirling his mustache, and listening to the new fiddler who came aboard with the last batch of recruits, playing "Carrie Bell." Now he sits in his chair again this evening, watching the sunset paint the western sky gold, crimson, purple. Listening to the fiddler below on the main deck shuffling through a slow, plaintive "Oh Susanna." He remembers where he was almost three years ago when he heard this song . . . with his West Irish selkie.

St. Valentine's Day evening. They are just finishing dinner in a dark corner of the Ebbitt Grill. The piano player's running through "Oh Susanna" when he tells Maude that he's leaving Washington to serve the South. He's going to catch the first train he can get to Montgomery where he hopes to meet with Jefferson Davis, get a ship and fight for his new country. He says that his wife, Anne, and the children will be leaving for her brother's house in Cumberland.

He's taking a slow sip of wine trying to calm the riot in his heart when her gaze slowly meets his.

"My god, Raffy. Would you look at me? Just look *at me?"*

He sees the lightning in her green eyes.

"Raffy, listen to yourself! Can't you see? You're killing me. Killing us. Snuffing us out like a . . ."

Her voice chokes. She rubs her eyes with the heels of her hands before continuing.

"And here I sit trying to hold back bloody tears. For what? For a man who wants to make himself a demon or an angel? Jesus, Mary, and Joseph, Raffy!"

He takes her right hand across the table. The hand on which she wears the silver band set with emeralds to match her eyes. The band he gave her for her twenty-sixth birthday almost a year ago when he first told her he would love her unto death.

Tears begin flowing down her cheeks. He laces his fingers through hers. Then he leans toward her across the table and begins wiping the tears off her face with his kerchief.

"This is the hardest thing I have ever done. Forgive me. Leaving you . . ."

Her body shudders. "I hope you die! Right here before God and the bloody Congress," she says. Then she hits him with a gale of red wine from her glass. . . .

It's past midnight, after he's been walking in the swirling snow for hours, when he shows up at the door to her room in the boarding house on H Street and begs her for forgiveness.

She stands in the doorway wearing the blue satin robe she has kept for his use, and she tells him to go away. But then, miracle of miracles, she reaches out, brushes the slush off his brows, cheeks, his mustache.

Later, after the apologies, after the lovemaking, he holds her and whispers, "My heart breaks from what I must do. Believe me, Lassie."

But, he says, his mind is firm in its resolve, he must serve his new country. It's a question of standing up for liberty against an oppressor. It's the American way. He begs her to let him do what he must. He swears that when the war ends he will come for her if she will still have him.

"Will you stand by me?" His eyes plead. . . .

***

The sun is down now. The fiddler has stopped. The manila a mere smoky stub. The stars are an immense quilt overhead. The evening watch has begun.

"Where are you? Where are you?" He doesn't realize that he's talking to the empty night, not his Irish selkie, or that just now Lieutenant Sinclair is looking up at him from the quarterdeck with a worried gaze.

He only knows that he never in all his loneliness imagined that the goddamned, awful Yanks would make such a fight against secession. That this war would last so long. That he would be condemned to wander the seas for this eternity. The wags who refer to him as the Flying Dutchman seem to have got it right. Surely, the end must be near. For the *Alabama*, his *kappal hantu*—his ghost ship—and for himself. The poet Tennyson had it right when he wrote, "Death closes all."

But . . . *but* Tennyson's Ulysses also said that, "something ere the end, some work of noble note, may yet be done."

He surely meant a battle. Where lies the Vanderbilt *or the* Wyoming? *Where lies my foe? Most Glorious Father, let him come. I pray let him come. Soon.*

45

USS KEARSARGE

Mid-March, 1864

At anchor. The ship huddles in the lee of high, white cliffs. Dover, England. The narrowest point of the English Channel. A northwest gale blowing. 0730 hours.

"Lord Almighty. Do I smell smoke, Luff?" Winslow hasn't yet had his coffee or eggs. He's still in his long johns as he stumbles to the door of his great cabin. Lieutenant Commander Thornton has come knocking.

"Yes, sir."

"Wood smoke?"

"Yes, sir."

"And this is a wooden vessel."

"Yes, sir."

"Have you come to tell me we're on fire, man?"

The ship tugs at her two anchors as a gust roars through the rigging.

"The number two and number three bunkers, sir."

"That damned coal we had to transfer in the rain two days ago."

"Afraid so, sir."

"Are we perpetually cursed?"

Thornton stares at his feet. It seems he doesn't want to answer, and Winslow hardly blames him. He knows the cause of the fire is really no curse. Even the freshest greenhorn on a steamer crew soon learns that if you tight-pack tons of wet coal in a close space, you are likely to touch off spontaneous combustion. But unless Winslow was willing to go without engines or heat from the boilers in this weather, the risk couldn't be helped.

The Frenchies and the Brits have tired of the *Kearsarge* standing guard over the English Channel now for months. First, Winslow penned in the CSS *Florida* at Brest. Now he's blockading the CSS *Rappahannock* at Calais, while waiting for the *Alabama* to come sailing under his guns. To thwart him, the French and English governments have given their support for the Rebs another turn of the screw. Not only have they been limiting Winslow's stay in their harbors to twenty-four hours, but they have made a rule that he can only enter their ports once every three months for coal. So . . . he has had to hire colliers to meet him in mid-channel to transfer fuel. In the worst possible conditions—fog, rain, wind.

And this is the upshot. Flames in the hold. It doesn't make sense to Winslow that water can be a catalyst for fire, but with mounds of stored coal, it is. And it's a devil of a fire to fight. Especially at sea.

"My men have battened a double layer of canvas over the bunker hatches," says Thornton. This is the standard approach to a bunker fire on board—try to cut off the fire's air supply.

"And . . . ?"

Thornton shakes his head. "No luck yet, sir."

"How bad is it, Mr. Thornton?"

"It's not getting any better."

The *Kearsarge* lurches, her bows caught by a gale of wind suddenly veering directly out of the north.

"The forward bulkhead on number two bunker is quite hot."

"Burning the wood, is it?"

"Afraid to open the hatch for a look, but by the smell of things . . ."

Winslow feels the pain behind his bad eye starting to scream. He knows that the only thing that stands between that burning wooden bulkhead and a ton of explosives in the powder magazine is a small storage hold for ship supplies.

"A fine mess we're in, Mr. Thornton."

"And there's one other thing, sir."

"Now what?"

"The English have sent a pilot boat out to us this morning from Dover."

"Probably not to invite us into the harbor."

"No, sir. The other thing altogether."

"They want us to leave?"

"Immediately, sir. They say we are anchored within the three-mile limit. That we are in sovereign waters of the queen. That we are in violation of their twenty-four hour rule."

"And where would they have me go to find shelter from this storm? At sea?"

"Beg your pardon, sir. But the officer who came out said he didn't give a good goddamn. Said the queen's shore batteries were prepared to use us for target practice."

"Here's what I say to that, Luff. Damn that man, and damn his queen . . ."

First things first. We don't quench that fire, it won't matter where our anchors are set.

***

The captain's great coat is soaked, water flowing off the corners of his beard in streams by the time he works his way forward from his cabin to the hatch leading down to the berthing deck. Despite the rain whipped by this frontal passage, smoke rises from the hatch in swirling clouds. The Jacks off watch have vacated their hammocks below and are sitting huddled together in their black oil skins, the bulwarks in the bows providing all the shelter they have from the wind and rain.

The soot-stained face of Chief James Haley emerges from the smoke. He's leading a gang of coughing men up the ladder, out of the miasma fuming below. The wind is screaming.

Winslow grabs Haley by the arm, almost asks, *Did you or one of your boys set this fire? Are you my true nemesis?* But he catches himself. "How's it look, Chief?"

Haley just stares at Winslow's destroyed eye and shakes his head. "Gaining on us, sir."

"Show me." Winslow pulls a kerchief out of his pocket, holds it into the driving rain until it's soaked, then ties it over his face and mouth and starts down to the berthing deck behind the chief.

On the berthing deck the visibility drops to less than fifteen feet. Empty hammocks swing like the shadowy wings of a flock of immense birds struggling to escape their cage. The air smells tart, sooty, hot. Between the groans of the ship and the sighing of the wind, Winslow hears a low roar. It's the fire sucking air through every hatch and crevice in the ship to feed itself. Touching the bulkhead between the berthing deck and the bunkers, he feels the skin on his right hand prickle with the heat. And this is only on the berthing deck. What must the heat be like in the storage locker on the deck below?

The captain is only five steps down the ladder to the storage locker when he sees flame. Blue and orange, bursting through more than a dozen holes where the bulkhead joins the cabin sole. Holes the size of thirty-two-pound cannon shot with fire trailing up the bulkhead in strange broad ribbons, flaring out as they hit the ceiling and lighting the room with a yellowish-red glow. The dry pine boards spark and crackle. Farther over near the starboard side of the ship, a jet of flames is shooting through a hole in the floor and is just now spreading to a barrel of salt beef. Compelled by a sudden burst of anger, Winslow strips off his great coat and beats out the fire on the barrel with the coat. Then he turns his head to the left and looks to the forward bulkhead separating this storage space from the magazine—all its explosive shells, its barrels of gunpowder.

If he wants, Haley could kill me here and now with impunity.

The captain frowns. "It's too late to cut off the fire's air."

"I believe so, sir."

"In ten minutes this fire's going to light up this whole room, Chief. And in twenty minutes we are all going to be blown to bits."

"We've got to try water."

Winslow thinks about the precious minutes it will take to rig the hoses, man the pumps. Thinks, too, about how only massive amounts of water might smother this inferno. If the crew can't lay on the water fast enough, it will only complicate the fire, make it a steaming inferno. *Is that Haley's secret plan?*

"What's on your mind, Chief?"

"How much water do we have in the tanks, sir?"

"At least ten thousand gallons."

Suddenly Winslow sees. The water tanks lie just beneath the magazine. If the stern-facing end of the tanks were tapped, water would spill aft in a torrent through the holes in the burning bunker bulkhead and douse the fire. "You want to flood the bunkers?"

"Don't you think it's our best chance, sir?"

The captain nods. "It is that, Haley . . . but can I ask you something? Why is it that you always seem to be around when things on this ship start to go to hell?"

"My old mom always said I have a nose for trouble."

"Is that why you helped to smuggle the Irish boys aboard back in Cork?"

Haley face turns pale. "Then you know, Captain?"

Winslow nods.

"What are you going to do to me, sir?"

"Can you put out this fire, man?"

"I'll give it me best."

"You love this ship?"

"Yes, Captain."

"And you fancy her catching Raphael Semmes and the *Alabama*?"

"Right-o, sir."

"Then flood the damn bunkers . . . we'll see about the other business. Later."

46

EASTERN NOVA SCOTIA
Early April, 1864

Maude wakes to the lurching of the wagon, hears the cries of her children and wonders if she has made a terrible mistake. Maybe she should have gone to England when she had a chance. Gone to James Bulloch. Gone in search of her Raffy.

After nearly three months of intermittent travel and searching for the Negro Promised Land, she fears that she, Cally, Virgil, and the toddlers will never find Lincolnville. They have been on the road now for a week since leaving Antigonish, where they found refuge from the winter blizzards in the basement of the Baptist Church for two months. In exchange for room and board, Cally helped the church women make hooked rugs. Virgil used his horse to skid timber. Maude taught reading classes for farm children. But one day a church elder said that American men had been seen in town asking after a red-haired woman with one black and one white baby. Even though Cally and Virgil had taken to pretending that little Levi was their own child with the Baptists, nobody believed the refugees would be safe for long in the church.

Since then travel has been tough, sometimes through snowdrifts three feet deep, sometimes—on the warmer days—deep mud. Once, during a thaw, they had to make a twenty-mile detour around a swamp that had gone boggy in the bright April sun. And now they are all beginning to wonder whether the stories of Lincolnville are just another cruel hoax played on fugitive Negroes desperate to find the new Jerusalem. Maybe it does not exist at all.

No one they have spoken with along the way, not even the black folks, has actually been to Lincolnville. And the directions that they have been getting are always vague and somewhat confusing. "Head on down to Guysborough," or "When you get to Melrose, ask people." But there is one common thread in all the advice they get. "Head east." Maude has the feeling that she and her companions are being sent to the farthest reaches of Nova Scotia, to the end of the earth as far as anyone on this island is concerned.

"Seems like there ain't nobody out here 'cept the moose," says Virgil.

He's a tall man with a thick beard on his thin, chocolate face. Rugged and handsome, to Maude's way of thinking, in his knee boots, overalls, and long beaver coat. But his frame sags as he holds the traces. His eyes stare ahead blankly at the wheel ruts ahead that lead through an endless cavern in the forest.

It's already two in the afternoon, and they have not seen a house, a barn, a person all day. This soggy wagon road through the pine forest and melting snow does not look like it has been traveled in a week.

"Maybe we ain't gone find a whole heap of blacks dem." Cally has her eyes squeezed closed as if in denial.

"But we aren't going to find any bloody white people neither," says Maude, thinking that for the moment, at least, she has shaken off the men Washington has sent after her.

"How much food we got left?" asks Cally.

"Keg of bread, half-barrel of water, and enough cod fish heads to get an army across the land of Egypt, I reckon." Virgil chuckles to himself. He's probably thinking about how those fish heads are going to smell in another day or two when they turn sour under the canvas tarp with the spring sun beating on it.

"Then keep going." Cally's voice is thick with conviction.

"Fine by me," says Maude, nuzzling her children against her as a dusting of snow filters down from the pines overhead.

She means it. If she can't be with her Raffy, she would rather die somewhere in these woods than go back to civilization. At least on this continent. That bastard who attacked her in Halifax was the last straw, she doesn't care if she sees any of her white brethren—Yank or Reb—for a long time, unless it's the sea captain who held her so tightly in Nassau and promised to carry her in his heart unto death.

***

After another night sleeping by a campfire and bathing in a sinkhole of fresh water, they come to a fork in the wagon track. One follows the coast east. The other turns away to the north.

Virgil stops the wagon at the intersection. "What's your pleasure, ladies?"

"That way," says Cally as if she has just caught a glimpse of paradise. "Look there. See?"

She points to the trunk of a tall spruce tree just beyond the turn in the fork on the track leading to the left—inland, north. Carved in its bark is the image of the Big Dipper with its lip pointing to Polaris, the North Star.

"Follow the North Star, follow the drinking gourd," says Maude, remembering the advice she heard Minty Tubman say so often to fugitive slaves.

"I'll be damned." Virgil has a grin on his face as big as a slice of watermelon.

***

It's three hours later when they first smell baking bread. Then they hear singing. When they crest a rise in the forest, they see spread out before them acres of cleared land, a saw mill, brick factory, what must be vegetable and tobacco plots emerging from the melting snow, pens for pigs, cattle grazing where the snow has melted, neat log cottages, and a log church. People are spilling from the front doors of the church. Mothers, fathers, children, grannies. All black, all singing. The song is "Swing Low, Sweet Chariot."

The forty-or-so citizens of Lincolnville gather around the travelers and hug them as if they are long-lost cousins. And the residents use the occasion of these new arrivals as a reason for a feast. On this first warm Sunday in April, the yard next to the church has lost the last of the snow. The citizens set up trestles laden with fresh bread, ham, roast chicken, okra, peas, turnips, current pie, apple cider.

Maude, her children, and her companions eat and laugh with their hosts as they relate to each other stories of their flights to freedom. A granny tells how Lincolnville is modeling itself on other Negro communities like Dawn and the Buxton Mission in Upper Canada. The village teacher shows newspapers for blacks called *The Voice of the Fugitive* and *The Provincial Freeman* that have inspired the settlers here and link them to blacks throughout Canada. The raven Obi jumps from shoulder to shoulder, jabbering like a magpie.

After the feasting and the talking, there's jigging to the music of men playing banjos, fiddles, concertinas, drums. The music shakes Maude's body like a thousand little flashes of lightning. And how she dances. With her toddlers. With Cally. With Virgil. With the citizens of Lincolnville . . . until well after dark. When the dancing finally ends, the preacher puts Virgil's horse in the community corral and beds down the travelers in the house of God.

Before Maude falls asleep wrapped in a fresh quilt, she hears Cally stirring beside her.

"What's the matter?"

"Nothin' . . . just nothin' at all. I know that if I die now, I been to Canaan, seen the dawning of a new day."

"Amen," says Virgil.

Maude hears herself sigh. For the first time in months, maybe years, everything feels nearly bloody right . . . even if it may not last. Even if Raffy is still lost to the world and her.

47

DISTRICT OF COLUMBIA
April 17, 1864

"What's so urgent, Major Allen? So secret, that you made me ride all the way out here on a Sunday morning?" Gideon Welles is wishing he was in the New York Avenue Presbyterian Church in Washington this morning with his wife, the president, and Mrs. Lincoln. With the crisp sunlight setting the stained glass windows on fire. He coughs into the elbow of his riding jacket, can't seem to shake this nasty spring cold.

"Certain things of import have come to light." Major E. J. Allen lights a cigar.

"Like?" The secretary of the navy sits his horse as it grazes in a small meadow by the Potomac's Great Falls. The water is swirling, roaring around the rocky falls in the middle of the river gorge.

"Ever heard the name Banks Howell, Mr. Welles?"

"As in Varina Anne Banks Howell Davis?"

"Exactly."

"Well?"

"Well, I thought you might like to know the name of the cheeky bastard who has been sending you those threats in red envelopes for more than two years." Allen hugs himself. There's a sharp north wind. The air has an uncommon chill for a late morning in April.

"Banks Howell? He's related to Mrs. Jefferson Davis?"

"Second cousin."

Welles thinks back on his secret visit to the office of Mr. George Washington Riggs's personal secretary a month ago, the place with its cache of red envelopes and stationery. "I thought you said Riggs's secretary was somebody named Spenser."

"Fillmore Spenser. I've dug deeper. It's an alias. The man is Banks Howell. From Charles County, Maryland."

"Wasn't Raphael Semmes born in Charles County?"

Allen nods. "It's the South down there . . . in all but name."

"Are you going to have this man arrested for treason as you did that Trowbridge fellow in New York?"

"I'm afraid you are not seeing the big picture."

"What?"

"You know that ship of yours that blew up two days ago in New York Harbor?"

"The *Chenango.*"

A terrible tragedy, an embarrassment. The side-wheel steam cruiser of eleven hundred tons, about the size of the *Kearsarge* and Semmes's *Alabama,* was only seven weeks old. She was on her way to join the blockade fleet at Hampton Roads when she exploded abreast Fort Richmond, rending her decks to pieces, killing two men outright and seriously injuring more than 30 of the 130 men aboard.

The *New York Times* reported that "many of the poor fellows were literally flayed alive, some of them being quite blind from the effects of the steam. Their shrieks and groans were painful beyond expression; great, stalwart men implored the surgeons to give them something to ease their pain. It was evident that several of them were beyond human aid and would find in death a speedy easement of their suffering."

"Her port boiler let go," says Welles. "Shabby construction."

Allen clears his throat. "Beg your pardon, Mr. Secretary, but it was no such thing."

"How do you know?"

"I know!"

"Damn it man, will you, for once, not play coy with me?"

Allen purses his lips, seems to be weighing his options. "Only the president knows this."

"What?"

"We've managed to get a really good man inside the Secret Line."

"A double agent?"

"Yes."

"What does this have to do with the *Chenango*?"

"My man says the Rebs blew it up."

Welles tries to imagine how a spy could blow up a boiler on a new ship. *It doesn't seem possible unless* . . . "He killed himself in the process?"

"No. He was bragging to his cronies in a Brooklyn pub two nights ago."

"How did he . . . ?"

"A thing called a coal torpedo."

"What?"

Allen explains that the South has taken the secret war in a new direction. They have gotten deeply involved in developing pyrotechnical devices including some weapons cooked up by a Cincinnati chemist going by the name of Greek Fire and this coal bomb called the Courtenay Coal Torpedo. It's an explosive device made to look like a lump of coal. When put in a fire . . . boom.

"Who's this Courtenay?"

"Thomas Edgeworth Courtenay. Inventor, *saboteur*."

"You've got him?"

"We believe he's fled for Canada."

"The bastard. Just a few chunks of that stuff in the right coal piles could do more damage than ten Raphael Semmes could even dream of."

Allen nods. "It seems that the likes of Richmond's bloody seahawk are quickly becoming unnecessary."

Welles feels his chest tightening. He thinks of Winslow and the *Kearsarge*'s long and lonely vigil in the English Channel. Could it be that Winslow's vigil has been all for naught, that the *Kearsarge* and the *Alabama*, like a hundred other warships built in the last three years, are becoming expensive, useless antiques? Is the day of yard-arm-to-yardarm naval combat rapidly drawing to a close? *Will this war be decided by legions of spies and innocuous-looking little bombs?*

The secretary of the navy is no lover of martial gallantry for gallantry's sake, but part of him has thrilled to the hunt for the *Alabama* and her preposterous Reb pirate. Part of him wants the epic ending, is sure that Winslow must dearly crave it by now, as well. And maybe Semmes does, too. All of them came of age in a more cavalier valorous world.

"Am I going to have the crews on all of my ships picking through every lump of coal in bunkers with hundreds of tons of fuel?"

"That may be necessary."

"Give me some good news, Major."

"We've all but got Banks Howell linked to Courtenay's attack on the *Chenango*."

"Really?"

Allen says he needs Welles to keep mum on this sabotage of the *Chenango* for a while. Let the world think it was a boiler failure. His Secret Service agents are close to putting the bite on a collection of Welles's favorite rogues. Now is not the time to raise fears of discovery among them.

"You mean the Iago conspirators."

"Call them what you want."

"But you're going to have soldiers detain them? Jail them?"

"You don't want to know. The president doesn't want to know."

"When?"

"The sooner the better, don't you think? Time's not on our side here. We think they are planning to kidnap Mr. Lincoln."

48

USS KEARSARGE
April 18, 1864

Ostend Harbor, Belgium. Noon. A gray wet day. Steaming into port between the stone jetties, a Flemish pilot in command.

For ten minutes Winslow has been watching a fishing smack ahead—a graceful, black-and-yellow *bisquine* with all upper and lower sails set on her two masts. And now he's concerned. She's laboring home with her catch under sail. The harbor pilot guiding the *Kearsarge* into the narrow, canal-like harbor has not slowed the ship properly, and now, just where the channel constricts, the warship is overtaking the fisher. She's bearing down on the sailboat as if intending to swallow it whole.

"My God, fellow, don't hit that smack." The captain's voice booms across the quarterdeck so loudly he feels that his dead eye might rupture. According to maritime law, the pilot is currently in command. It is not Winslow's place, after hiring a pilot, to second-guess the man. But damned if something is not patently wrong here.

The pilot is a sallow fellow of about forty in a blue suit, perched on the horse block. In response to Winslow's shouts, he mutters something dismissive and unintelligible—probably Flemish—in the direction of the captain. He has his eyes locked on something or someone ashore to port.

The *bisquine* is so close under the warship's bows that only the topsails are visible when the pilot calls to the quartermaster to reverse his engines and put the helm hard over to port.

The engine room signal bell clangs. Machinery deep in the hull grumbles. The screw ceases turning for some seconds, then beats astern, churning up a great bubbling of water around the *Kearsarge*. The stern starts to skid to starboard just as the ship overtakes the fisher. Winslow dashes to the rail, sees the bows of his vessel just miss—by less than ten feet—running right over the *bisquine*. The ship's starboard whisker stay snags the clew of the fisher's main topsail. For a second the *bisquine* is caught in the *Kearsarge*'s bow rigging and is being dragged along, nearly submerged, by the forward motion and side-slipping of the ship. But then the main topmast on the fisher carries away, topples. And the broken workboat breaks free.

It's all over in an instant. The fishermen making obscene gestures, shouting up English curses—fucking Lincoln, fucking *yanquis*—as their little boat crashes alongside the warship's open gun ports and, finally, falls astern.

Now with the helm hard over, the *Kearsarge* is yawing sideways in the channel while still moving forward at two knots. Heading right for a pedestrian bridge extending from the eastern bank.

"All astern *full!*" Winslow screams his orders.

The quartermaster clangs the engine room signal bell. The hull shudders as the engineer pours on the steam to stop the ship. The pilot puts both hands on his hips, stares dumbly ahead at the people on the bridge. Cyclists and the driver of a baker's wagon laden with fresh *baguettes* abandon their vehicles, leap for the water. An instant later the ship plows through the bridge, strikes bottom, lurches to starboard. Stops. The foredeck of the *Kearsarge* is a jumble. Shattered wood from the bridge, bicycles, hundreds of loaves of fresh bread, a dog cart spilling a cask of ripe and crumbling cheese.

Standing on the stub of what's left of the bridge, two *gendarmes* point right at Winslow with extended arms and blow into their preternaturally shrill whistles.

My God, thinks Winslow, *am I now to be under arrest?*

***

"I believe it was intentional," says Lieutenant Commander Thornton. "No pilot in all my years at sea has shown such total disregard for the restrictions of a channel . . . nor such ineptitude with ship handling."

He's seated at the wardroom table with the *Kearsarge*'s full complement of officers, the captain, and the local United States consul. Fearing that at any moment he may be dragooned ashore by local authorities, Winslow has already convened an accident investigation. It's night. The ship's still aground, held more or less upright in the mud by guys set out from the mastheads to distress anchors and stayed with pennant tackles. The tide has just started to come back in. It will be hours before the crew can even attempt to refloat the ship. On shore hundreds of gawkers have gathered to look at this stellar example of American seamanship.

"Reb agents have been most active in this port of late," says the consul. "It is not beyond the realm of possibility that the pilot has been bribed to contrive this mischief."

"What recourse have we?" asks Winslow. "That ignoramus showed not the least remorse."

"Claims it was the ship's fault. Claims she did not respond to his commands," says the second lieutenant, who was officer of the deck at the time of the accident.

"The pilot guild is backing their man," says the counsel, "and so are local officials. They're putting all the blame on the ship and the crew."

"Another damned dirty trick." Thornton's face is red. He reminds everybody at the table of all the wild goose chases they were sent on a year ago back in the Azores, the continuing diplomatic problems arising from the Irish stowaways last fall in Cork, the mysterious bunker fires off Dover about a month ago that may not have been spontaneous combustion after all. And now this.

Winslow feels his wrecked eye throbbing, the pain running right through his skull, across his shoulders, and down into his belly. He wonders once again if he's got an enemy agent in the crew, whether Chief Captain of the Fo'castle James Haley can be trusted despite his quick thinking and hard work in dousing the bunker fire.

"Something stinks to high heaven," he says. "But let's look to the facts and to the mission, men."

He says that the *Kearsarge* has all but been banned from both British and French ports. If she is to continue her watch in the English Channel, then these little ports in Belgium and the Netherlands must serve. The ship cannot now pick a fight with the Brussels government.

"I think the cost of repairs to the bridge and the fishing smack is something I can cover out of my funds," says the consul. "I'm with the Captain. Let's pay the bill and eat humble pie."

In other words, there's no advantage in giving the Rebs and partisan newspapers another chance to cast this ship in a negative light. Another chance to let local officials and enemy agents deter the *Kearsarge* from her mission. Dirty tricks will not force her to quit her watch on the channel at a critical moment.

Winslow's back stiffens, his good eye turns on the consul. "Is there something I do not yet know of?" He asks if France has finally given the Rebs' *Rappahannock* permission to sail from Calais.

The consul says he has no news on the Confederate cruiser interned down the coast. "But I have more interesting news. We have word from a ship just in from Cape Town. Raphael Semmes was there some three months ago and was heading back this way. It would seem he could be here any day."

Winslow feels his cracked lips smile. The pain in his belly softens a notch. His endurance and his patience may yet be rewarded. James Haley may yet get to prove his worth at the fo'castle guns. Let the Rebs try as they may. They cannot stop this Jacob's appointed rendezvous with his Esau.

The Lord is my shepherd. I shall not want.

49

CSS ALABAMA
April 23, 1864

Fifteen degrees south latitude, thirty degrees west longitude. About 300 miles off the coast of Brazil. Westbound. Two bells into the mid watch. Broad reaching under a full course of sail. Enemy in sight.

At last.

The *Alabama*'s 294th chase. Soon to be her 68th prize, her 53rd floating bonfire.

He has been dreaming of almost nothing but this encounter since leaving Cape Town more than a month ago. *Alabama* is more than three months without a prize. She's falling to pieces. Her crew's bored, surly. And now, finally, comes this chase under a bright moon.

Most merciful and benevolent creator of all things.

Only the steward Bartelli knows that the captain has been drinking since dinner, is well into his second bottle of the floral-scented Stellenbosch white wine from South Africa that he has come to favor. Only God knows what haunts the captain as he sits in his chair here alone on the windward wing of the bridge deck, watching his tired ship loping after the Yank ahead. Semmes can't shake Maude's lavender scent from his mind nor the words of the poet he has been reading much of this last month. The one who desired for his epitaph the words "Here Lies One Whose Name Was Writ in Water." The tragic boy John Keats. Dead at twenty-five, ravaged by consumption. The magician who wrote as if he were here. On this ship. At this time, this place.

. . . tender is the night,
And haply the Queen-Moon is on her throne,
Cluster'd around by all her starry Fays

The moon tonight is so full, so brilliant, that the sea glows a pale and misty silver. The large American bark—a crisp, black specter, five miles ahead—clearly knows that she's being chased and has set staysails and stunsails to get away.

As Semmes looks on, he thinks of perhaps the most painful and romantic of all Keats's poems. It haunts the mariner, speaks to him. "Ode to a Nightingale." A nocturnal rhapsody to misery and impossible longing.

My heart aches, and a drowsy numbness pains
My sense, as though of hemlock I had drunk . . .

Yes, *Alabama*'s gaining on the Yank. Not as quickly as she would have in times gone by, but like an old hound, Semmes thinks. A seasoned hunter drawn to the chase and the scent of game by instinct and habit, perhaps for the last time. . . . Dying a bit, feeling that frozen pain in the lungs settling into every crevice of the body with each new moment in pursuit, each fresh gasp for breath. While the lines of Keats's poem weave themselves into new and dark yearnings.

O . . . That I might drink, and leave the world unseen . . .
Fade far away, dissolve, and quite forget . . .
The weariness, the fever, and the fret . . .

Lieutenant Kell has come onto the bridge. He keeps a respectful distance from his captain, confers with the officer of the deck, Lieutenant Armstrong. They are on the leeward wing of the bridge, more than thirty feet away, talking over the chase and the possibility of getting up a boarding party if and when they finally overtake the Yank.

"The men are restless, tired too, sir." Semmes hears Armstrong say. "The doctor says sickbay is full."

"Scurvy?"

"Among other things. This cruise has been . . ."

Kell says something Semmes can't quite catch, possibly the word "epic."

"Can we wait until after daylight, sir? For the men's sake?" asks Armstrong.

"Jesus! Is this a ship of war or . . . ? What have we become, man?" asks Kell.

Semmes feels the luff's fatigue, his frustration. This once fine and lively ship has become, as Keats says, a place

. . . where men sit and hear each other groan;
Where palsy shakes a few, sad, last gray hairs,
Where youth grows pale, and spectre-thin . . .

Kell throws up his hands, his long shadow blackening the deck in the moonshine.

"Come, Mr. Kell . . . talk to me."

"I'm afraid I'm just in a foul mood, sir."

"Have you been thinking on your family?"

"Aye, sir."

For just an instant, the flaming hair of a West Irish selkie flashes through the captain's mind, vanishes. "Missing loved ones may well be the hardest part of the service. Harder than the battle. Am I right?"

"Permission to speak plain, sir?"

"As always, Kell."

"We all just want to go home."

"It's only natural, man."

"Still . . ."

"Still the only route home for the warrior is battle . . . or death."

"Aye."

"Then we must fight."

"Yes, sir."

"But are we able? The ship? The men? Can we find the fire we had when we defeated the *Hatteras*?"

"There's only one sure way to find out."

Semmes sees Kell's gaze settle on the dark phantom they're chasing, thinks he knows what's on the luff's mind. "You want to stage a full battle drill? Against this Yank merchantman? All guns blazing?"

"That would be the thing, Captain."

"A test? For the ship and crew?"

"Aye."

Semmes feels something flare in his chest. "Then you better ring up the engineer and tell him to lay on the goddamn coal. We can't catch that fast bastard out there under sail alone."

Not anymore.

***

"Well, Kell, was that satisfactory?" Semmes asks.

The luff smiles, gives his captain a nod. It's a mild tropical afternoon, and Kell's sweating as he fetches the deck from the Jacob's ladder slung on the starboard side of the *Alabama*. He's just back after inspecting the damage his gunners have done during the last two hours to the once-proud bark *Rockingham*, hailing from the Yankee heartland of Portsmouth, New Hampshire. She was bound from Peru to Cork with a load of guano. Now her crew is prisoner on the *Alabama*, her stores plundered, her hull and rig a shattered wreck waiting for the torch.

A ship full of bird shite, thinks the *Alabama*'s captain. *The perfect reflection of Abe Lincoln's rotten Union . . . blown to bits by my gunners.*

"Fifteen large holes from the hundred-pounders in what would have been her boilers, engine, magazine if she were a Yank steamer, sir." Kell is now walking aft on the quarterdeck of the *Alabama* with Semmes.

"Our gunners were fast and accurate."

"I doubt any of Gideon Welles's lackeys could do better."

"The boys seemed to get a charge out of playing with their guns." Semmes twirls the tips of his mustache, holds his eyes on the wreck of the *Rockingham.*

"They sense what's coming, sir."

"You think they'll fight, then, when the time comes."

"Every man jack of them, Captain."

"But we've got a problem."

"The ammunition, sir?"

Semmes says that by his count at least a third of the explosive shells that the *Alabama* fired into the *Rockingham* failed to detonate.

Kell thinks some of the fuses must have gone bad.

"Have your best gunner's mates and a pair of officers go through our munitions. Heave every suspicious fuse overboard."

"Yes, sir."

"Every shot must count if we enter a fight."

"Of course, sir."

"But, Kell . . . what think you of the powder itself?"

The luff winces. "I did not like the sound of it right much."

Semmes has been thinking the same thing. The shells that exploded made a dull thud, not the sharp ear-piercing report of fresh powder.

"I fear the damp has not done it any good, to be honest, Captain."

"But will it serve, Luff . . . if our gunners are quick at their jobs and our aim is true?"

Kell closes his eyes for a second. He's thinking or wishing on something.

Semmes grabs him by the elbow. “But will the powder serve?”
“I believe so, sir . . . if the fight comes soon.”
Aye, there's the rub.

50

LINCOLNVILLE, NOVA SCOTIA
Mid-May, 1864

Maude's getting what she tells herself are funny feelings.

For more than a month she, the children, and Cally have been living with an old granny who everyone calls Miss Venus. They have been helping her every morning get in her vegetable plot now that the ground has truly thawed and the air feels and smells like Galway in springtime. Almost every afternoon they meet with about a dozen other women in the church to spin wool and knit sweaters, jackets, hats, and blankets for next winter. Little Fiona and Levi play with five other toddlers, while the women of the village take turns watching over the brood. Virgil has become Lincolnville's hostler, using his horse, Willie, to do all the heavy lugging as the men clear more land for plantation. He lives with a group of young men known as "The Uncles."

Maude, Cally, and the children still see a lot of Virgil. Almost every night he has been coming to Miss Venus's cabin to sit outside with his friends under the stars and visit. On such nights of late, Maude has been getting her feelings. They aren't exactly bad feelings—just an uneasiness, a melancholy that makes her poor company—so she takes her leave. Heads off to put the children and herself to bed. Both Fiona and Levi are still nursing before they go to sleep. It takes almost an hour to get them fed and in bed before Maude can slide under her own blankets. But Virgil and Cally seem to go on for hours. Maude can hear their talk and laughter, murmuring like waves pulling rocks off a steep shore. Their voices remind her of Ireland and home as she nods off to sleep.

But tonight when Virgil comes by just as Maude and Cally are finishing the supper dishes for Miss Venus, something's different . . . and Maude's getting her funny feelings again. Especially after Cally tosses down her apron and asks Maude, "Will you excuse us? Virgil and I gots to go for a little walk."

Maude sees the hostler's eyes grow wide, wonders what's the matter. But she smiles and waves them off. "I must write to my sailor."

So while Cally and Virgil head off down the road toward the church, Maude grabs a candle, pen, and paper. She sits down at Miss Venus's table and thinks about how to begin another letter to her Raffy. Not to tell him about all the daily events that have made her feel so welcome here in Lincolnville. Not to tell him about how the children romp around in the fresh green grass and make her laugh at their delight of every new thing they discover in the world. Not even to tell him that she still fears that there are vicious, dark men chasing her.

She needs to tell him about this abiding longing she feels for him that won't go away. Tell him that she hopes he is well and still remembers his selkie. She wants to find the right words to ask him if his service and his war will soon come to an end, if he's returning to England soon. Wants to ask him if he would welcome her and the children there.

But she hasn't even written the first word of her letter's greeting when Cally pokes her head in the door and asks, "Hey, child, can you come outside?"

In the glow of the candlelight, Maude can see a rose glow running up Cally's neck and into her chocolate cheeks. Something's different.

"We have something to ask you," Cally says.

Virgil's face beams a watermelon smile.

Cally casts a shy look at the man beside her. "Maybe you better sit down," she says to Maude.

"What's bloody come over you two?" Maude's hands are on her hips. She's not going to move an inch unless someone tells her what's going on.

Well . . . you know Virgil and I been spending some time together . . ."

"She's the apple of my eye." Virgil's words seem to pop as they come out of his mouth. He takes Cally's hand.

"He be the one and only," she says as she nuzzles to his chest.

I should have seen this coming, Maude thinks. *But what do you say when your best friends tell you they're sweet on each other?* She tries to speak, but those funny feelings are rising in her throat. All she can do is fold Cally and Virgil in her arms.

"How would you like to be a god mammy?" Virgil asks.

Maude pulls back from her hug, looks her friends in the eyes. *What are they trying to tell me here?*

Cally's eyebrows curl up . . . then just about leap off her forehead. "Virgil and I gone get married."

"We having a baby, Maude. We want you to be the god mammy."

Maude thinks her heart must have stopped for a second because she can feel nothing, hear nothing but the distant hoot of an owl.

"I'd be most honored," she says at last.

"This be heaven on earth." Cally has tears on her cheeks.

Virgil looks down into her big brown eyes and clasps her tight to his chest.

Maude smiles and smiles for them, but her heart lets out a little cry. Unlike Cally, Maude's arms are empty after all. She has no man of her own.

And what she sees now only makes her feel less secure. Four shadowy figures are coming up the moonlit road on horses. As they move closer, she can see that one of them is wearing a red shirt. She thinks it's a shirt that she recognizes from her days visiting at the home of Varina Davis back in Richmond. A Rebel's shirt.

51

CSS ALABAMA
Early June, 1864

Off the Lizard. Southern approach to the English Channel. Ship jogging northwest under topsails alone. 0345 hours.

"Wretched, wretched English Channel," Raphael Semmes grumbles to himself as he stares into the black fog. He hears the steep seas building and crumbling around the *Alabama*, feels her rolling awkwardly. Knows he's in a mariner's purgatory, caught between a fierce spring tide ebbing south out of the channel and a building sou'west half-gale.

"Beg your pardon, sir." It's Pills Galt, the paymaster, once the ship's surgeon. He's been sailing with Semmes since they left New Orleans together on the *Sumter* three years ago. "I'm speaking as your old friend and physician now. You've got to get some rest. You've been on the bridge for twelve hours."

"The enemy is abroad, man, I can smell him."

"You have a cold and a fever, Captain."

"Would you have me retire to my cabin when the hour of my ship's need approaches?"

"I think that we want you alert and rested when that moment comes. Let Mr. Kell take the watch now. I think God would have it thus."

Semmes feels a rattling in his lungs, a sudden urge to throttle someone . . . his friend will do. "Are you suddenly getting pious with me?"

"I only meant . . . you cannot drive yourself this way, sir, day upon day. It's unnatural."

Semmes's skin bristles, his head burns. "Unnatural? I'll tell you what's unnatural. The way you, Dr. Llewellyn, and that black Nancy-boy, David, have been carrying on. You think I don't know you've got him wearing dresses down there in sickbay when no one seems to be around."

The paymaster throws up both of his hands in front of his face, palms out. An instinct for self-protection.

"My God, I must be crazy to let the three of you go on like that for so long. I have half a mind to . . ."

Galt's face sags with surprise, pain. It's the look of a man who has just taken a sword through the heart.

Semmes sees the wound, feels it, too. Knows he has crossed an unspoken line. "I'm sorry, Pills."

"You wouldn't understand."

"How would you know?!" The words burst from Semmes's throat. This must be the fever talking.

There are tears in Galt's eyes.

"It's right hard to even dream of a personal life when at sea . . . let alone have one," says Semmes.

Galt brushes away a tear, gazes away into the fog. "We all know you have suffered, sir. . . . I was in Nassau with you two summers ago when we were waiting for a new ship. When the young miss came for you. When we got orders back to England to get the *Alabama*. Remember?"

Maude has fallen. She has tripped on the coral shore after running from him when she learned he was going to leave her for a new ship. He's at her side now. Galt's easing her pain with laudanum. An old black woman's here, too, tending to Maude with compresses, an herbal tea to strengthen her and staunch the blood leaking between her legs.

"It was a hard time you had of it, Captain."

After she has told him about the baby in her womb, he walks silently beside her as she's carried on a cot aboard a schooner bound for the Savannah River. Her bleeding has not stopped. Galt says she needs better medical attention than she can get here in the islands. She may yet require hospitalization, lose the baby, die from her hemorrhaging.

Semmes sighs, can't rein in the urge to confess. "Sometimes I wish I had gone off to Brazil with her, Pills."

"She did seem a most rare flower, sir."

As he's about to let her go, she pulls him down to her on the cot. Embraces him, asks if he's giving up on their love. His eyes leak tears. "I do not think I could live even an hour without holding you in my heart."

"I miss her right much."

Galt reaches out, nearly touches his captain's arm, seems to think better of it and scratches at his beard. "Is there not a good chance that you may reunite with her . . . in England or France, sir? This cruise draws to its conclusion."

Semmes looks away into the fog. The dawn has begun to lighten the infernal night. And now there's a dark shape looming out there off to port. A ship. Possibly a Yank. Bearing down on the *Alabama.*

"Things may not end as we wish, my old friend," he says. Then he adds something that sounds like a man bracing himself for the apocalypse. "Look to your loved ones."

***

The dark shape in the fog is not the feared *Vanderbilt,* the venerable *San Jacinto*, the luckless *Iroquois,* or any of the other two dozen ships that Gideon Welles has sent in Semmes's wake. No Yank. It's an English pilot schooner offering her services. And after the pilot has been brought aboard, hired, and has debriefed the captain as to the current state of affairs in England and the Confederacy, Semmes staggers off to his cabin.

He now knows that the enemy's USS *Kearsarge* has been watching the channel with vigilance for months. He also knows that England's sympathies for the South are no longer what they once were. The British government has stopped the release of the rams built for Richmond in Liverpool. Other Confederate cruisers, the *Florida*, *Georgia*, and *Rappahannock* have found a more welcome reception in France, sought shelter of late in ports on the coasts of Normandy and Brittany.

For Semmes the decision of where to go next to repair his ship and pay off his crew is clear. He has told the pilot to steer him to the nearest French harbor that can handle him. So the *Alabama* turns for Cherbourg. Her captain is feeling an extreme need to pray for deliverance.

The dawn and the fog freeze his cabin in faint, hazy light. The shadows of sails and masts vibrate and sway through the skylight, cast vague shadows on the cabin sole that swell and fade with each roll of the ship. Semmes pictures valkyries swooping in toward the *Alabama.* He falls on his knees before the little shrine he keeps to the Virgin Mary, murmuring his pleas to his God and the Holy Mother. His forehead and cheeks burn with fever. His chest aches from trying to breathe. The cabin swirls about him. He's reciting his twenty-first Hail Mary when the first ghost appears.

She's a dark-skinned mulatto from the Street of Women in Santo Domingo, looking at him askance, an eyebrow cocked. Arms just folding across her chest. Bare shoulders, breasts showing through a gauzy white dress. Black eyes. Long, straight dark hair. A headband with three hawk feathers like the spikes on a crown. Silver and gold lines painted on her high cheeks, forehead, chin.

"There be a terrible dark cloud over your ship, Captain," she says. "Drowned men swarming all around."

He sees the *Somers* awash in monstrous seas. His first command. His lost ship. His disgrace. Men clinging to anything in the wreckage that will keep them afloat.

The air's filling with the shouts of swimmers, calling the names of their shipmates for comfort. Calling his name. Begging for mercy. But these are not the voices from that terrible accident eighteen years ago. These are the voices of the *Alabama*. Kell's voice, Sinclair's voice, Galt's voice. Bartelli's voice, the boy David's voice. "Save us, Captain."

But how, Heavenly Father? How, sweet Mary full of grace? Where lies the glory?

52

DISTRICT OF COLUMBIA
June 5, 1864

Lincoln waves a confidential report from E. J. Allen in his hand. "According to this, all of General Grant's soldiers and all of your ships, Gideon, don't amount to a hill of beans."

The president is at his most private post. The White House roof this morning is an excellent place to witness the blossoming of a Sunday in June. Gideon Welles and E. J. Allen stand at his side, watching the golden sun soaring above the Capitol. The mist rising off the Potomac. The river just now looking like a sheet of copper.

"Grant's march on Richmond, your endless hunt for Raphael Semmes have become mere sideshows. The real war is being fought behind closed doors and in dark alleys by accountants and lawyers and bankers . . . and the shady agents of these rascals in fancy suits and silk petticoats. My enemies are legion."

Welles nods glumly. He knows the report outlines a multitude of threats to the president, including rumors of a Confederate plot to kidnap him. The document cites suspicious Freemasons, domestic financiers, international banking families like the Rothschilds, American businessmen, Copperheads, Radical Republicans, B'nai B'rith, Jesuits, Knights of the Golden Circle, Judah Benjamin's Secret Line.

And then there are the known rats in the cabinet. Seward, Stanton, Bates, Chase. And their cronies like George Washington Riggs, Rear Admiral Wilkes, Senator Hale.

Lincoln wields the report as if to drive off a swarm of gnats . . . chase them across the river to Alexandria, Virginia. "If this nation is to survive, you must separate the merely unhappy factions in this report from the dangerous ones. We are, after all, a democracy that holds the freedom of speech dear, gentlemen. And we do not have the resources to thoroughly monitor all those who simply oppose us."

"Yes sir, but . . ."

"But . . . yes, *but*. But once the names and shapes of our gadflies are as clear to us as the face of Raphael Semmes and the look of his hell ship, then you must by every means rid Washington and our beloved country of them once and for all."

"I believe we are making good progress on that score," says Allen.

He notes recent successes. Charles Wilkes has been convicted by a court martial of ignoring orders and violating military protocols. He has been suspended from national service for at least two years. Concerned citizens and party members in New Hampshire (with some prodding and secret support from Allen) have vowed not to renominate Hale to run in the fall elections for the Senate. Allen's sources say that Salmon Chase has decided not to run for president and will resign his post as secretary of the treasury before the month is out.

"I intend to make this resignation easier for Chase," says Lincoln. "I have given out in certain circles familiar to him that if he tenders me his resignation, a position on the court may well open to him, possibly chief justice."

Welles finds himself taking a deep breath, relishing the crisp air. It's good to see that Lincoln has been planning his own initiatives to cleanse the government. Just as he has, the president finally permitted a court martial to cleanse the navy of Wilkes, just as he cleansed the army with his appointment of Grant as general-in-chief back in March.

Allen says that the South's Secret Line and the Knights of the Golden Circle have grown vastly more sophisticated in causing terror since the days of Rose Greenhow and sending threats to Welles in red envelopes.

"We used to think this Iago business was coming out of, what did you call it, a *cabal*, Welles? In Washington and Richmond."

"Used to?"

"Here's the news from a number of good men and women whom we now have on the inside. It's coming out of Canada. The Rebs have set up an entire shadow government up there in Toronto."

Lincoln's eyebrows raise.

Allen says the architect of the operation is a Captain Thomas Hines. Among the other conspirators are military officers in civilian clothes and politicians, such as Jacob Thompson, who was secretary of the interior under President James Buchanan, and Clement Clay, former U.S. senator from Alabama. They're ostensibly commissioners sent to Canada from Richmond with public roles as their cover. And there are other Reb politicians involved, including George N. Sanders, who has been party to secret Confederate operations in Europe, and Clement L. Vallandigham, once a powerful member of Congress from Ohio. He claims he has 300,000 Sons of Liberty ready to follow him in an insurrection.

"You mean all of these devils in Washington are just agents? Not the ring leaders?" says Lincoln.

Welles pictures Banks Howell, George Washington Riggs, Senator Hale, Charles Wilkes, Seward, Stanton, Chase, Bates.

"It's entirely possible."

"How can you be sure?"

"Semmes's tart will help us there."

"She's in custody?"

"I should think yes, by now."

"Still in Canada?"

"Where else?"

"But aren't the Rebs after her, too?" Welles again.

"And we're her only safe way out. . . . What's the matter, Mister Secretary? You're looking a little pale."

"That wench . . . she . . ."

"I say, I think she's going to hand us enough information to bring down more than a dozen rascals we've been suspecting for a long time."

"How do you know she's going to cooperate? The last time she left one of your fellows back in Halifax with his teeth all over the floor, didn't . . . ?"

"I cannot hear these things, sirs. You'll excuse me." Lincoln turns, heads for the stairs leading down into the attic. The country lawyer in him tells him that he must protect himself from charges of unscrupulous, secret activities. He must have no knowledge of details concerning Allen's dirty tricks.

But the president pauses at the top of the stairs. "Listen to me, gentlemen. Our citizens cannot fathom the depth of this secret war, cannot appreciate its private little victories. We will lose this coming election and the war . . . unless we give them a military victory to cheer about."

"Yes, sir."

"Can't you catch Raphael Semmes, Gideon?"

"We've heard no news of him for nigh onto four months."

Lincoln actually growls before turning to the stairs again.

When he's gone, Allen licks his lips, flashes a wicked smile at Welles. "I think I know a way that I can save your job for you."

"Do I even want to know?"

"This time we're doing things differently with Semmes's red-haired slut, my man. We're going to snatch one of her babies. You know what the thought of a lost child will do to a mother?"

The secretary of the navy pictures the president two years ago. His little Willie dead. Lincoln's wearing a tattered maroon dressing gown, slippers down at the heels. Weeping into his hands. . . . *And my poor lifeless little Hubert, my flawless four-year-old, gone off to Connecticut, too, in a box for burial with only his mother at his side.*

"We get our hands on one of her urchins, and I believe she'll sing like a bleeding skylark. And then I think she'll lead us straight to Semmes once we turn her loose. He'll be yours for the killing."

Welles's chest starts to convulse. A great barking cough breaks from his throat.

Allen tosses his cigar off the roof, grabs the secretary by the elbow. "Are you all right?"

"Let me be, villain."

53

USS KEARSARGE
June 12, 1864

"Sound the recall gun, Luff." Winslow's voice is shaky. "We must have the men at liberty back aboard."

He has sought out his executive officer on the wharf this warm Sunday afternoon. Thornton's supervising a gang of Jacks unloading a new trysail and a new topsail just brought down to the wharf in two drays from a local sail loft. It is only the ordering and buying of locally made sails like this that has induced the Dutch government to allow the Yankee warship in their port here on the River Scheldt for more than a day or two, but now the captain of the *Kearsarge* reckons he will need no more of Holland's *largesse*.

"We're leaving, sir?"

"I aim to get underway *post haste*."

Thurston gives his commander an inquiring look, has no doubt taken note of the warble in Winslow's voice. "Is this serious, Captain?"

He passes Thornton the telegram that has been tucked deep within the inside breast pocket of his jacket. Watches as Thornton reads. Sees the luff's face turn pale, a slight tremor in the hand begins to shake the coarse yellow paper as he rereads the message. It comes from William Drayton in Paris. He's the U.S. minister to France, and he has just heard from his coastal spies in Normandy.

"At last," Thornton is talking to himself.

"My long-lost brother Esau has come."

"In Cherbourg? Arrived yesterday? The *Alabama*?" Thornton questions the details of the telegram as if he still needs confirmation. As if he's not sure that he ever truly imagined that Raphael Semmes's ghost ship could be real.

"Can you believe it?"

"My mother always told me good things come to those who tarry, sir."

"How long has it been, this wait?"

"Nigh on a year and a half, sir."

"Sometimes it has seemed an eternity."

"But we have always been ready, sir. Are most ready now."

Winslow knows what his luff means. Only yesterday he had called the crew to quarters off Boulogne for target practice. They had fired thirty-five shots at a makeshift floating target. James Haley and his crews on the forward Dahlgren pivot gun and the Parrot rifle had scored hit after hit. And the powder in both the guns and the projectiles had a nice snap when it went off. The flooding of the number two bunker during the coal fire off Dover seems not to have affected the shells or powder stored in the nearby magazine.

"Have the engineer get up steam as soon as you've fired the recall gun, Luff. I want to be at sea before sunset."

"Do you think Semmes intends to leave the *Alabama*?"

Winslow looks down the river with his good eye, gazes out to sea. He remembers 1846 again when he and Raphael Semmes were assigned to the *Raritan* after both men had lost their respective ships in freak accidents. Remembers how they teased each other to keep their spirits up.

Shall we have a duel at sunrise . . . ?

I prefer we meet at noon, good sir.

"Would it not be like that old fox to try and sneak off into the night the way he left the *Sumter* two years ago in Gibraltar?"

"I knew him as a man of honor."

"Then you think he will fight us, sir?"

"Mark my words, Luff. The seahawk will come, I believe. As soon as he can . . . probably at high noon . . . unless he learns of the chain mail shirt protecting *Kearsarge* beneath her plain black skirt."

"You must speak to the crew. They must hear your certainty, your confidence. It will rouse them for the battle."

"First I must speak privately with James Haley . . . and with my God, Mr. Thornton."

Yea, though I walk through the valley of the shadow of death,
I will fear no evil: For thou art with me;
Thy rod and thy staff, they comfort me.
Thou preparest a table before me in the presence of mine enemies. . . .

***

"Let me get right to the point." It's late afternoon, and Winslow has James Haley seated opposite him at the chart table in the great cabin.

"Yes, sir."

"You are a damned fine gunner . . . but you're Irish born and bred."

"Sir?"

"I've a mind to pay you your wages and let you ashore this afternoon with no questions asked."

"This is about them bloody stowaways back in Cork, ain't it, sir?"

"Among other things."

"You think I might have played double with you?"

"Only you know that. But now we go to battle, and this ship seems to have had more than its share of mischief."

"You think I'm to blame?"

"Those stowaways were not just a problem for this ship. They cost the United States of America dearly."

Haley understands, Winslow does not need to further explain how the newspapers and the Tory politicians used the *Kearsarge*'s illegal shipping of Irishmen in Cork to fuel anti-American sentiment in England.

"Don't send me ashore, Captain. I really want a piece of Raphael Semmes."

"Then you owe me an explanation about why you helped those stowaways. . . . Why you helped James Bulloch, a known Confederate agent, gather those men."

"All right, sir . . . I guess the horse is out of the barn."

"Excuse me?"

"I'm going to tell you what I ain't told another living soul, Captain."

"To the point, man."

"It has to do with a lass, sir."

"A woman? Recruiting the stowaways has to do with a woman?"

"Me young cousin, sir. Maude from the West Country."

"I don't understand."

"She's in America now. . . . Or, at least, I think she is."

"So?"

"So somehow when we got to Cork back last fall, this James Bulloch fellow comes up to me in a Casement Square pub, sir. Says he knows me, from back in the day when he was in our navy before the war."

"What's this have to do with your cousin?"

"He says he knows her, too. Says she's in a bit of trouble in America, sir."

"What kind of trouble?"

"He didn't exactly say. But he said she's friendly with Raphael Semmes, and he sort of winks. Then he asks me if I know that Semmes is a married man."

"Strange."

"Aye, right strange, sir. The whole thing—him bumping into me, so to speak, him knowing me cousin Maudie and her troubles. It all seems like too much of a coincidence."

Winslow feels the pressure building behind his dead eye. "Maybe it wasn't a coincidence, James."

"I don't follow."

"Maybe he got his hands on a crew manifest for the *Kearsarge*. Maybe he knew that sooner or later we would come to Cork. Maybe he was waiting for you, thought he could use you."

"You mean, he was laying for me, Captain?"

"The Rebs will stop at nothing to get the upper hand on us."

"He was a right dodgy bastard."

"How so?"

"He said he was in a position to help Maudie with her Semmes problem . . . or not."

Winslow sees where this story's leading. "He'd help her, if you helped him with the stowaways."

"Aye. In a nutshell, Captain."

"He was blackmailing you."

"Me cousin's a sweet young lass, sir. I know what I done helping them wretched fellows aboard was an awful thing, but I was in all hell of a jam. And I got the idea Maudie's life could hang in the balance."

"You have feelings for her?"

"I ain't seen her in fifteen years, sir. But once a long time ago, I . . ." His voice cracks.

Winslow shakes his head. His dead eye is throbbing now, a blistering, white pain. Of all the crazy stories. . . . "So is this why you claim to want a shot at Semmes so badly?"

"It's not just a claim, sir."

"The proof's in the pudding, man."

"Take me to that bloody son of a bitch . . . sir."

54

HALIFAX, NOVA SCOTIA
June 12, 1864

Maude has been more than two weeks on the run in the wagon with church folk and Virgil and Cally hiding her and the children, shepherding them by night from one house of worship to another. The man in the red shirt and his comrades never more than two or three days behind.

This morning she's in Halifax, her friends gone back to Lincolnville. She's just blocks from a ship to England, to freedom, to her Raffy. This week's packet for Liverpool, the Cunard Lines' Royal Mail Steamship *Europa*, is only hours from sailing. As a way of wishing her Godspeed, Cally and Virgil have purchased her and the children tickets with money given by the kind citizens of Lincolnville.

But now, before the Sunday morning call to worship, right as she should be heading for the *Europa* with her children and bags, she fears that she cannot leave the safety of St. Paul's, the big Georgian Anglican church on Prince Street. For the past three days she has been hiding on the bottom level of the four-story belfry with her toddlers, thanks to the rector and the sexton, waiting for the last possible moment to make her dash to the Liverpool mail packet.

"I'm bloody surrounded by villains," she says to herself as she looks down on the streets of Halifax.

From the bell room at the top of the belfry, she can see the man in the red shirt grazing his horse on a green to the north, can see his three traveling companions with their horses lingering on each side of the church building. Up here the damp east wind whirs through the wooden louvers and makes her shiver despite her heavy wool shawl.

She's descending the three tiers of steep ladders to her children napping in a nest of blankets in the bottom room of the tower, when she hears the organ music stop abruptly in the church, right in the middle of playing "Amazing Grace." It's a little after ten in the morning, and the organist has been practicing for an hour already for the eleven o'clock service.

"Get out of here with that gun," she hears someone shout from down in the sanctuary. The voice has the thick brogue of the sexton.

There's some sort of scuffle, then running on the stairs below. The door to the tower bursts open.

"Be nice, Red, and nobody will get hurt." The man has a pistol aimed at her.

But this is not the man she expected, not the man in the red shirt. The man she could swear she saw stealing in and out the back door of the executive mansion of the Confederacy in Richmond several times like a rat. This is another man altogether, another nightmare. He's dressed in a brown suit like a Sunday churchgoer. But he has the long, lean body, the fish-white face, the scraggly little beard around his mouth that she remembers from that horror back in January at Widow Todd's. Fewer teeth though.

Maude grabs a mop from the corner of this storage room.

"Don't make me play rough, you saucy witch."

She remembers who sent this bastard and why. *They want you alive and well . . . back in Washington.*

"I come to help you, Red." He takes two steps toward her, toward the babies just starting to wake in their blankets against the south wall. He moves to the center of this room that is more than fifteen feet across.

She waves the mop in front of her, threatening him to back off as he starts to move toward her. "I don't need your kind of help."

"There are four Rebs outside like to see you dead. But I can get you out of here."

"Leave me alone, you filthy sod." She's shouting, but she's also thinking. Realizing that she's only beginning to understand why the Rebs would be looking for her, too. Realizing this broke-tooth son of a Yankee dog might be telling her the truth.

"Come on now. Don't make this hard on yourself." He sighs, gums his pursed lips. "Don't make this hard on your children."

"Leave my children out of this!"

"Not a chance," he says. He looks to Fiona who is just rising to her knees, staring back and forth between him and her mother with wide blue eyes.

"Don't you bloody touch her!"

But he does. In one swift move he snags the little girl by the hair and drags her against his knees.

It's at this same moment that she flings down her mop and grabs the bell rope feeding up through the tower floor to the belfry. And pulls with all her strength.

By the time the Yankee agent understands what's happening, the three bells are already clanging with ear-splitting intensity. And both little Fiona and Levi have begun piercing shrieks.

"Stop it or I'll kill her." He's screaming. "I'll kill them both."

He's dropped to one knee and is reaching for Levi with his pistol hand when she catches him under the chin with a brutal kick and the hard toe of her boot. His head snaps back with a terrible crack. He's tumbling to the floor when she scoops up her children and dashes down the stairs.

When she gets to the nave on the ground floor she finds the rector in his white vestments bending over the sexton who is sitting on the ground with a huge, red lump rising on his left temple.

"I'm sooo sorry." Her whole body is trembling as she clasps her children to her breast. "But . . . I need to get to my ship. And there is a man in the tower and at least four more outside who . . ."

The rector takes her by the elbow. "Come, young lady. They dare not harm you when you're with a priest."

"You bloody well think?" The words just snap off her tongue.

55

CSS ALABAMA
June 14, 1864

"Look, sir. I believe that's Winslow." Kell is on the quarterdeck with Semmes. The *Alabama*'s lying to her anchor behind the breakwater at Cherbourg.

The masts and yards—sails tightly furled—of a mighty ship of war are just now looming out of the channel fog above the eastern entrance to Cherbourg's breakwater. Her funnel trails a cloud of thick gray smoke.

In his prayers, Semmes's daily counsel with himself and his God have so often come from his much-loved Shakespeare. But the words no longer come just from *Hamlet*. No longer does Semmes simply tell himself that *readiness is all*. Recently, he has been hearing verses from *The Tragedy of Macbeth* echoing in his brain. Hears them now as he looks on the *Kearsarge* for the first time. Hears himself reciting the lines of the Second Witch in Act IV.

"By the pricking of my thumbs, something wicked this way comes."

Kell squints his eyes at his captain, clearly does not get the reference to *Macbeth*, but catches the dark tone.

Semmes feels his face wrinkling into a somber half-smile, the wings of his mustache flicking as he heads forward and up the ladder to the bridge with his binoculars in hand. "Here comes my old friend." *Perhaps my fate.*

His mind mangles a line from *Macbeth.* "Fortune, on this damned quarrel smiling, shows like a rebel's whore . . ."

***

It's six bells into the morning watch. *Alabama* has been in Cherbourg since the 11th of June. Has landed her prisoners from two prizes. The final ship, the bark *Tycoon*, Semmes seized and burned just south of the equator on April 27. She was the 295th vessel boarded by *Alabama*'s crew. The last of Semmes's more than 85 conquests, *Alabama*'s 69th prize, her 54th to go down in flames. The last prize.

Unless, thinks Semmes, *the* Kearsarge *is to be the grandest of them all.*

Two days ago the captain of the *Alabama* had been waiting for word from the French authorities here in this naval port as to whether he might dry-dock his tired ship for a major refit. He had been thinking that he would pay off the crew and give them some months of shore leave. Thinking, too, that he would give himself a chance to search out his flame-haired Irish selkie if she has come to England, come under the wing of James Bulloch, as he counseled her to do so long ago back in Nassau.

But all his plans changed when word came to him from the South's agent in Cherbourg that the *Kearsarge* was known to be coming here to trap him. Changed most certainly when he learned that his former shipmate John Ancrum Winslow was in command. Months ago Semmes decided that he was finished running from the Yank navy. And certainly he will never run from Winslow. There's something providential about this reunion. He's thinking of *Macbeth* again. *I dare do all that may become a man; Who dares do more, is none.*

The *Kearsarge* has now turned toward the *Alabama.*

"Look you, Kell. Is that not Winslow there on her bridge deck?" Semmes points to a stocky figure. "I believe my friend has put on right much weight."

"But he has kept his girl looking fit," says Kell as he surveys the *Kearsarge* through his binoculars.

The men of both ships have gathered at the rails of their vessels to take measure of each other.

"There appears to be something wrong with his right eye. He's wearing a patch."

"A sister ship to *Wachusett* and *Tuscarora*, sir. She mounts one less gun than *Alabama*, but those two eleven-inch Dahlgrens are most lethal."

Semmes seems not to hear, continues talking about John Winslow, not his ship. "Sea service will make invalids of us all."

The *Kearsarge* has stopped her engines, lays to abreast the *Alabama*, not seventy-five yards to port.

"Look at her filthy smoke, sir."

"It fits that hard scowl he does wear upon his face." Semmes and Winslow are now staring at each other through their binoculars.

"He's got a right nasty load of wet coal aboard."

"A fat paunch and a pirate's patch."

"Aye, Captain."

"But old John is here for us, is he not?"

Kell nods. "With one hell of a ship . . . sir."

Semmes drops his binoculars from his face and turns to his luff. "My God," he says, suddenly picturing nights of mirth with Winslow in the wardroom of the *Raritan* off Veracruz while they were at sea during the Mexican War. He hears his friend's rich laughter in his head. "I just remembered something I have long forgotten. Winslow's from North Carolina."

"He should have been our comrade in arms, sir."

"It's too goddamn late for that, isn't it?"

***

Semmes has sealed his challenge in an envelope, passed it off to his steward Bartelli to be sent ashore with the mail boat.

Now he sits at his desk and lights one of the last of his much-loved Cuban cigars as he waits for Kell to arrive at the great cabin for a conference. The captain feels something like the easy breathing, the giddiness and surety of his youth again as he thinks on the letter that he has just penned and sent to the Confederacy's agent in Cherbourg, Mr. Bonfils.

Sir: I hear that you were informed by the U.S. consul that the Kearsarge was to come to this port solely for the prisoners landed by me, and that he was to depart in twenty-four hours. I desire to say to the U.S. consul that my intention is to fight the Kearsarge as soon as I can make the necessary arrangements. I hope that this will not detain me more than until tomorrow evening, or after the morrow morning at the furthest. I beg that she will not depart before I am ready to go out.

I have the honor to be, very respectfully, your obedient servant,

R. Semmes, Captain

He's sucking on the cigar, running his right thumb along the edge of the dress saber that Bartelli has sharpened, polished, and left for his inspection when Kell appears, closes the door behind him instinctively.

Semmes nods for the luff to take a seat across the desk from him. He knows that Kell and the crew were expecting to get paid off and leave the ship here with no further obligations.

"I'm going out to fight the *Kearsarge*. What do you think?"

"I'm not sure it is the thing to do, sir. But . . ."

Semmes glares, asks why not.

Kell says that he is no longer as confident in the ship's gunpowder as he was back in April. He worries that the powder has gone foul. He reminds Semmes that one out of three shells fired at the *Rockingham* failed to explode.

Semmes raps the desktop with the hilt of his sword, says he's aware of that. "But one lucky hit could do the trick." He adds that the *Alabama*'s seven-inch Blakely rifle on the foredeck and her eight-inch smooth-bore swivel gun are capable of sinking any wooden ship in the world.

"That goes for the *Kearsarge*, too, sir. She carries two eleven-inch pivots. She's a man-of-war, built to fight. The *Alabama* once had the speed on her, but now . . ."

Semmes raps the desktop again. "In a fair fight I can win."

Kell looks at his hands, says nothing.

"I see nothing rash in offering battle to Winslow. Our ships are well matched. We carry one gun more than the *Kearsarge* . . . though she throws a little heavier broadside."

The luff is still staring at his hands.

"Kell."

"Yes, sir?"

"Have you any other concerns about the state of our ship and her crew?"

"The men are willing, even anxious to meet the enemy, sir. They will follow you to the gates of hell."

"Will you?"

"I am most ready."

"Then do not fret, my loyal friend. Notify your men. Go. Clear the ship for action."

Kell rises from his chair, salutes when Semmes stands, too.

"What's done is done."

"Sir?"

"May God defend the right among us . . . and have mercy on the souls of those who fall."

56

USS KEARSARGE
June 18, 1864

Winslow's on his knees, kneeling before the crucifix on his cabin wall, his eye patch flung on his berth. On this gray June afternoon even three whole teaspoons of laudanum stirred into a glass of watered-down Flemish *rouge* is not enough to stop the burning behind his blind eye. It's racing down his neck, spreading like fingers in his chest. He feels his stomach rise and fall with the ship in the waves. They start to breed in the late morning, propagating all afternoon in the channel, especially when the tide turns against the onshore winds.

"Damn him, Lord, but he does dally."

He's talking about Semmes. It has been four excruciating days of waiting since his brother Esau implored him not to leave, proposed a duel. Begged him for the honor of doing battle. And still the *Alabama* tarries in port. Winslow can easily imagine why. He hears the words of the English captain on the *Diomede.*

Balls. Brass balls. Never seen anything like him. Acts like the world's his oyster.

Winslow knows Semmes is carefully sending all of his gold and pirate booty ashore, topping off his water tanks and coal bunkers to make *Alabama* a low, thin target, shielding her vitals with hundreds upon hundreds of tons of coal. Knows, too, that Semmes is no doubt consulting with the Rebel naval *attaché*, George T. "Terry" Sinclair, an armament expert, about the best uses of his shot and shell. He may even be trying to smuggle fresh powder and shells aboard against French prohibitions. And today there has been much coming and going between the Reb cruiser and the British steam yacht *Deerhound* that arrived yesterday. *Surely there's mischief afoot. Now the battle will be delayed until the morrow. The Lord's day!*

"It reeks, Dear God, to high heaven. Does it not?"

If Winslow is expecting an answer from his Savior, none comes. But he continues with his catechism . . . his mind needs to unpack its burdens.

"Help me, most heavenly Father, in this my hour of need."

There's a low groaning deep in the ship as she pitches, then rolls in the building waves.

"Who truly is this brother I seek? This brother I must now fight?"

His memory opens. He sees again the twists and turns of the friendship and long ordeal that have finally brought him to this confrontation.

He's walking side by side with Semmes in Tampico. A band plays "Blue-Eyed Mary" in the plaza. They followed a trail into the hills, confessed to each other that they believed in the same three things. That human freedom is an inalienable right. That honor and duty go hand-in-hand. That nothing can touch a man's heart so deep as his wonder at womankind and his bond with his shipmates.

He asks again the old questions. "What if I must find Raphael Semmes not to kill him, but to save him? What if I must face his guns—not to make war, but to secure peace? Must one of us lose? And who will it be?"

He imagines a falcon overhead. Twisting in gyres. A vague recollection is taking shape. *Beneath the circling hawk a canary flutters among the cattle in the pasture. Falcon and canary. Predator and prey. Both winged creatures. Both free and admirable. Brothers of the air . . . but with different destinies.*

"Am I ready?"

He closes his eyes, thinks on the sheathing over his ship's chain-mail armor. Feels not smug joy, but a hot brand of pain in his eye. He sees the topsides of the *Kearsarge* fitted with chain plating, covering a space amidships nearly fifty feet in length by six feet in height. Sees Azorean carpenters building a wall of fresh planking over the chain, painting it black like the rest of the ship. He hears the elder Dabney ask, "You aim to snare Semmes with a wolf in lamb's clothing?"

But what if the famous Rebel corsair has a surprise, as well, for me?

"You haven't been yard-to-yard with that ship," the captain of the *Diomede* had warned him. *"She's a sinister-looking thing."*

"Does he have the speed on me?"

"The Lairds . . . must have put some brilliant engines in her because Diomede *is no slouch for speed. Yet* Alabama *had better than a knot on the man-of-war."*

"How shall I engage him?"

"Your man Semmes could have sailed rings around me firing continuously with those swivel guns of his. A ship like that, like your Kearsarge, *too, will change everything they ever taught us about naval battle tactics."*

Now there's a voice in his head. The captain of the *Diomede* yet again. *"What are you going to do when you catch up with that wildcat?"*

Pain rips through Winslow's head in starbursts. But he hears himself say what he has said before, "I must find my brother's weakness . . . before he finds mine."

The *Kearsarge* groans. The cabin sole seems no more stable than a breaking sea beneath his knees.

"But just look in a mirror, man. You wear your weakness on your cyclopean visage. How can you think he has not already seen your ruined face, has not already understood the pain it visits upon you? Sees how easily he may apply several more turns of the screw? Can you stand it?"

Something heavy like the weight of a man pins him down. Then it is a man . . . wrestling with him in the darkness. Crushing him, bending him. Blasting hot breath on his neck. A claw tears at his hip.

"Mercy," he says.

Someone or something touches him on his shoulder, but he dare not open his eyes. "There's a divinity that shapes our ends, Rough-hew them how we will."

"Mercy."

"By your sword you shall live, but your brother you shall serve."

"This is too much for one man to bear." Winslow squeezes his eyes even tighter.

He's praying that his Lord, his all-knowing Savior, will give him strength when the image of a young man—with the body of a broken boxer and a face burned into a pulpy, purple mass—fills his mind. Smiles.

"Few people even remotely suspect what men like you and me are capable of. You show them, sir. You can yet save your brother. You can crush your enemies."

"Let us hope," he says. His good eye bursts open, takes in the room as if seeing it for the first time. Everything looks luminous. Wet and red.

57

ROYAL MAIL STEAMSHIP EUROPA
Early morning, June 19, 1864

She still can't believe that she has made it this far without the American villains dropping a net over her or her children. Even here, seven days at sea, on the Cunard liner *Europa* from Halifax to Liverpool, she keeps looking over her shoulder for shadowy Yanks or Rebs.

But so far none have appeared. The ship has cleared the ice belt and the cold fog off the Grand Banks and Newfoundland. She is now steaming easily under fore-and-aft sails to steady her. The Gulf Stream current and a light southwest wind are boosting her toward England, the sound of wind and waves subdued beneath the grinding and constant whooshing of the side wheels. *Europa* will be in Liverpool within three days.

And so will I, thinks Maude. *The Holy Redeemer willing.*

She's standing with her back leaning against the foremast of the ship, hands on her waist, facing in the direction of England. Smiling at the thought that her Raffy may well be there already, or will be soon. In Halifax last week she saw newspapers reporting the *Alabama* had been sighted off Cape Town, heading north into the Atlantic. Sometimes her old worries that Raffy will not accept her children keep her from sleeping. But then she remembers his plaintive love letters. Each one. Most of all she remembers the fury with which he made love to her two years ago in Nassau . . . and his pledge that St. Valentine's night in her Washington boarding house when he held her so tightly she could hardly breathe, nuzzled the hollow between her neck and shoulder.

"Pray for me that I can do what must be done to bring this secession conflict to a quick end. Then I swear with all the fire in my soul, I will make my peace with Anne and come to you as an obedient servant if you will still have me."

She and her two children are not among the 140 first-class passengers with luxurious deck, or 'tween deck, private cabins. Maude and her little family are traveling in steerage, a dormitory for about 40 poor passengers beneath the captain's cabin in the stern of the ship. In steerage the air stinks of coal smoke, lubricating grease, fetid socks and clothing, vomit, rotting baked goods, sweet meats brought aboard by her cabin mates, the stench of dirty diapers, two toilets shared by forty people.

But up here on deck, especially alone in the forward part of the ship, she feels as privileged and free as the gentry promenading around the deck or lounging on their chaises back aft with cups of tea, glasses of wine, Scotch whiskey. It's a bright morning. She can feel the sun and the warm breeze raising the color in her cheeks, bringing out the patch of freckles across her nose. Her children have taken their breakfast milk from her, consumed a small bowl of porridge with a bit of apple sliced in. And now they are down in steerage, playing with wooden blocks of assorted shapes under the guidance of a teenage French-Canadian girl.

She doesn't know why—maybe it is this growing nearness to her old Irish home, to England, to her seahawk—but her mind keeps drifting back over what an odyssey the last three years have been for her. She's thinking about all the women, white and black, that have saved her from ruin, helped her on her way. She misses them, and now she closes her eyes. One by one, the faces rise before her. Rambling Rose Greenhow, poor dead Fiona O'Hare, Varina Howell Davis, Minty Tubman, Cally, Lincolnville's old granny Miss Venus.

They are swirling around her, beginning to hum a low and hypnotic ululation, when she thinks she hears footsteps at her back.

Her eyes burst open. She looks quickly astern. No one in sight. Just the deck of the steamer bathed in the brilliant golden light of early morning, the sails looking pink, dark curls of coal smoke trailing from the funnel.

She turns again to look forward, thinks about Raffy and feels the sudden urge to climb the ladder to the fo'castle deck, go all the way into the bows. And she does. When she's there among the machinery of the anchor windlass, she steadies herself, bracing her legs apart and grabbing the thick iron cable of a head stay. She can feel vibrations surging through it with the rhythmic churning of the side wheels. A jib sail, its belly full of wind, groans nearly overhead. The bows crash and hiss through the dark blue waves. The ship rises, falls. Her knees and legs tighten to meet each surge. It's like riding a horse.

Surely Raffy must know the peace, the power, the thrill of this place, she thinks.

She remembers predawn aboard the whaler *Jacqueline B* bound for Canada, before she was caught as a stowaway. The wind light and fish fresh like this. Carolina warm. A crescent moon hanging overhead, and the morning star winking on the horizon. She had felt close enough to Raffy to touch his soul. She wondered if even then he was under this same sky, smelling this same fragrant breeze, hoping that somehow, some way, it would carry him back to her.

And now she pictures him here, standing even thus on his beloved *Alabama*, escaping the endless decision making, the frustrations, the loneliness, the terror of the job he has done so well for all of these days, these years. Surely he's dreaming of a homecoming, of leaving this sea with some small measure of honor. Maybe he, too, closes his eyes like this and imagines that seaside cottage in Brazil. . . .

It's like that little hut in Nassau, the one where she loved her Raffy nearly to death. Just one room. Clean, freshly painted in pinks and blues. Windows wide open to the trade winds. Scents of acacia, bougainvillea drifting in. Hummingbirds darting among the blossoms outside. Two children playing in the yard—a little girl with red hair in braids and a dark-skinned boy with the brightest eyes and the biggest smile in all the world.

She's there on the porch swing, nestling against her lover's chest, safe in the cove of her hero's arms, when she hears footsteps again. This time there's no mistake. They are mounting the ladder behind her.

When she turns, she sees a man standing not six feet away, smiling at her. He's not wearing a red shirt this morning. He's got on a brown sweater. But he's the same man who came looking for her with three friends in Lincolnville, who surrounded her at the church in Halifax. The Reb.

"What do you want?" She feels something already starting to melt beneath her left breast.

"I promise you I will not harm your children."

58

THE ENGLISH CHANNEL
Morning, June 19, 1864

Sunday. Haze burning off. 10:45 A.M. A calm morn tending to blue skies, just the slightest westerly breeze. The *Alabama*'s four miles beyond the Cherbourg breakwater. Steaming northeast. The French ironclad gunboat *La Couronne* and the British yacht *Deerhound* are trailing astern . . . to bear witness to the coming battle.

Semmes stands on the starboard horse block arrayed in his best dress uniform, gold epaulettes and cutlass scabbard sparkling in the sunlight. His eyes have never looked so blue, his face projects confidence, ease. But the waxed tips of his mustache twitch. The crew is at general quarters, sailors in their Sunday muster togs, gunners stripped to their waists. As per orders, the deck crew lies resting on the sanded planks at their fighting stations.

"She still seems to be running away from us, sir," says the quartermaster speaking from the helm of the *Alabama*.

"Don't you believe it," says Semmes. "Winslow just wants to draw us offshore to make certain we are well beyond the French three-mile limit."

He does not add what he's thinking. *He wants me to fight him where neither of us can easily flee back into the arms of France if we are mortally wounded. He wants a fight to the death.*

Semmes has been trying to clear his mind of home, of family, of everything except the battle to come since he saluted each of his officers individually as they joined him at the evening mess last night in the wardroom. After the mess he had gone ashore and prayed at a chapel for God to stand by him one more time, prayed for one more lucky Sunday. One like the Sundays when he escaped the Federal blockade at New Orleans in the *Sumter*, christened the *Alabama*, seized the *Ariel*, defeated the *Hatteras*.

Just a half hour past he had saluted the cheering crowds of French gathered on the shores of Cherbourg to watch the coming battle. Then he had mounted a gun carriage back aft and invoked the glorious history of this ship one last time before his assembled crew as he urged them to gallantry today. During her cruise, *Alabama* has escaped the guns of twenty-five ships sent after her by Gideon Welles. Her pursuit has cost the U.S. Navy over $7 million. She has destroyed more than $15 million worth of Yankee shipping.

The captain has urged his men this morning to think on nothing but their duty. And yet his mind drifts. Terry Sinclair arrived yesterday from Paris bringing with him a batch of correspondence. Among them a heartbreaking letter passed on by James Bulloch in England from Maude. A letter posted in Halifax last January. Its sentences have been running riot in his brain, will not let him set them aside.

My Dear Sweet Raffy,

I pray with all my soul that this letter finds you safe and in good health. I yearn to tell a thousand things, but my time is short, and I do not know when I will again be able to send you my next letter.

The Yanks are after me. They have pursued me all the way to Canada. I think they believe that they can find you by capturing me. It is only for this reason that I will not come to England and Mr. James Bulloch, as I most thoroughly desire, unless I think it is safe to do so.

But now is not that moment, my dear. I am bound into the Canadian wilderness with two friends. At best, my trek will finally lead me to safety and put me in a position from which I can come to England and you eventually. At worst, I shall distract the Yanks for a while and buy you perhaps a little more time to bring your cruise to a safe end.

Do not fear for me. I carry you in my heart, in my soul. And I give you back your own words as my most ardent pledge of my abiding and eternal love. No matter what will come to pass, know my darling gladiator that "you are my sun, my moon, the stars that guide my course."

Look for me among these most glorious heavenly bodies, and on your soft green seas. Look for me there, waiting for you.

Always and forever,

Your Loving Selkie

He's still rolling over these last words in his mind when Kell says, "See, Captain, how he comes!"

A mile and a quarter ahead the *Kearsarge* is leaning in a sharp right turn and charging straight toward the *Alabama*. Astern the French gunboat has stopped to mark the three-mile sovereign limit of its country, and now the *Deerhound* is peeling away to windward.

Semmes looks at his watch. It is 10:57. "Are you ready, Mr. Kell?"

"Aye, aye, sir. Ready and willing." Kell's broad shoulders flex, a boxer stepping to the center of the ring.

"Then you may open fire at once." His words sound neutral, controlled . . . but his soul's thinking on Winslow's Carolina roots and shouting, *Bring it on, you traitorous son of a bitch!*

***

At three-quarters of a mile from the *Kearsarge*, the *Alabama* shears to port and fires two broadsides with extraordinary speed.

Winslow, standing atop an arms chest near the rail well aft on the quarterdeck, hears his brother's shells buzzing overhead, sees the fore topmast backstay part with a sharp whipping of the mast. There's no other damage.

"Continue holding your fire," he says calmly to his luff, Thornton. "He's not yet in range of our Dahlgrens."

In his mind, Winslow is remembering the ease with which his ship plowed through the pedestrian bridge back in Ostend, and he thinks that if he can get close enough he will drive his bows right through the *Alabama*. The shipwrights at the Portsmouth shipyard in Kittery, Maine, have made the *Kearsarge* a rugged vessel. With the ships now closing at full speed, a combined velocity of over twenty knots, ramming the Reb would deliver a mortal blow.

But he fears that at this range, and with this head-on course, Semmes's third volley might rake his decks with devastating damage to his men and guns.

The ships are just half a mile apart.

"Hard to port, Quarter Master. Fire at will."

The *Kearsarge* is sheering off to port, her gun crews just getting off their first salvo, when Semmes's guns roar again. Their aim is high and wide.

"Hit, sir," says Lieutenant Commander Thornton. He's pointing to the enemy's forward pivot port. There's smoke and debris on the deck, at least two men down. A small fire starting.

Winslow sees a chance here. "Now bring her hard to starboard."

By turning back toward the *Alabama* he hopes to cross her stern and rake her with a full starboard broadside. He can already see that he has the speed on Semmes. He knows that after raking her he can seize the weather gauge and draw alongside her at close quarters. Then he can force her into a running battle as she flees offshore, north into the no-man's land of the channel.

Semmes seems to immediately realize Winslow's intent and throws *Alabama* into a tight turn to starboard, too. The ships begin to orbit each other in clockwise fashion at half-mile range. Semmes has avoided Winslow's attempt at raking fire, but he has committed himself to this circling. Any attempt to break from the circle, to run to the safety of the French three-mile limit, will expose the *Alabama* to another opportunity for *Kearsarge* to rake her at close range with those killer Dahlgren pivots.

Both ships are spitting fire, belching gun smoke. The *Alabama* rapidly, but still not yet finding the range. The *Kearsarge* gunners are working much more deliberately. But Winslow can see that James Haley and his crew on the forward pivot gun have the enemy clearly in their sights as a shell takes out the *Alabama*'s spanker gaff, the tangled gear falling almost on Raphael Semmes's head, the Confederate Stainless Banner now trailing low in the air from the sagging wreckage.

A circling battle. This is not what Winslow had imagined in his year-and-a-half of planning to meet his Esau. Pure sailing ships could never have fought thus. But with steam power, gaining the weather gauge is of little consequence. Everything depends on the speed of the ships, the accuracy of the gunners, the ability of the ships to withstand persistent and devastating barrages. In the sailing navy, most naval battles last a few brief minutes before someone strikes his flag and surrenders. *Kearsarge* and *Alabama* have already been at it for more than a quarter of an hour.

The ships are starting into their third circle. Winslow has realized his advantages in the fight. Because he has the speed on the foul-bottomed Confederate, he can tighten the radius of the circle, bringing his Dahlgrens into increasingly more accurate and lethal range. And he is now seeing the value of his ship's chain mail shirt. The seven-inch shells from the enemy's Blakely rifle are bouncing off the sides of the *Kearsarge*.

But then comes the fizz and sizzle of a hundred-pound shell. It bursts through the engine room skylight. Another shell ruptures the starboard bulwarks just thirty feet in front of Winslow. It explodes on the quarterdeck wounding three of the crew on the after pivot gun. A third shell tears through the Yank's funnel, spilling black smoke over the after end of the ship.

Winslow's choking, groping with his arms to clear the soupy air for a better vision of his ship and his enemy, shouting for the fire brigade, when he feels the *Kearsarge* jerk violently beneath his feet. He's down on one knee, nearly tumbled off his post on the arms chest, when he hears someone shouting to Thornton. "They got our rudder, sir!"

59

DISTRICT OF COLUMBIA
Morning, June 19, 1864

"If I do not return from visiting General Grant, gentlemen, then there are things you must know. Must do in my stead." Lincoln's voice is flat, resolute.

He's walking with Welles and Allen into the White House stables. Pausing at a stall that holds a chestnut pony with a hay belly, he fishes in his jacket pocket. Comes up with an apple, offers it with an open hand to the animal. Then he presses his head to the forehead of the pony, closes his eyes.

Welles feels himself wince. He has seen Lincoln rub foreheads with this pony before. It was Willie's pony. Dear, sweet Willie. Taken so young. The president is still grieving.

The secretary of the navy feels as if he has just been struck by something cold and hard at the back of his neck. He knows that the Republican Convention in Baltimore two weeks ago has taken its toll on the president's energy. Knows that Lincoln has barely escaped a tough contest for the nomination from radical Republicans and their candidate, the explorer General John C. Frémont.

And General Grant is in a tough fight, too. He has laid siege to the railhead at Petersburg, Virginia, with an army exceeding 50,000. But Lee's generals are putting up a tenacious defense. During the first four days of battle, Union casualties have exceeded 11,000, with as many as 2,000 men killed or wounded. Now the president aims to leave Washington and visit Grant at his headquarters in City

Point to assess the chance for a military victory over Lee . . . and the costs of this battle to the nation.

But Welles senses that his president is getting at something even darker than the ongoing battle when he speaks of not returning.

"What are you trying to tell us, Mr. President?"

Lincoln scratches his beard with a bony finger. "I'm saying that Mrs. Lincoln has been having more of her premonitions."

Following Willie's death, Mrs. Lincoln held séances to contact the boy's spirit. For these séances she brought in famous spiritual mediums like Nettie Colburn. One medium, Cora Maynard, has been claiming that Lincoln wrote the Emancipation Proclamation with the help of spirits she channeled, telling him the Civil War would not end until the slaves were freed. And Lincoln has spoken before to Welles and Allen of spiritual experiences of his own. Before his 1860 re-election, he saw two images of himself reflected in a mirror. One was pale and seemed to disappear when he looked at it. His wife said she feared that this was a sign he would not survive a second term as president.

Allen clears his throat. "Excuse my bluntness, Mr. President, but Mrs. Lincoln is sometimes a woman who wallows in romantic poppycock. Do not be taken in by such . . ."

Lincoln stiffens. "She is the First Lady, man. I am sure you do not aim to insult her."

"It is my job to look out for you, Mr. President. And I just thought . . ."

"Why don't you shut up, Major."

60

THE ENGLISH CHANNEL
Late-Morning, June 19, 1864

On the *Alabama,* men are cheering. The Blakely rifle's shell has struck the enemy's sternpost.

"Splendid, splendid!" Semmes's voice rings out.

It's a killer shot, a shot to so disable the enemy that she will now be a sitting duck. But the shell, visibly lodged in the sternpost of the *Kearsarge*, fails to detonate. Rotten powder. The rest of the *Alabama*'s broadside hits catch the enemy amidships and do nothing but throw up small clouds of splintering wood.

"Look, Kell. Our shells cannot penetrate her. They are just bouncing right off her side."

"So it's true, sir?"

Semmes looks incredulous, blurts, "What do you mean?"

Kell reminds Semmes that they had heard a rumor some days ago from French spies who believed that Winslow had draped his vitals with anchor chain and hidden it beneath fresh planking.

For just an instant, Semmes feels a heavy blow strike deep in his bowels, has a terrible sense of something overlooked, something pushed out of his mind and forgotten because of honor, because he refused to believe the straightforward Winslow could be so devious. Refused, too, to renege on his oh-so-public challenge to the Yank traitor.

But now is not the moment for recrimination or doubt. He's hearing his own mouth denying any knowledge of Winslow's chain mail skirt when a deafening explosion rocks the *Alabama* just forward of the mizzen mast, blasting over the ship a storm of metal and wood and blood.

The breeze has begun to build, and the smoke clears quickly. The wrecked deck is burning, and the fire crew is already at the leaping flames with its hoses. Semmes sees that the after pivot gun has suffered a nearly direct hit. There are eighteen men down. The only thing left of Midshipman Anderson is his mutilated leg. And now the captain notes that his own right arm is torn open, bleeding in pulsing spurts.

He thinks how Horatio Nelson took a musket ball to his right arm at the Battle of Santa Cruz de Tenerife, immediately had the arm amputated and was back giving orders in half an hour. So he shouts to the nearest quartermaster to bind his wound and sling his arm. Tells Pills Galt who rushes to his aid that he would rather die at his post than go below to sickbay. . . . *Fair fight or foul, Nelson would spit in death's face.*

He orders one of the thirty-pounders secured and its crew transferred to the all-important pivot gun. But before the new gun crew can revive the pivot, another onslaught comes thundering across the water. The enemy's forward Dahlgren has totally found its mark and is just raining hell on the seahawk, walking its aim incrementally forward along the lower planks of the Rebel's topsides with each new firing. The first shell damages the rudder, and Semmes orders his deckhands to rig relieving tackle to steer the ship.

Alabama is burning now in three places. The deck crew is heaving fire buckets of water on the flames that the men on the hoses can't reach.

Then two shots bore through the *Alabama* at the waterline. One explodes in the engine room and blows a hole right through the spar deck. Another passes through the surgeon Llewellyn's operating pit in the ward room, taking with it his operating table and patient. Kell reports that the surgeon and his nurse David are wandering around below decks with stony looks in their eyes, blood splattered not just on their aprons, but on their faces, hair, hands. The black gang and engineer Miles Freeman in the engine room are up to their waists in water, the boiler fires are going out. There's no way to shore up the great rents in the hull.

Semmes seizes the tips of his mustache with both hands, twirls them viciously. Bites down on the inside of his cheeks until he tastes his own hot, bitter blood. *This is the end. Let Winslow go down in history as a butcher. I will not.*

"Men aloft, Mr. Kell. Set all sail. Shift your guns to port. Make for the coast." Semmes is resorting to what he knows best. Sailing. Running.

The ships are beginning their seventh orbit, when the *Alabama*'s forward batteries get off a final salvo. One shot parts the stops on a second Stars and Stripes furled at the main truck of the *Kearsarge*, and the flag bursts open in the fresh onshore breeze.

Goddamn Winslow would rub my face in that hateful rag, Semmes is thinking when Kell comes jogging up to him from a survey below decks.

"How bad is it, Mr. Kell?"

"We can stay afloat perhaps ten minutes."

Semmes can see that Winslow is now turning to cut off *Alabama*'s flight back to the safety of France. The Confederate cruiser is doomed. Not just this sinking ship, but her crew. The seahawk has no doubt that Winslow and his bloodthirsty bosses will make a spectacle of punishing him, the officers, and men of the most successful commercial raider in history.

Then he thinks on how much he really abhors the thought of hanging, how much he owes this loyal crew, and decides to play his last ace.

"Cease your firing, Mr. Kell. Shorten sail. Haul down the colors. Prepare to abandon ship. And when all is ready, sound the signal guns . . . and pray that *Deerhound* is listening carefully."

61

DISTRICT OF COLUMBIA
Late Morning, June 19, 1864

Lincoln wheels away from Willie's pony and starts to walk farther into the shadowy stable. He glares at Allen with an immense blackness such as Welles has never seen. "Perhaps you do not yet know the things that I know!"

Welles can tell an explosion of some sort is coming from the president. The secretary tightens his jaw, his fists. His eyes narrow as if to absorb an actual blow.

Lincoln says the magnificent hero of Gettysburg, Colonel Joshua Lawrence Chamberlain of the Twentieth Maine, has been severely wounded.

"By God, Chamberlain took a shot through the hip and groin at Petersburg. But Grant writes me that Chamberlain did not fall. The man drew his sword, stuck it into the ground. Propped himself thus, gentlemen . . . until the blood just ran out of him."

"He's dead?" Allen asks.

Lincoln waves his right arm wildly as if to drive off swarming wasps, miserable thoughts, phantoms. "The First Maine Heavy Artillery lost over six hundred of nine hundred men," he says. "In one assault. Imagine!"

Welles knows this is a new low for the Union. Never has the army lost so many men in one unit in a single event.

"And now . . ." Lincoln squeezes his mouth beneath a huge hand. "I have news from Seward and his man in Halifax. Raphael

Semmes's Jezebel, it seems, has gotten away once again. So, Major Allen, there goes your best hope of quickly unraveling all the Confederates' hocus pocus, am I right?"

Allen clears his throat, speaks softly. "I just heard about this, sir."

"Damn it all, man. How can one woman evade a slew of your agents? Is she some sort of phantom?"

"I have no idea how such things occur, Mr. President, but I assure you that it will not happen . . ."

"For just once, stop making me promises that I fear you can never keep."

"I'm so sorry, Mr. President. If we don't have that moll, then the Rebs surely must, and I fear that they are planning . . ."

"Listen to me. Both of you! Last night Mrs. Lincoln and I both had horrible dreams. She woke me as she fled from our bedroom calling out Willie's name. She said she could hear him crying for her."

Allen shoots Welles a skeptical look.

"But I could not rise from bed to comfort her for some minutes," says the president. "I, too, was beset with ghosts. In a dream I was just waking from, I saw legions of our torn and bloody boys in uniform marching up Pennsylvania Avenue, into the White House."

"Mr. President?" Welles feels chills rising in his arms, back.

"They paraded right through my office, beckoning me with fractured limbs and broken smiles to follow them." The president closes his eyes, tilts back his head. "Mrs. Lincoln believes that God's telling me that my days are numbered. The woman cannot stop weeping."

Allen opens his mouth to speak, but the president cuts him off. "Sometimes I feel that Mrs. Lincoln may be more right than we know."

"It pays to be cautious," says Allen. He seems to realize he must yield to these premonitions for better or worse.

"Since Willie's death, Mrs. Lincoln has been much consumed with grief. I, too, have sometimes . . ."

Allen stiffens to attention. "You can tell her that we are going to take great care with your travel arrangements and your movement in Virginia, Mr. President. I am going to double your personal guards and accompany you myself."

Lincoln gives a tight-lipped smile. "Would you please just leave me alone?"

***

Welles and the president have returned to the stall of Willie's pony when Lincoln speaks again.

"If something is to happen to me, Gideon, look to my boys. Robert is a man. He is nearly finished at Harvard and will make his own way in the law, I am confident. But Tad, Tad is just a special little boy. He still—God bless him—thinks his father some kind of immortal."

Welles sees the pleading and a frank sadness in the president's eyes, knows his friend and leader craves comfort. "You are much loved by your sons, Mr. President. And by the nation. You know you can always count on me in all things."

"Good Gideon. . . . There is more that I must ask of you."

"Yes, sir."

"Catch Semmes. Bring that bandit to justice no matter how long it takes. We must not let him sail off to some Rebel Valhalla with impunity . . . and . . ."

Welles feels a darkness creeping over him.

"And one last thing, Gideon. Write down everything that has transpired these last three years . . . so that someday the world will know what villainy we faced here . . . and what horror."

"On my honor, Mr. President," says Welles.

There's a hollow tone settling into the secretary's voice. He's heard it more than once before of late. It's as if something inside him has begun to say its farewells to the commander-in-chief. And say farewell to this monumental, thankless, man-killing job. If it were not for this great, gaunt, vulnerable man standing before him, he would be off with his family to little Connecticut on the evening train. Today.

He doesn't like the eerie feeling that surrounds him here in Washington, seems to haunt him daily. So . . . at this moment he is most sincerely hoping that Lincoln has finished with all of this talk of the dead. Welles has lived with death for far too long and in far too much abundance, he thinks. He's not even sure that he would any longer relish the sight of Raphael Semmes hanging from the yardarm of Winslow's *Kearsarge.* There must be a better way to restore order . . . and peace. *But what, Oh Lord my God? How?*

The president is once again pressing his forehead to that of Willie's pony. He's weeping silently. Welles inhales, tries to catch his breath. But something seems to be ripping his lungs from his chest.

At the far end of the stable a Negro hostler oiling riding tack is singing in a low, faint voice. The song is a spiritual called "Ezekiel Saw the Wheel."

62

THE ENGLISH CHANNEL
Noontime, June 19, 1864

Two guns sound from the *Alabama*. Pop-pop, in quick succession. This is not the heavy rumble of the pivot guns or the thirty-two-pounders. But the lighter note of bow chasers.

"That rascal's firing on us again!" The quartermaster shouts to anyone listening. The bile in his voice is a clear mark of his disbelief. The Rebel wreck, her decks nearly awash, has already struck her colors, surrendered. The men of the *Kearsarge* are already starting to assemble boat crews to send to her rescue. But now she fires again?

Winslow, distracted momentarily by the onset of excruciating pain behind his bad eye did not see, barely heard the shots from his enemy. But he does not take the time to wonder why Semmes would fire his guns after striking. He just knows from hours spent playing cards with the man that Semmes is a gambler and a man of bluffs and subterfuges. And after a year and a half of waiting for this slippery fellow, John Ancrum Winslow has had enough.

"Who does he think he is?" The pain is searing Winslow's brain. "Fire at will. Silence him once and for all, Mr. Thornton."

Five guns erupt instantly.

But no sooner does the broadside thunder toward *Alabama* from a mere 400 yards away, than Winslow realizes that he had previously ordered all his guns reloaded with devastating antipersonnel grape shot because he had anticipated a close-quarters fight near the end. Now he has fired point blank on defenseless men. And on the *Alabama* he sees the crew stand, turn, and face the withering blast—lambs defiant in the face of slaughter—in the brief seconds between the flaming of his cannons and when the grape cut them down. And someone is waving a white sheet over the Confederate's stern. *Oh most merciful God . . . brother, forgive me!*"

***

It's about twenty minutes after noon when Raphael Semmes stands on the stern of his ship with the cold June water of the channel just starting to wash over his bare feet. Many of his crew are standing around him, stripped to their waists or small clothes, waiting for him to lead them on this final foray. *Alabama*'s a wreck from stem to stern. But the fire crew has extinguished the last of the flames aboard.

At least she will not burn to death, thinks Semmes. He cannot think God would be so cruel to annihilate his bride with the fire on which, for two years, she has thrived.

Guns and gear are settling aft and falling through holes in the deck and torn bulwarks as she settles, starts to raise her bows before her final stern-first dive. Bartelli and seaman Michael Mars have just rescued Semmes's journals from the flooded great cabin. Two of the ship's best swimmers, Mars and Quartermaster Freemantle volunteer to keep the journals safe and dry. A boat is launched and sent to the *Kearsarge* with Master's Mate Fullam, Pills Galt, and the most severely wounded.

"All hands overboard and save yourselves," Kell's voice booms.

Bartelli the steward urges Semmes, stripped to his pants and service vest, to don a life vest. But before the captain of the *Alabama* agrees, he unbuckles the dress saber at his waist and raises it over his head at arm's length. For several seconds it towers above the assembled crew, then Semmes sends it wheeling through the air as best he can with his good left arm. It sparkles in the air, strikes the water, is gone. No Yank will ever claim the prize.

"Into the water, boys." Semmes's voice is sure, but his mind's in riot, riddled with Macbeth's words of agony. *I have almost forgot the taste of fears . . . I am in blood . . . Nought's had, all's spent . . .* Riddled, too, with a prophecy by a hoodoo girl in Santo Domingo. *The saints dem done told me dead spirits . . . have laid claim to your soul. Drowned men. You gots to get clean.*

There is only one way.

Semmes and Kell mount the taffrail and leap.

Hitting the water, submerging, he sees the *Somers* yet again awash in foaming seas. Men clinging to anything that will keep them afloat. *The air filling with the shouts of swimmers, calling the names of their shipmates for comfort. Begging their God for mercy. . . .*

Rising to the surface he finds himself side by side with Kell, pushing a grate for flotation. The men around him are not screaming, cursing. Everyone seems calm. Off to windward, the sleek *Deerhound* has turned toward the Confederate wreck. She's less than a mile off and she's steaming this way fast. His last ace. Help on the way. Salvation.

He feels odd. Not like waking from a nightmare exactly, but more like the time when he fell from a bolting horse at the age of twelve. He was knocked cold by the side of the C&O Canal in Washington. Waking up, he had stared at the sky and the trees. Everything seemed oddly brilliant.

So it is now. He barely feels the cold of the water starting to creep under his skin, slow his muscles. The noonday sun is crisp. The air swells in his lungs. And loyal Kell is at his side, waving to the *Deerhound.* The *Alabama* rears, head high, and starts her downward slide beneath the waves.

"Shite," he says. Then, "Godspeed."

He turns away, lets his mind drift. To a red-haired Irish selkie with green eyes and freckles across her nose. To a one-room cottage, all pinks and blues. Windows wide open to the scents of acacia, and bougainvillea. . . .

***

It's 12:24 when Winslow sees the *Alabama* raising her bows to the sky. Her main topmast goes by the boards. Her funnel tumbles. Another mast comes crashing down. And then she sinks into the deep blue channel, a whale gone submarine.

Winslow's dead eye and the guilt in his heart are riddling him with icy pain. Most of his ship's boats have been damaged in the battle and his crew is terribly slow in launching boats to rescue all those men in the cold water. He knows that they have at best forty-five minutes to an hour before they freeze to death in this water. So he has paroled Master's Mate Fullam and his oarsmen who have brought over some of the wounded Rebs to return to the wreckage of the raider and rescue all the men they can. He wishes he could go with them.

I have won the battle, but I have not yet saved my brother.

When the *Deerhound* comes alongside asking if she can be of assistance, he shouts to her captain, "For God's sake, do what you can to save them!"

He's picturing drowning men. Feeling his brother Esau's uncontrollable shivers . . . and his sorrow in losing such a noble ship and loyal men.

But as he stands on the bridge of *Kearsarge* watching the rescue, he's starting to get the feeling that there's some funny business afoot. The *Deerhound* seems exceedingly fast and selective in the way she's picking up survivors. Two French pilot boats have arrived on the scene as well. Suddenly, in the midst of the rescue, with men still bobbing in the water, the *Deerhound* is recalling her small boats, seems to be getting up steam, edging off to leeward.

"I believe the yacht aims to leave us, sir . . . and take the survivors," says Thornton.

Winslow pulls his long glass to his good eye, squints. It cannot be possible that she would not bring the *Alabama*'s men back to him. It would be the natural thing. He has doctors, he has ample food, shelter. And he is the victor here. But it does indeed look as though she's already heading north toward Southampton, toward England, as she retrieves her boats.

"They must have Semmes and Kell. They must have most of the officers, sir."

Winslow finds himself suddenly craving a glass of red wine with three heaping teaspoons of laudanum. "What would you have me do?"

"Fire on her, Captain. Stop her before she gets away."

"After all the trouble we have already stirred up with the English, you would have me fire on a British yacht that has just performed a crucial act of mercy?"

"But it's Semmes, sir. He's escaping."

Winslow hears a voice rising through the pain in his head. *By your sword you shall live, but your brother you shall serve.*

"I believe he has found my weakness . . . just as I have found his."

"Sir?"

"Let be, Mr. Thornton."

"Sir?"

"God has given me this day my brother's ship . . . and given Raphael Semmes his life back."

Thornton looks deep into Winslow's good eye, seems to understand for the first time that his captain has never been moved by blind allegiance to a government, but by a fundamental trust in righteousness and a higher power.

"Amen, sir," says Thornton. There's a note of admiration in his voice.

"Aye. Amen, Mr. Thornton. Our boats return. Let us go give succor to those who suffer, to our brethren."

EPILOGUE

SOUTHAMPTON, ENGLAND
June 21, 1864

"Walk with me, Raphael. We should talk." The chief Confederate spymaster in England, Naval Captain James Bulloch, has a pale, somber look on his face as he exits the hack that has just rolled to a stop at the curb.

It's seven in the evening. The light of the day's going fast as a heavy fog creeps up from the Solent, spreads into the River Test and River Itchen that form the delta of this seaport. Semmes is sitting on the bench in front of his temporary lodging at Kelway's Hotel, number 6 Queen's Terrace. He has been waiting on Mistress Coster to open her little restaurant on the first floor for dinner. Trying to tally up his dead and wounded, reckon what they call in the service the "butcher's bill." Wondering once again if he has the courage to be a good Roman and fall on his own sword. But, of course, the sword is gone. A pistol must serve.

But now the strapping spy with the dark whiskered cheeks and shaggy brown hair has interrupted, wants a walk in the park across the street.

Semmes rises from his seat, looks deep into the eyes of this younger, more vigorous, man. "I lost nine men killed in action. Another twenty-one wounded. We must make arrangements to get their wages to their survivors. Then I must . . ."

"Raphael, please! Let's walk. I need to tell . . ."

"I'm not sure of the drowned. Some of the men seem not to have made it to France or to . . . Winslow's ship." He cannot say *Kearsarge*. It sticks in his gorge, makes his eyes water.

"Raphael."

"Did you know that Kell and I found poor Doctor Llewellyn drowned beneath a makeshift raft of shell boxes? Dead. The man could not swim. He gave his life preserver to one of the wounded, and . . ."

Bulloch looks at the dithering little man before him in a plain brown suit. Semmes looks shrunken to half the size he was when Bulloch bid him farewell as he began his cruise on *Alabama* almost two years ago in the Azores.

"I'm sorry, Raphael. Do you really want to know about the dead?"

"It's my duty, I must make what amends I. . . . Just tell . . ."

"By the count of my men here and in France, sixteen men died in the water. Among them your steward, Bartelli, and a young black."

"David White, the surgeon's helper. . . . Good God."

"Now he goes with Llewellyn . . . for eternity."

"They were at my side just before we all went into the water. They never told me that they couldn't swim. Bartelli, too. I would have gladly given up my vest. I . . ." His words are clotting in his throat.

"I most earnestly wish it were not my lot to visit you with such tidings, but . . ."

Old Beeswax sees that Bulloch's face has grown even paler than when he arrived. "There's more grievous news, isn't there? That's why you came."

"Please, Raphael, walk with me."

"No, goddamn it. I will not move one wretched inch from this spot until you tell me what you came here for."

"Oh, Christ."

"Speak man."

Bulloch tilts his head back, seems to be looking at something a thousand yards overhead. "The Royal Mail Steamer *Europa* arrived in Liverpool this morning."

Semmes looks baffled.

"A woman you know was on the passengers manifest. Maude Galway . . . with two children."

Semmes feels his heart beginning to pound.

"We believe she was coming to England to search for you."

"Was?"

"Why don't we sit down on the bench?"

"No. For God's good sake what has happened, James?"

Bulloch heaves a deep breath and blurts, "We lost her, Raphael."

"What do you mean? We . . . ? Where . . . ?"

"It seems that she disappeared from the ship some three days ago. A French girl was watching her children one morning when your Maude went on deck to take some air and she . . . she never came back to steerage for the children. She must have had some kind of accident, fallen . . ."

"Shut up. Jesus Christ, shut up." His voice is choked with tears.

"I'm so sorry, Raphael. I would give anything not to have to . . ."

"Get out of here!" Semmes drops onto the bench in front of Kelway's Hotel as his upper lip and the impossible white mustache begin to quiver. His eyes leaking.

"I believe we can lay this loss, too, at the feet of the Yanks," says Bulloch as he turns away, hails a passing cab. There's something rushed, hollow in his words. Possibly fraudulent.

For just a second Semmes has the briefest suspicion that Bulloch is not telling him the whole truth. But then his skepticism, his weariness, sinks beneath a sob. Semmes covers his face with his hands. Tears boil down his cheeks. Would that he had already put that pistol to his head and pulled the trigger.

But he can do nothing but sit here on this bench, his mind unraveling. He remembers Maude on that spring day when first he met her five years ago, when he sliced a sprig of apple blossoms from a tree outside the Smithsonian castle with his saber, presented them to her with a courtly bow. But he can't picture her. Not the color of her flouncy dress, not the symmetry of her face. He only sees pieces of her. The flaming hair drawn back in the silver combs he gave her, the long muscles in her neck, the freckles across the nose. Those green eyes. But try as he will, he cannot bring them all together into a whole. Nor can he hear in his mind the note that was the liveliness in the husky voice of his West Irish selkie. Gone. Like the *Somers,* the *Sumter*, the *Alabama*. The *Golden Rocket* and all those other Yankee ships. All gone. As if they never were.

These disconnected pieces and Maude's sweet letters are all that he has left of her, of love. Of youth. Of vain gallantry, too.

If only he had his sword or a pistol right now . . . how easy it would be at this juncture to yield to Lady Macbeth's death wish, and yield, too, to her withering pronouncement that life is a tale told by an idiot, full of sound and fury, signifying nothing . . .

His mind lurches, totters. He's doubling over, head and shoulders folding into his belly when he hears Tennyson's words seeping from some fissure in his head. That poem. The one that has so often seemed to inform his life, his choices, "Ulysses."

The long day wanes: the slow moon climbs: the deep
Moans round with many voices.

He's sinking. Going down inexorably toward these flagstones beneath his feet, toward the earth, the grave. Yet something deep in his core is reaching out wildly for a handhold. For some shred of hope or dignity for a tired and bloodied man. For some sign from the Almighty.

His heart grasps for words. His mind stretches for the great Ulysses' final vision in Tennyson's poem. His exit lines. His defiance and hope.

Tho' much is taken, much abides; and though
We are not now that strength which in old days
Moved earth and heaven; that which we are, we are . . .
Made weak by time and fate, but strong in will
To strive, to seek, to find, and not to yield.

He wipes the tears from his eyes and cheeks, rises to his feet.

Yes, the seahawk thinks, *the Holy Savior has decreed it. Death will come. But not here, not now. Not by my own hand. I was not born to yield, even to death. In the end Winslow must have seen it, too . . . when I stood up to his dastardly salvo of grape shot after* Alabama *had struck her colors.*

The moment Kell and he have so long talked of has come at last. It's time they truly turn toward home, time that the seahawk return most resolutely toward his family. Toward Anne, toward their children. Begging their love and understanding for all that he has done and all that he has been in this most horrid war. Waiting God's judgment. Packing titanic memories in his humble, ghostly heart.

Historical Notes

After his brief stop in Southampton, Raphael Semmes stayed for three months with the family of Rev. Francis Tremblett at his London home and elsewhere. During this time Semmes and Tremblett's daughter Louisa, a young woman in her twenties, developed a deep, possibly romantic, friendship.

To avoid Federal spies, Semmes escaped to the Continent for seven weeks and traveled under the alias of Raymond Smith with Louisa, her brother, and three friends. On October 3, 1864, Semmes made his way back to the South. He was promoted to the rank of rear admiral in February 1865, and for the last months of the war he commanded the James River Squadron. It eventually scuttled the vessels and joined what remained of Johnston's army in North Carolina and Lee's army in the final, futile defense of the Confederacy. Lee surrender to Grant on April 9, 1865. John Wilkes Booth shot Abraham Lincoln five days after Lee's surrender.

Following the war, Gideon Welles had Semmes arrested for treason in December 1865. He spent four months in a Federal jail before being released by President Andrew Johnson. After his release, he rewrote his memoirs, taught philosophy and literature at Louisiana State Seminary, and worked as a newspaper editor, as well as a judge. Eventually, he settled with Anne at their home in Mobile, surrounded by his children and grandchildren, and continued his legal career. Semmes died in 1877 after eating tainted shellfish. As Semmes, ever the Latin scholar, might have written in summation, *sic transit gloria.*

Hailed for his victory, John Ancrum Winslow was nevertheless chastised by Secretary of the Navy Gideon Welles for failing to pursue the yacht *Deerhound* and letting Raphael Semmes escape to England, and he was also reprimanded for paroling the survivors whom he captured from the wreck of the *Alabama.* Eventually, Winslow and the *Kearsarge* returned to the United States, and Welles grudgingly promoted Winslow to the rank of commodore. Eventually, Winslow attained the rank of rear admiral and commanded the Pacific Squadron, in spite of his persistent health problems and age, until shortly before his death in 1873.

Chief Captain of the Fo'castle James Haley won a Medal of Honor for his role in sinking the *Alabama.* His fo'castle gun crews were credited with delivering mortal blows to the Rebel cruiser. Haley was cited for "marked coolness and good conduct and was highly commended by his division officer for his gallantry and meritorious achievement under enemy fire."

Abraham Lincoln's "Old Man of the Sea," Gideon Welles, was at the president and Mrs. Lincoln's side following the shooting at Ford's Theater, and Welles's description of Lincoln's final hours offers a heart-wrenching eyewitness account of the tragedy. He served President Andrew Johnson as secretary of the navy until 1869, when they disagreed over reconstruction policies.

Welles finally returned to "little Connecticut" to write and edit his famous diary and other books about the intrigues he had witnessed in Washington. In 1878, he died from a streptococcal infection of the throat.

Like *Southern Seahawk* and *Seahawk Hunting,* the first two volumes in this trilogy, this novel is set against the backdrop of real events in the American Civil War. The naval action, infighting in the Lincoln cabinet, political intrigue in the office of the secretary of the navy, the clandestine operations of secret agents like the Confederates James Bulloch and Federal Allan Pinkerton (alias E. J. Allen) are well known. Likewise, Harriet "Minty" Tubman's work as a conductor on the Underground Railroad. Specific locales used in this novel—such as the Ebbitt Grill and the Willard Hotel in Washington (which are still in operation); the homes of gentry and churches in South Carolina; the Africville neighborhood and St. Paul's Anglican Church in Halifax; the escaped slave village of Lincolnville, Nova Scotia; Kelway's Hotel in Southampton, England; and the Federal and Confederate executive mansions—have been the subject of analysis by scholars and Internet coverage.

All of the major historical figures in this novel—Raphael Semmes, Gideon Welles, John Ancrum Winslow, William Seward, Abraham Lincoln, Charles Wilkes, Allan Pinkerton, Rose Greenhow, Varina Davis, Harriet Tubman, John P. Hale, John Wilkes Booth—were real people. The dates, places, and action of all major war-related events in this novel are drawn from actual occurrences as revealed through the journals, published memoirs, and correspondence of the characters. Semmes's *Memoirs of Service Afloat* and *The Cruise of the Alabama and the Sumter*, *The Life of John Ancrum Winslow*, as well as the three-volume diary of Gideon Welles have been invaluable research tools.

Biographers have often revisited the lives of Semmes, Winslow, Welles, Lincoln, Bulloch, Wilkes, Seward, Greenhow, and Pinkerton. Among Semmes's biographies, Stephen Fox's *Wolf of the Deep* stands out for its deep and meticulous research, as well as its courage to air guarded secrets about the man the Semmes family often refers to simply as "The Admiral." Specifically, Fox documents that Raphael Semmes's wife, Anne, bore a daughter, Anna, in 1847, who could not have been fathered by Semmes. He was away fighting the Mexican War during the time of conception. Fox also details the existence of a "romantic connection" between Semmes and the young English woman named Louisa Tremblett, a relationship that persisted through years of correspondence.

These discoveries led me to make an intuitive leap and imagine that Raphael Semmes may well have had a mistress at the outset of the Civil War. Maude Galway is that character in my novel and is an entirely fictional creation. Maude burst onto the page the day that I began to draft the first book of this trilogy. I immediately liked her spunk, admired her loyalty to her man. So she stayed, blooming in *Southern Seahawk* and evolving further in *Seahawk Hunting* and in this volume as well. Fictional flesh and blood, heart and soul. She is an emblem for the many women caught in the deadly web of the War Between the States. These women kept company with secret agents and played crucial roles as spies on both sides of the Civil War—often with great risk to themselves.

—Randall Peffer